## Books by Katy Swann

*Dominion*

The Ultimatum
Behind The Scenes

*Boundaries*

To Love and Submit
To Love and Trust
To Love and Obey

*Anthologies*

Over the Knee

*Single Titles*

Kneel for You

Behind The Scenes

ISBN # 978-1-78686-078-1

©Copyright Katy Swann 2016

Cover Art by Posh Gosh ©Copyright 2016

Interior text design by Claire Siemaszkiewicz

Totally Bound Publishing

Published in 2016 by Totally Bound Publishing, Newland House, The Point, Weaver Road, Lincoln, LN6 3QN, United Kingdom.

Dominion

# BEHIND THE SCENES

KATY SWANN

# Dedication

This is for all the dancers out there who work so hard to be the best they can. I write from personal experience. I suffered an injury when I was younger that stopped me from dancing so I know how devastating it is to lose your dream.

# Chapter One

Evie Lloyd smiled happily as she basked in the electrifying atmosphere buzzing around her. Below, thousands of adoring fans sang along to the stomping anthem being performed by the band on the distant stage. Normally she'd be one of the sweaty bodies trying to avoid being crushed in the crazed mosh pit, but not tonight. Tonight she was in a private VIP suite sipping champagne while enjoying a privileged view of the concert. The music was loud, the crowd ecstatic and the beat pulsed as the deep bass shook the floor of the massive arena.

She turned in her seat and glanced behind her. Some of the other VIP guests were mingling, not taking the slightest bit of notice of the concert, while others danced in the small space between the seats and the bar at the far end. The suite was large enough to accommodate about twenty people, with one end opening out to the arena. This had several rows of seats where the guests could sit comfortably and watch the event while being waited on hand and foot. Evie smiled. She could get used to this.

"So, are you coming to the wrap party?" She could only just hear the question over the noise of the music and crowd. Christina, her best friend, had been trying to convince her all evening to come along to the nightclub in central London where Decadence would be celebrating the end of their European tour after tonight's gig. But arrogant rock stars and their tarty groupies were so not her thing.

She shook her head and shouted her reply. "No thanks."

"Oh, go on," coaxed Christina, giving her a friendly nudge.

Before she could reply a waiter appeared and filled their glasses with more sparkling champagne, then offered a platter of tempting canapés. Picking up a smoked salmon blini, Evie decided to change the subject.

"Thanks for inviting me to the gig tonight. I hadn't realized the offer of a free ticket included this VIP suite as well."

Christina grinned. "It's cool, isn't it? Aaron, the lead guitarist, is a friend of Marco's. Apparently they used to be in a band together years ago. Anyway, it was Aaron who arranged this for Marco and his guests."

Marco was Christina's Dom and trainer. He owned an exclusive BDSM hotel and club in Kent that was rumored to have the best dungeons in the country. According to Christina, Marco had taken pity on her when her moody boyfriend had dumped her and left her on her own at a beginner's BDSM weekend at the hotel. Marco and Christina weren't romantically involved, though, and Evie had wondered a couple of times if her friend liked him more than he liked her. She hoped not, because she'd hate for Christina to get hurt.

"Aaron is sexy, don't you think?" shouted Christina.

Evie nodded. Yes, he was actually. He was by far the best-looking member of the band, although the lead singer, Hunter, usually stole the limelight. Aaron was tall, really tall, and built like a tank. In the band's videos, his strong muscles rippled across his broad chest and shoulders as the camera zoomed in on him. His long dark-brown hair was his trademark, along with the impressive tattooed sleeve that covered almost the whole of his right arm.

Christina nudged her again. "He's a Dom, you know," she said in a raised voice.

"Really?" Evie studied the tall guitarist on the stage below more closely. She wasn't at all surprised. Aaron Holmes screamed 'Dom'. From his powerful stance to his dark, authoritative eyes, Evie had no problems imagining him with a submissive kneeling at his feet. *Mmm, now that's a sexy thought.* She wasn't about to let Christina in on that little fantasy, though, because her friend was notorious for matchmaking. The last thing she wanted was to be faced with the humiliation of being rejected by someone like Aaron Holmes.

Rock stars went for rock chicks—beautiful, skinny and glamorous. She was none of those things. She didn't have an inferiority complex, but she was realistic enough to know that her tall, curvy figure, unruly, wavy hair that turned frizzy in the rain and paler-than-pale skin weren't what rock stars went for.

And, anyway, she couldn't stand arrogant men, and everyone knew that people in the music industry were far too full of their own self-importance to carry their fame with dignity. No, the last thing she needed was for Christina to start meddling in her non-existent love life with that lot. Another change of subject was called for.

"So, how's it going with Marco?" The current song was building to a crescendo and she could hardly hear herself speak over the noise.

Christina frowned and leaned closer. "Pardon?"

"Marco," she shouted. "How's it going?" As she spoke, the heavy song finished to rapturous applause.

When the cheers had died down and the opening chords of a softer, quieter song started, Christina shouted back, "Really well. He says I'm a natural submissive, albeit a bratty one."

Evie laughed. Now why didn't that surprise her? Christina would have to be pretty brave to want to be trained by Marco Alessi. He'd been a well-known singer once and still looked every bit the rebellious rocker. Although his black hair wasn't as long as Aaron's, it was still wild and untamed, and his tribal tattoos revealed a darker side to his character. And those eyes. He had the blackest eyes she'd ever seen, set in a rugged, stubble-covered face. He wasn't classically handsome, but he had charisma by the bucketload and Evie could well understand why Christina was so taken with him.

"He's a bit scary, don't you think?"

"Scary? Nah, Marco's a pussycat," said Christina with a casual wave of her hand.

"Am I, now?" A deep voice over their shoulders made them turn around.

Neither of them had known that Marco had sat down behind them and they both jumped when he spoke. Evie realized that, even over the sound of the music, it had been clear what, and who, they'd been talking about.

Evie grinned as she watched the flush on Christina's face drain away. *Pussycat? Yeah, right.*

Marco reached forward, took a handful of Christina's hair and tugged. When her head was tilted back far enough that she could look up into Marco's face, he growled, "Pussycat, eh? I'll show you who's the pussycat later, kitten."

Christina grinned up at him and giggled. "Yes, Sir."

As Marco effortlessly exerted his command over Christina, something stirred deep inside Evie. A memory of having her hair pulled just like that made little butterflies tingle in her belly. She recalled how good it had felt to surrender to a Dom. It had been nearly two years since she'd last done that. Was she envious of Christina? Maybe.

Marco let go of Christina's hair, his expression becoming serious. "Listen, there's been a change of plan," he said, his deep voice easily carrying over the music. "The wrap party is going to be held at Dominion now."

"Why?" asked Christina.

"Security reasons." Marco's expression was grim and he didn't elaborate any further.

"Evie," exclaimed Christina, "why don't you come with us, then? You said yourself how much you'd love to go to Dominion. Well, now's your chance."

"You're more than welcome to come," added Marco with a warm smile. "You can come in our car and of course you can stay over if you wish. We've got plenty of rooms."

"Well…" Evie faltered. Although the idea of mingling

with rock stars didn't appeal to her, the possibility of going somewhere like Dominion was too good to miss. She might not get another chance. *Maybe it wouldn't hurt...*

Christina must have sensed her hesitation, because she put her arm around Evie's shoulder and said, "You're coming, end of discussion."

"God, you're bossy," groaned Evie, although she was secretly glad that she'd had the decision made for her. If left to decide herself, she might have insisted on going home to her empty flat for another lonely night. A visit to an exclusive hotel, which just happened to be renowned for its impressive dungeons, was far more exciting. And maybe she could ask one of the Dungeon Monitors to top her? It had been a long time since she'd last felt the kiss of a flogger.

She grinned back at Christina and nodded her agreement.

Christina squealed gleefully and threw her arms around her. "Yay! If you're lucky, Ross or Andre might be there," she said, with a conspiratorial wink.

When Evie looked blank, Christina rolled her eyes and added, "They're long-time members and help out regularly as DMs. They're both shit-hot Doms and I'm sure they'd be more than happy to give you a good seeing to."

Evie laughed. "I'm not that desperate, you know. Just keep me away from those musicians and I'll be fine."

Their conversation ended abruptly when the crowd exploded with cheers as the band finished their song. The whole arena shook as feet stomped and 'Decadence' was chanted by the adoring fans. The band ran off the stage, leaving the audience wild with cries for their return, and when they did reappear, the roar was deafening.

"Thank you, London," Hunter called and waved. "Here's our last song of the night and it's dedicated to all you fucking awesome people out there. Goodnight."

As the band launched into their final number, Evie's eyes were drawn to Aaron, strutting around the stage as if he owned it while playing a catchy guitar riff. God, he was hot. Even from the vast distance to the stage, she was aware of his black leather trousers clinging to his muscular thighs. He was wearing New Rock boots — big, heavy and sexy as hell. *Oh, to kneel in front of those boots*. Evie shook her head to rid herself of the thought. No, she was definitely not going to harbor any secret dreams about Aaron Holmes. She might very well get to meet him later and she'd be damned if she was going to make a fool of herself by acting like a gushing fan ready to throw herself at his feet.

"Okay, ladies," said Marco, leaning over the row of seats behind them. "We need to make our way backstage before the mass exodus at the end of the gig."

As Evie rose and followed Christina toward the exit, she couldn't help but turn and glance back at the band one more time. Her stomach flipped at the realization that she was going to be partying with them in a private club. Then she gritted her teeth when she envisioned them flaunting a carefully selected bunch of groupies. No, she would absolutely not have anything to do with those guys tonight.

* * * *

"Hey, Kev, go and get those little tarts at the front of the stage. One of them flashed her fucking tits at me. She's fucking gagging for it."

The crude words were the first thing to greet them as Evie, Christina and Marco pushed open the door to the green room backstage. Evie frowned. *How vulgar*. Her opinion of rock stars sank to an all-time low and she briefly regretted her decision to come to the wrap party. But Christina had told her on the way down that, as far as she was aware, the only member of the band who was into BDSM was Aaron. Hopefully, then, the other band members would stay away from the dungeon while they fucked their groupies somewhere else.

A bodyguard, or whatever he was, nodded at the drummer and left the room with a sleazy grin on his face. Maybe it wasn't just the musicians who got to use the groupies.

They'd barely stepped into the room when Marco's phone rang and, as he answered it, Evie and Christina waited near the door where the drummer was chatting to the keyboard player.

"That's Jaymz, spelt J-A-Y-M-Z," whispered Christina, scowling at the obnoxious-looking drummer. "He thinks that changing the spelling of his name makes him more irresistible to the fans. He's a pretentious git," she snarled. "The other prick with him is Jona, the keyboard player."

Evie smiled. It seemed she wasn't the only one with a distaste for uncouth rock stars.

"Are we gonna take 'em back to the party?" asked Jona, before downing the best part of a whole bottle of beer.

Jaymz pulled the ring on a can of cider and sneered. "Yeah, although it's now gonna be at some fucking kinky shithole in the middle of fucking nowhere."

"Well, in that case we'd better make sure we bring plenty of chicks to last the night then," said Jona. He belched loudly then grinned. "We can always tie 'em up to stop 'em from escaping."

Jaymz laughed as he shook his head. "Nah, I'm not into that kinky shit, man. I just wanna spread their little legs and shag 'em, one by fucking one."

"What a couple of dickheads," growled Christina, scowling openly at them.

"Yeah." Evie glared at the two assholes and sighed. This was going to be a long night.

To distract herself from the obnoxious musicians, she decided to take in her surroundings. There were about fifteen or so people all standing chatting among discarded clothes and various music paraphernalia. To their right the bass player chatted to a well-dressed man and in the far corner Aaron Holmes and Mike Hunt, or Hunter as he was known, were talking to a beautiful, petite, dark-haired woman. She was the epitome of the type of woman Evie imagined rock stars would go for. Everything she wasn't.

She wondered for a brief moment if she was Aaron's girlfriend. She didn't follow the band's personal lives and had no idea of their romantic involvements.

Christina must have seen where she was looking because she whispered, "That's Fabiana, Hunter's wife. She's really nice."

"Oh." For some bizarre reason, Evie was ridiculously relieved to hear that the woman wasn't Aaron's wife or girlfriend, but the thought was soon quashed when she reminded herself that she could never be in that kind of league anyway.

Marco finished his call and turned back to her and Christina.

"Sorry about that," he said, glancing around the room. "Just checking with Cleo that we can accommodate the party without too much disruption to the regular members. Come on."

He took a light hold of Christina's arm and began to lead them across the room toward Aaron and Hunter. "Who's Cleo?" whispered Evie.

"She's the house Domina and runs Dominion with a rod of steel," answered Christina with a giggle. "She's also my other trainer. If you thought Marco was scary then just wait until you meet Cleo."

As they neared Aaron and Hunter, Evie seemed to shrink as her gaze drew upward. Aaron Holmes was even taller in real life than he appeared on stage. Hunter was a whole head shorter than his bandmate, and he wasn't exactly short.

She watched in silence as the musicians greeted Marco with friendly handshakes. Christina gave Fabiana, Hunter and Aaron a friendly hug then turned to Evie.

"This is my friend, Evie Lloyd. She's coming with us to the wrap party tonight, although she took a bit of persuading."

Both Fabiana and Hunter greeted her warmly before Aaron turned his dark eyes on her. Suddenly her world stood still. She was trapped, powerless to look away as he held her prisoner with his omnipotent gaze.

"Well, hello," he said, in a deep, rich voice. "It's nice to meet you, Evie."

Somehow she managed to drag herself out of the hypnotic trance he'd put her in and attempted to fix a detached expression onto her face.

"Hi," she replied, trying to look as casual as she could. She glanced down at his extended hand, momentarily breaking the intense eye contact, and shook it. His grip was strong—of course.

She expected him to have lost interest as she pulled her hand away and returned her gaze to his face, but was surprised to find that he was still studying her with that same look of authority that he had before.

"Evie's a sub," blurted Christina.

Evie glared at her friend. Why the hell had she just said that? It made her look bloody desperate. And, anyway, it was none of his damn business.

"So I see," said Aaron, his eyes still fixed on her.

Huh? How the hell could he tell if she was a submissive or not? Then she remembered looking down at his hand for a split second when they were being introduced. How fucking presumptuous of him to assume that she had lowered her eyes in submission. It was the typical arrogant rock star mentality. He probably thought she was desperate to fuck him. Her frown deepened as she opened her mouth to put him straight.

"Christina," scolded Marco, interrupting Evie before she could make some sort of angry retort. "Behave yourself or I'll gag you right here in front of everyone."

Christina just giggled. "Yes, Sir," she sang, with a deliberate note of provocation.

God, she was really setting herself up for punishment later. If what Evie had heard about Marco Alessi was true, there was no way he was going to let Christina get away with such a bratty attitude.

Aaron grinned as Marco cupped his hand over Christina's

mouth, silencing her before she could get herself into any more trouble.

"Do you see what I have to put up with?" said Marco, with a good-humored shrug. "Somehow I have to turn this impudent sub into a perfect house slave."

"What, Christina?" Evie feigned disbelief and looked at Marco in sympathy. "You'll be lucky."

Aaron laughed and looked like he might say something but before he could, a woman approached him from behind and tapped him on the shoulder. He turned around and greeted the glamorous lady waiting to talk to him, and Evie knew she'd been forgotten.

That, concluded Evie, was the end of that little encounter with the great Aaron Holmes. She dragged her eyes away from the back of his head as Marco told them they needed to make a move. The car was waiting and he wanted to leave before the rest of the entourage to make sure his staff were ready for the unscheduled guests.

She wondered if it was too late to back out, but Christina had taken her firmly by the hand. There was no way her friend would let her change her mind now, so she followed as Marco led them out of the room and along several corridors to the back exit.

Christina chatted nineteen to the dozen on the way down, but Evie wasn't listening to anything she was saying. All she could think about was Aaron Holmes—his firm grip, his captivating gaze and the silent command for her compliance. But she was deluding herself. She might like to think that he wanted to dominate her but she knew that, in reality, someone like him would never be interested in her. She knew that. So why was her tummy somersaulting and her head spinning at the thought of seeing him again at Dominion? As she climbed into the car and strapped herself in, she vowed to stay strong. There was no way—*no way*—she was going to make a fool of herself with that man tonight.

# Chapter Two

Aaron Holmes smiled at the record company's press officer and thanked her for her time. He turned around, but Marco and the girls had already left. Shame. Christina's friend had intrigued him and he'd been hoping to chat with her a bit more. Her reaction when she'd assumed that he believed she'd lowered her eyes in submission was hilarious. Of course, he hadn't really thought that, but he did so love teasing pretty submissives, and this one was cute as hell. She didn't need to know that Marco had already mentioned Christina was bringing her submissive friend to the gig. This was going to be fun.

He rejoined Hunter and Fabiana, who had moved away and were chatting quietly. Fabiana looked worried and Hunter was trying to comfort her.

"You okay?" Stupid fucking question. Of course she wasn't okay.

Fabiana nodded and smiled bravely, but she didn't fool him.

"Listen, mate, I'm sorry about messing everyone around with the venue," said Hunter, a deep frown etched on his handsome face.

"Hey, nothing's more important than keeping safe. And, anyway, it suits me," said Aaron with a grin. He'd been dreading the wrap party until it had been moved to Dominion. A bit of kink would round the evening off very nicely.

Hunter laughed. "Yeah, I bet it does."

The door to the green room opened and Aaron glanced over in case Marco and the girls had returned. But it was one of the roadies with six giggling girls in tow.

"Oh no," groaned Aaron. "Here we go again."

Aaron glared across the room as Jaymz and Jona crudely greeted the girls with leering jibes about their tits and asses.

"I'm sick of those two sleazebags," said Hunter quietly.

"Yeah, I was hoping they would just take the girls back to their hotel, but they've said they're coming to the party," growled Aaron. *They'd fucking better keep out of my way.*

He watched as Jaymz put his arm around one of the girls and groped her breasts. The girl didn't seem to mind until she looked up and saw Hunter and himself. *Uh-oh!*

She screamed. "Oh my God, there's Hunter and Aaron Holmes."

He automatically fixed a well-rehearsed smile onto his face as the girls rushed over, leaving Jaymz and Jona looking like they might like to kill their bandmates. This always happened. Jaymz and Jona would score the girls, but as soon they caught sight of Hunter and Aaron the girls lost interest in the other two. But Hunter was married and Aaron didn't do groupies. Jaymz and Jona were welcome to them.

Levi, the bassist, looked up and grinned when he saw the girls. He was openly gay and thought it was hilarious how Hunter and Aaron always got stuck with the groupies. He usually disappeared with his boyfriend shortly after a gig finished so didn't have to fend off the screaming fans.

Aaron smiled his obligatory smile and signed the CD sleeves the girls had brought. Then he signaled to the other end of the room and called, "Hey, Jaymz, come and get your 'guests'."

Jaymz looked seriously pissed off as he slithered over and tried to convince the girls to leave Hunter and Aaron alone. Thankfully Bill, their manager, saved the moment by announcing that the tour bus was ready and it was time to leave.

"Do you want to come in the car with us?" asked Hunter. He didn't like traveling on the bus and insisted on driving himself whenever possible.

"Thanks, mate. That would be good." At least he wouldn't have to listen to Jaymz spew his crap to impress the girls on the journey.

As Hunter took Fabiana's hand and started to leave, Aaron grabbed his sleeve. "Hey, shouldn't we wait for security?"

"Fuck them," growled Hunter. "I'm not going to creep around like a mouse because of some fucking nutter."

Aaron sighed as he followed the couple out. He understood Hunter's insistence that he wasn't going to allow one person to violate his freedom, but this was a little more serious than the ardent attentions of an overeager fan. After all, threats to their safety shouldn't be taken lightly.

They slipped out and made their way to the private underground car park that was usually reserved for the musicians and their crew. As they crossed the large, empty space, their footsteps echoed against the concrete walls and floor. Dark shadows loomed from behind thick pillars and distant sounds from outside gave the place a creepy and isolated feel. For the first time, Aaron became aware of how easy it would be for someone to get to them if they were determined enough.

He shook off his unease. He wouldn't be surprised if this latest scare would be the final nail in the coffin for the band. He knew Hunter was close to quitting. If that happened he didn't know what he'd do. They'd have to find a new singer and that would be a nightmare. Finding Hunter after their previous singer had left had been bad enough, and the thought of going through all that again filled him with dread. But Decadence were at the top of their game with number one albums and sell-out tours. Could he walk away from that?

Now wasn't the time to speculate on the future of the band, though. They had the end of a tour to celebrate. No faceless hotels, screaming fans or sleazy bandmates for the next few weeks. In the meantime, he'd concentrate on writing new songs and try to forget about the dark threats hanging over them. So far Hunter was the only target, although that was bad enough. He liked and respected Hunter, both as a musician and as a friend, and hated to see the stress this was putting him and Fabiana under.

As Hunter drove the car away from London toward Kent, they all seemed to relax. Tonight, he resolved, they would enjoy themselves. Hunter and Fabiana would undoubtedly disappear to their room straight away, and he had a feisty little submissive to find. He hadn't forgotten about Christina's cute friend. He hadn't topped a girl for nearly a month. He could do with the rush of adrenaline that he could only ever get from the surrender of a submissive. And, tonight, he knew exactly which submissive he wanted over his knee.

* * * *

Evie's jaw dropped as the car pulled up outside an enormous mansion. It was huge, very old, but well maintained and stunningly beautiful. Not at all what she'd been expecting.

After driving for over forty-five minutes, Hunter had finally turned into a narrow gravelly road. It was dark and she hadn't been able to see much at first, but when they had cleared the shadows of some tall trees and the house had come into view, its size and grandeur had stunned her.

In complete awe, she couldn't drag her eyes away from the massive building as she climbed out of the car. It was illuminated by bright floodlights that cast eerie shadows down from high turrets and buttresses. Mesmerized, she stared up then jumped when she spotted a pair of sinister dark eyes glaring down at her. But she smiled as she realized they were just the hollow eyes of one of the many creepy gargoyles grinning cheekily from their high perches.

Marco led them up lichen-stained stone steps to a grand arched doorway, and as Evie stepped over the threshold, she couldn't help imagining that the house probably had an interesting and checkered history. *It may even be home to a ghost or two?*

Inside was just as impressive. A welcoming fire roared in a stone hearth in the large entrance hall. At one end of the hall a grand sweeping staircase rose to the upper floors and two wood-paneled corridors fed off from either side into other areas of the house. Evie tried to take in as much of the incredible room as possible – the opulent décor, the tangy smell of smoke with a subtle hint of beeswax lingering in the background and silence broken only by the crackling fire and creaking floorboards as they crossed the large space.

Marco stopped by a wooden door set in a heavy stone-arched frame. "This leads to the East Wing," he said solemnly. "We normally keep it open on weekends, but as there will be vanilla guests from the wrap party staying in other parts of the house, it's going to stay shut tonight. We don't want any unsuspecting strays accidentally wandering into the play areas. Our members pay a lot of money for privacy and exclusivity and wouldn't appreciate the intrusion."

He keyed in a code on a discreet device attached to a paneled wall and the door opened. He ushered them through it then closed it carefully again and continued. "The wrap party will take place in the West Wing, which is where we hold our business conferences during the week. It's my aim to keep the two events completely separate."

"Good," said Evie, thankful that she wouldn't have to mingle with the musicians, especially now that she knew what sleazebags they were.

Marco led them down a wide corridor until they arrived at an open door. Evie smiled as she recognized the sounds spilling out from the room – the sounds of a dungeon. Low music, murmured voices and the slap of leather hitting flesh. Oh, how she'd missed this.

As she stepped into the room she gasped. This was the most unusual dungeon she'd ever seen. Set in a large, stately room with embossed wallpaper and crystal chandeliers, it was elegant and spacious. It didn't have the dark, more intense feel of a regular club playroom, yet the equipment scattered around the room left her in no doubt as to its purpose.

Large gilt-framed paintings hanging on the walls drew her attention. Each one featured a naked or semi-naked woman in a submissive pose. They were tasteful and beautiful.

The equipment appeared impressive too. Obviously sturdy and of high quality, there was no shortage of places to play. Two solid wooden St. Andrew's crosses padded with black leather adorned adjacent walls and several spanking benches had been placed strategically around the room.

She couldn't help noticing that people weren't queuing up to use any of the equipment. Even though there were a good forty or so guests in the room, there was enough space to comfortably accommodate them all. While those not playing lounged in leather sofas or Queen Anne-style armchairs, others watched a flogging demonstration on a small stage.

A male sub locked into a cage in the corner of the room kneeled in the confined space while his Mistress spoke to him through the bars. In another part of the room a pretty young woman was suspended from a mechanical hoist in the ceiling, her wrists bound in strong leather cuffs.

A shiver of excitement ran through her as she imagined herself draped over one of those benches, or even helplessly stretched and bound in those cuffs. Her heart suddenly beat a little faster as she recalled how it felt to be at the mercy of a Dom. A slow-burning need started building between her legs as the desire to submit intensified.

She watched longingly as a smartly dressed man tied a woman to a nearby spanking bench. Unlike most of the Doms in the room he wore a formal suit rather than leather or latex, but he had such an air of authoritative control that his smart attire only added to his sexiness.

She smiled happily. This place was even better than she'd imagined. It was perfect—the people, the atmosphere, the surroundings. *Oh yeah, this is one cool dungeon.*

Before she'd managed to take it all in, Christina whispered in her ear, "I'll ask Marco to take you down and show you the other dungeons later."

Evie laughed. "What, there's more?"

Christina nodded, her eyes sparkling. "Oh yeah, this is just the half of it. The downstairs dungeons are real. They were used as prisons in the old days. There's even an old cell down there."

"Wow!" Evie shivered. *This place just gets better and better.*

At that moment a tall, beautiful woman with flame-red hair approached them. She kissed Christina softly on the lips before asking Marco, "Has she behaved herself?"

Marco appeared to consider the question carefully. "Mostly," he replied gravely. "Although, she seems to think I'm a pussycat."

Evie giggled. She'd *known* that was going to come back and haunt Christina.

The woman laughed and affectionately tugged Christina's hair. "Does she now?"

Not giving the woman a chance to say anything else, Christina pulled Evie forward and said, "Cleo, this is my very bestest friend, Evie. Evie, meet Cleo, my wonderful, sweet and kind trainer."

Cleo smiled and reached out for Evie's hand. Instead of shaking it though, Cleo raised it to her lips and softly kissed the back of her hand. "I'm very pleased to meet you, Evie."

"You too." Evie flushed. She'd never met a woman quite like Cleo before. Charming as well as beautiful, she also carried an air of danger and Evie resolved not to cross her. Ever.

Cleo looked back at Marco and grinned. A look of cunning evil flashed across her face. "Would you like me to take our little kitten upstairs and get her suitably attired, Marco?"

Marco nodded, his black eyes flashing with sparks of

humor, and said, "Yes, you do that while I get Evie a drink."

As Cleo marched Christina out of the room, Marco looked down at Evie and smiled. "So, Evie, are you hoping to play tonight?"

"Well, it's been a while, but…I guess…" She paused, feeling awkward. She wasn't used to this anymore. *Oh heck, might as well just say it as it is.* "Yes, Sir."

"Good girl," said Marco. "I much prefer a direct and honest answer."

Her blood warmed at his approval. There had been a time when pleasing a Dom had meant everything. It had been her choice to reject the BDSM lifestyle in order to settle down and become a 'nice' respectable woman. Now she knew she'd been wrong. She'd never be that normal vanilla girl that Vince had worked so hard to mold her into. She was kinky through and through and now that she had finally accepted that, she was damn well going to enjoy herself.

"Follow me," said Marco and headed off toward a door on their left.

He walked in large strides and she had to be careful not to stumble in her high-heeled boots as she tried to keep up. A few people stared as she passed them and she frowned. Had she grown horns or something? Then it dawned on her. Everyone wore fetish gear. She was wearing casual jeans and a T-shirt. Well, how had she been to know she'd end up in a BDSM club?

She followed Marco into a room that led directly off the main dungeon.

"This is the chill-out room," he said when they reached a small bar at the far end.

She looked around and smiled. It was nice. Lots of comfortable-looking sofas, dimly lit lamps and scattered rugs—very home from home. A man wearing a leather kilt and waistcoat was cuddling his sub on one of the sofas nearby. It looked like a tender aftercare moment and she quickly averted her eyes, careful not to intrude on their privacy. On another sofa, six people chatted and laughed, while another small group was catching up at the bar.

"Did you go to the Red Dungeon last week?" asked one willowy Domme standing by the bar.

A man, also a Dom by the look of it, shook his head. "No, we couldn't get a babysitter. Was it any good?"

Evie turned her attention back to Marco, as he asked her what she'd like to drink.

"Just a Diet Coke, please," she replied. If she was going to play a little later, she wanted to keep a clear head.

As the bartender poured her drink, Marco nodded at the high stool next to her and she climbed onto it without hesitation.

"I'm going to introduce you to Ross later," he said, sliding onto the stool next to her. "He's a little busy right now, but he'll look after you. He's a dungeon monitor and a trusted friend. Now, about your outfit…"

"Ah, yes, I'm sorry, but I didn't know I'd be coming here so I haven't got anything to change into." She shifted in her seat, aware that she looked painfully out of place in her street clothes, and hoped Marco wouldn't be too hard on her.

Marco smiled, his eyes darker than ever. "I could insist that you strip and remain naked all evening," he said in a low voice.

Was he serious? Something about Marco Alessi scared her shitless. She knew from Christina that he was a formidable Dom and, even though Evie wasn't his submissive, he still commanded her with effortless control. Could she obey him if he ordered her to strip?

"But," he continued as visions of herself wondering around in the nude burned her cheeks, "as I'm feeling generous, you can choose an outfit from a small selection we keep in the Ladies' cloakroom."

"Thank you," said Evie with relief.

"Do you have a safeword?" he asked as the bartender placed her drink in front of her.

She nodded her thanks and turned back to Marco. "Well,

it used to be chili, but that seems a bit silly now."

"Not at all. If it's what you'll remember when you're under duress then it's fine. Just make sure Ross knows. We use the universal color coding here. You know, green meaning everything's fine, yellow for slow down and red for stop. Ross will have a chat with you about your limits before you start. Do you have any questions?" Marco stood and held out his hand.

"No, thank you, Sir." She took the offered hand and slid off the stool. Despite her earlier excitement, nerves now fluttered through her stomach. Christ, was this real? She'd gone from attending a concert with Christina to discussing safewords in a posh BDSM hotel with a Dom who, quite frankly, was scary as hell.

As she followed Marco's directions to the cloakroom, her head spun with a mixture of nerves and excitement. What would this Ross be like? Could she submit to someone again after all this time? Not for the first time that evening, she wondered what the hell she'd gotten herself into.

# Chapter Three

Evie sat back and watched Ross in action. When she'd returned to the dungeon moments earlier dressed in a tiny black PVC dress that left very little to the imagination, Marco had pointed out the DM who would be topping her later.

She'd been surprised and very pleased when Ross had turned out to be the sexy man dressed in the suit. There were no armbands, special T-shirts or tags marking him out as a dungeon monitor—he just looked like a regular guy. Well, a very good-looking and well-dressed regular guy. Marco had explained that, because Dominion was a private club and most of the guests had been members for years, there was no need for a DM to stand out. Everyone knew who they were. In fact, there was no need for a dungeon monitor at all really, but Marco liked to have someone in each room anyway just to ensure all was well.

Ross was still flogging the woman on the spanking bench, so Evie relaxed into the comfy sofa Marco had taken her to, sipping her drink and admiring the way Ross worked. He knew how to wield a flogger, that was for sure. The long leather tails landed expertly on the woman's exposed bottom with a loud slap followed straight away by a soft groan from the sub. Every now and again he'd stop and rub his large hands over the girl's red skin, soothing it before resuming the beating.

As Evie watched she became more drawn into the scene. Ross was completely focused on the sub, keeping an eye on her every flinch and checking she was okay at regular intervals. He was a good Dom, she could tell. So much so that she wouldn't have a problem trusting him when Marco handed her over to him.

When Marco had pointed him out earlier, Ross had just slipped his jacket off and had been draping it over a nearby chair. Then he'd rolled up his sleeves, exposing strong, sculpted biceps. Now those muscles flexed as they danced to the movement of his arms while he continued to flick the heavy flogger over the woman's body.

The more she observed, the more she wanted to be that girl. Her heart hammered painfully in her chest as excitement and longing built to an unbearable intensity. She could almost feel the sting of the leather as it thudded against the woman's skin and she shivered in anticipation as she tried to remain patient. It would be her turn soon. *Not soon enough.*

Marco, who was sitting next to her, glanced at her and grinned. "Does watching that scene turn you on?" he asked.

Damn, she'd forgotten how blunt Doms could be. She knew better than to lie though, so she nodded and said, "Yes, Sir."

"If you're good, Ross might let you come later. Would you like that, Evie?"

Her cheeks flamed at Marco's crude question. Ross was a very attractive man. He had sandy hair, blue eyes and a lean bod. He also had a commanding air about him that made him look stern and authoritative. Although she wouldn't want full-on sex, she could easily imagine herself letting go enough to come under the command of a man like that.

"Evie, let me warn you now, if Ross asks you a question he'll expect an answer. Just like I do."

Ooh, there was that stern Dom voice again. "Er, yes, Sir. I'd like that."

One of the things she'd always loved about D/s was the subtle humiliation of having to answer a question truthfully, no matter how embarrassing that might be. She was well aware that Marco was making sure she was getting into the right headspace for her imminent scene, and it was working. The need to kneel before a Dom and relinquish her control intensified. Bloody hell, how could she ever have thought she could live without this?

Finally, Ross put down the flogger then massaged the girl's trembling shoulders. He whispered something in her ear and she nodded. Evie fidgeted with her hair as her impatience grew. He'd undoubtedly take the girl away for some aftercare before he would be finished with her. He'd want a break himself then, before they could start their scene, they still had to have that chat about limits and safewords. It would be a while before she got what she so badly wanted and needed.

As Ross helped the young woman off the bench, Christina reappeared with Cleo, and Evie's own needs were temporarily forgotten as she snorted with laughter.

Christina was on her hands and knees being led by Cleo on a leash attached to a diamante collar. She wore a headband with kitty ears attached and had long black whiskers drawn across her face — even her nose had been painted black. As she crawled, little bells jangled as they swayed from clover nipple clamps, but the funniest thing was the tail between her legs. It looked like it was secured by a butt plug seated deep in her ass, and Evie had no doubt that Christina would be feeling it very intimately every time she moved.

Christina must have heard Evie laugh because she looked up and glared at her, her face crimson. Marco chuckled as Cleo tugged on the leash and brought Christina to rest at his feet.

"Hello, kitty," he said with a deep laugh. "Don't you look cute?"

Christina scowled and Cleo tugged on the leash as Christina emitted a low growl.

Cleo laughed. "Pardon, kitty? Marco didn't quite hear you."

With her face now a deep puce, Christina gave Cleo a death-defying glare before looking up at Marco and saying, "Meow."

"Our little kitten is going to crawl to every Dom here, rub herself up against their legs and greet them with a sweet 'meow', aren't you, Christina?"

"Yes, Mistress…I mean, *meow*."

Damn, she shouldn't laugh, but seeing Christina resemble a ferocious tiger instead of the cute cat she was supposed to be was so funny she couldn't stop another giggle from escaping.

Cleo turned her sharp green eyes on her and smiled darkly. "Well, well. Do we have another pussycat here to keep this little one company?"

The blood drained from Evie's face. *No way!* "I'm sorry," she muttered, hoping to God that Cleo had been joking.

Thankfully, it seemed that she had, because Cleo sat down next to Marco, crossed her legs and shooed Christina away. "Off you go, kitty, there's a good girl."

Evie remained silent as Christina crawled across the floor. The first person she reached was Ross, who had his arm around the sub he'd just scened with. Christina stopped by his feet, rubbed her cheek against his leg then looked up and said, "Meow." Ross smiled, reached down and patted her head before walking off with the sub. Christina looked across at Marco and Cleo as if awaiting further orders. Marco nodded and she turned and crawled toward someone else who wasn't in the middle of a scene.

"I've got a nice little treat lined up for her later," drawled Cleo to Marco.

"Oh yeah? What's that then?" he replied with a wicked smile.

"It involves licking up cream." Cleo licked her luscious red lips and grinned.

Evie looked away before Cleo saw the blush creeping up from her neck. This was getting a little too personal for her liking. She looked around the large room, hoping for some sort of distraction. The flogging demo on the stage had finished and the small crowd had dispersed. She turned her head to the right and froze when her gaze settled on the door leading out of the dungeon. Standing in the doorway, completely filling the frame, was Aaron Holmes, and he was looking right at her.

* * * *

Aaron couldn't decide which looked funnier — Christina crawling around on all fours pretending to be a cat, or her friend Evie's face when she'd seen him just now. He was beginning to get the impression that Evie didn't like him very much. Well, that wasn't going to put him off, so he gave her his best Dom glare and strode over to the sofa where she was sitting with Cleo and Marco.

"Hello, mate," said Marco. "Is the rest of the entourage here?"

Aaron shook his head. "Nope. I came with Hunter and Fabiana in their car. They've already gone up to their room."

Evie rose and turned to Marco and Cleo. "Excuse me, I'm just off to the Ladies'."

She didn't even look at Aaron as she passed him and headed toward the cloakroom. Her sexy little ass wriggled as she walked and Aaron's cock twitched in response. Her aloof indifference to him was rather refreshing and, instead of putting him off, it made him want to know more about her.

"How is Hunter?" asked Marco when Evie had left the room.

Aaron frowned and sat down in the space next to Marco that Evie had just vacated. "Still a little shaken, but he's putting a brave face on. Fabiana, on the other hand, is distraught." Aaron fought to control his anger as he spoke. If he caught whoever had done this he'd —

"If they need a little privacy and security they're welcome to stay here for as long as they wish," said Cleo. "And when they find the bastard who sent the notes, just send him to me. I'm in the mood for an intensive CBT session," she added with a growl.

Aaron laughed. "Cleo, you'd be welcome to him. You can inflict as much cock and ball torture on him as you like, as far as I'm concerned."

"Assuming it's a man, of course," said Marco quietly.

They all turned to Marco and stared at him. He had a point. There was nothing in the notes to suggest it was a man—they were jumping to conclusions. It could just as easily be some crazed female fan.

"Well, whether it's a man or a woman, they'll be lucky if they can still walk by the time I've finished with them," said Cleo with a lethal injection of venom in her voice.

Aaron grinned. He sure as hell wouldn't want to be on the receiving end of Cleo's wrath. "Well, you'd have to make sure you get them before the police do, then."

Cleo opened her mouth, but before she could speak, Ross strode up, his face tense.

"Hey, Ross," Aaron said, and shook hands with his friend. "Everything all right?"

"Hmm, not really," replied Ross. "Caroline seems to be suffering from sub drop."

"Really?" Caroline was a sweet little house slave, well used to the effects of a hard flogging. It wasn't like her to have a negative reaction after a scene, so Aaron could well understand why Ross was concerned.

Ross nodded. "Yeah, she's tearful and can't stop shaking. I don't want to leave her alone so I'm afraid I'm going to have to let down the other young lady."

Marco nodded. "Of course, mate. Go and take care of young Caroline, don't worry about Evie."

Aaron raised his eyebrows. "Evie?"

"Yeah," said Marco as Ross turned and left. "Ross was going to top her tonight. She hasn't been on the scene for a while so I thought he would be a good choice for her. Not too intense."

"I could do it," blurted Aaron. Despite her chilly response to him, Evie fascinated him. He sensed that beneath the cool exterior hid a warm and passionate woman whose need to submit went deeper than just the occasional spanking. He'd welcome the opportunity to top her and give her what she so clearly yearned for.

Marco studied him for a moment then grinned. "Actually, that's not a bad idea. I was going to offer to do it, but I think I scare her a bit. Okay, but go gently."

Aaron nodded and grinned. A hit of adrenaline surged through his veins as he imagined Evie on her knees in front of him. Better still, draped over his knee with her bare bottom braced for a good spanking. His cock stirred under his tight trousers. For a night that had started off on such a downer, it sure as hell was looking up.

A few minutes later Evie returned to the room, chatting amiably with a tall Domme. She looked relaxed and at ease and when the Domme said something Evie laughed. But then she looked across the room and saw Aaron sitting with Marco and Cleo and the smile froze. Damn, what had he done to offend her?

She approached them slowly, avoiding eye contact with Aaron, and headed straight for Marco and Cleo. There was no room on the sofa for her to sit down so she stopped in front of Marco with an uncertain look on her face. Aaron's natural instinct was to stand up and offer her a seat, but Marco would want her standing in front of them as he addressed her, so he didn't move.

She shifted from one foot to the other, as if aware that the game was beginning. Aaron was tempted to reassure her with a smile, but he kept his expression stern as he silently assessed her.

"Evie," said Marco, his voice solemn. "Ross is no longer available to top you tonight."

Her face dropped for a split second, but she seemed quick to compose herself again. "That's all right. I'm a bit tired anyway," she replied, a little too hastily.

"But," continued Marco, not looking too pleased at the interruption, "Aaron has kindly offered to take his place."

"Oh."

Was that anger he just saw flash across her face? *What the fuck?*

"Is there a problem, Evie?" asked Marco in a low and even tone.

"I, er..." She looked at the three of them, her fingers clenched into tight fists. She genuinely seemed to be struggling for the right answer.

Poor Evie. They'd be looking pretty intimidating right now, what with Cleo's sharp eyes, Marco's firm, set jaw and his own confusion all aimed right at her. This didn't feel right. It was pretty clear that Evie didn't want to submit to him and he had no intention of topping a sub who wasn't completely willing, whatever her reasons. This had to stop right now.

"Evie," he said and stood up, "no one is forcing you to do this. If you don't want me to top you, that's fine. But I would appreciate a little more courtesy."

He nodded to Marco and Cleo then turned back to Evie. "Goodnight," he said politely and walked away. He didn't want Evie to be any more uncomfortable than she already was, so he figured it was probably best that he made himself scarce. He headed toward the chill-out room, smiling a quick greeting at an older couple he recognized.

"Hi, Aaron," called Pete, one of the regular players, as he crossed the room to the bar. "Come and join us." Pete was with a group of friends, all of whom Aaron knew and liked. But he wasn't in the mood for socializing. Apart from the fact that he was exhausted from the gig, those notes Hunter had been receiving were still playing on his mind.

He declined Pete's invitation, sat down on a bar stool and asked the bartender for his usual beer. As he waited, Mimi, one of the house slaves, approached. When she reached him she sank to her knees before him and waited for permission to speak.

"Yes, Mimi?" he asked affectionately. He liked the pretty sub who was always so eager to please.

"Master Marco asked if you would like to scene with me

tonight, Sir," she said demurely. She'd been well trained—everything about her was beautifully poised and graceful.

He grinned. Trust Marco to want to sort him out. But he really was tired so he leaned forward and kissed Mimi on her slightly parted lips.

"Thank you, sweetie, but not tonight. I'm just having a quick beer before I head off to bed."

"Yes, Sir," she said after a split second's hesitation and rose elegantly back to her feet. Then, before she turned to walk away, she winked at him and said, "If you change your mind..."

He laughed. "Yeah, yeah, I'll know where to find you."

When he was alone again he took a large swig of beer. Mimi had looked surprised when he'd declined Marco's offer. In fact, he was a bit surprised himself. He'd been in the mood for some playtime earlier, so why the hell had he just sent Mimi away?

"Meow." Something brushed against his leg and he looked down to find Christina kneeling by the stool and smiling up at him.

He grinned back and motioned for her to stand up. Christina glanced at the door then back at him, clearly not sure if she'd be allowed up, then she shrugged and stood up anyway.

"Don't worry," said Aaron, helping her up. "I'll tell Marco that I ordered you to join me for a drink."

"Thank you, Sir." Christina slid onto a bar stool and grimaced as she put pressure on the plug.

"Comfortable?"

"Perfectly, thank you."

She stuck her chin out defiantly and glared at him. He glared back until they both laughed at the same time. That was what he liked about Christina. Even though she tried so hard to be a good submissive, there was always a stubborn little streak that would get her into constant trouble. Her sense of humor was infectious, though, which was why she'd undoubtedly get away with more than most. Marco

33

had his work cut out training this one.

He ordered her a sparkling water then narrowed his eyes at her. "So, what did you do to deserve this punishment?"

Christina rolled her eyes in indignation. "Well, Evie said that she thought Marco was scary so I said that he was a pussycat really and *he* overheard me."

Aaron laughed. He could just imagine Christina's face when Marco had made it clear that he'd heard what she'd called him.

"Don't you start. Evie thought it was hilarious too when Cleo brought me down dressed like this."

"Talking of Evie, have I done something to offend her?"

Christina looked surprised at his question. "Not that I'm aware of. Why?"

Aaron shrugged. "I just get the impression that she doesn't like me very much."

"Really? Well, as far as I know she hasn't got a problem with you. I can't think why she'd let you think otherwise. Shall I ask her?"

"No, it's not a big deal. I was just curious, that's all." Aaron finished his beer and decided to put Evie to the back of his mind. Shame, though, she was a sexy little thing and he would have enjoyed a scene with her.

They chatted a little longer and, when Christina had finished her drink, she slid off the stool and reached up to give Aaron a peck on the cheek. "Thanks for the chat. I guess I'd better get back to being a perfect kitty cat."

She'd barely sunk back down onto her knees when Marco strolled into the room.

"Ah, there you are, you can take a break now. Evie's waiting for you next door." Marco stroked the top of her head and she flashed him a quick smile before scrambling back onto her feet.

"Thank you, Sir," she said sweetly before heading back to the playroom.

"She's a cute one," mused Aaron as he watched her disappear around the door.

Marco's face softened. "Yeah, but she needs a firm hand," he growled, trying in vain to keep a smile at bay. "Join me for a drink?"

Aaron nodded. "Yeah, thanks." He had been about to head up to his room, but it would be good to catch up with Marco. They didn't get much time to chat these days.

Marco ordered a couple of beers and they headed toward a vacant sofa at the far end of the room. The music was low so he could still hear the thuds, slaps and sensual moans coming from the dungeon. Maybe he would find Mimi later. It wasn't sex he particularly wanted, but perhaps a good flogging scene would be just what he needed to unwind.

"I don't suppose this is quite the wrap party you'd imagined?" said Marco as they sat down.

"No, thank goodness," sighed Aaron. "I'd much rather be here. I dread to think what it's like in the West Wing right now." He shuddered as visions of Jaymz and Jona screwing the groupies they'd brought with them flashed through his head. Not for him!

He and Marco settled down for a chat about the old days, reminiscing about the time they were in a band together. As Marco explained why the life of a musician didn't lure him anymore, Aaron spotted Christina and Evie walk into the room. Christina, although back on her feet, still wore the cat outfit, including that sexy tail.

As they crossed the room to the bar Evie turned and met his gaze. A deep flush crept up her cheeks and she quickly looked away again. Aaron frowned. *Forget her, she doesn't like you so fucking get over it.* But he couldn't help wondering what the hell he'd done to make her so angry. Because she'd definitely been angry when Marco had told her that he had offered to take Ross' place. The fact that she didn't find him attractive didn't bother him in the slightest, but it did bother him that she acted as though he'd done something wrong.

He returned his attention to Marco, but not before resolving to find out exactly what Evie's problem was.

# Chapter Four

Evie nodded her thanks as Christina handed her a glass of Coke then followed her friend as she headed toward a quiet corner. They found a vacant sofa generously piled with plump cushions and sat down.

Christina moaned as she shifted her weight. "Damn plug," she groaned. "Marco won't let me remove it. It's fine when I'm standing, but fuck it's uncomfortable when I sit down."

Evie grinned. "I can imagine. Sorry I laughed before, but you did look funny."

Christina rolled her eyes and laughed, her earlier annoyance apparently forgotten. "I know. To be honest, even though I was pissed off it was kind of sexy at the same time, but don't you dare tell Marco that."

"I won't. Your secret is safe with me." She winked as she raised her glass to meet Christina's in a toast then took a sip of her drink. "It's nice in here," she said, glancing around her. Despite her annoyance at Aaron Holmes, the room's warm atmosphere thawed a little of the frost still chilling her from earlier. Although it wasn't huge, there seemed to be plenty of room to accommodate everyone. Nobody stood around looking for somewhere to sit and there was no long queue at the bar. It was relaxed and informal. The dark, electronic sound of Blutengel played through hidden speakers, not so loud she couldn't hear anything else, but with just enough volume to add to the friendly buzz.

Christina nodded. "Yeah, this is my favorite room. At two o'clock they put food out on that counter over there. Warm bacon rolls, pastries and hot chocolate. Everyone seems to congregate here around that time, it gets really crowded, but it's nice."

"That's fantastic, I always used to get hungry after a scene," said Evie, her mouth watering at the thought of a bacon roll.

Christina laughed. "Yeah, you and just about everyone else here."

Evie sighed with contentment. Although it had been a while since she'd last been in a BDSM club, she felt incredibly at home here. Unlike some clubs where she'd felt awkward and intimidated, this was friendly and comfortable. If only she could have had just a teeny little scene everything would have been perfect. She looked across the room and frowned when her gaze settled on Marco and Aaron sitting on a sofa almost directly opposite her and Christina. They were deep in conversation and didn't seem to notice her hostile glare.

It was his fault that she hadn't gotten her flogging. If only he hadn't tried to take over...

"So are you not playing tonight then?" asked Christina.

Evie's frown deepened. "It seems not."

"But why? I thought you were quite keen on the idea?"

"I was until Aaron fucking Holmes tried to barge his way in," snapped Evie, surprised at the intensity of her irritation.

"Huh?"

"I was really looking forward to Ross topping me, but then that arrogant sod tried to muscle his way in. He had the cheek to tell Ross and Marco that *he* would top me instead."

The anger thumping through her veins intensified and she threw Aaron another fiery glare across the room. He glanced up at that same moment and frowned when he must have spotted the furious glower aimed at him. *Well, fuck you, Aaron Holmes.*

Christina stared at Evie incredulously. "But why is that such a problem? I thought you fancied him?"

"I do...did until he started throwing his weight around.

He thinks he can do what he wants because he's famous. How dare he assume I'd rather be topped by him than by Ross?" she said angrily.

"No, Aaron's not like that," cried Christina, still looking shocked by Evie's reaction. "When he's at Dominion he wants to forget that he's famous. He hates it when people treat him differently. And, as for the scene tonight, he was only offering to help after Ross bailed."

"What?"

Christina wriggled in her seat then turned her attention back to Evie. "Marco told me Caroline wasn't well after their scene. He said Ross wouldn't be able to scene with you because he needed to look after her. Aaron offered to step in so you wouldn't be let down."

"Oh." *Shit, have I misjudged him?*

"He's a good guy, Evie. He's not like Jaymz or Jona. In fact, he can't stand them. And I'll tell you something else, he's a shit-hot Dom, I've seen him in action."

Evie laughed. "That may be so, but he's still way out of my league."

"Don't be stupid... Oh shit, Marco's coming over." Christina straightened in her seat, groaning as she most probably put pressure on the plug.

Marco strode across the room and stopped in front of Christina, folding his arms across his chest as he looked down at her. A shiver ran down Evie's back as Marco's powerful form cast dark shadows over both of them. How could someone so terrifying be so sexy? He was way too scary for her, although she couldn't deny the strong submissive instinct he brought out in her. Christina was one brave woman to want to be under his command.

"Christina, go to the dungeon and wait by the bondage chair," he growled, sounding every bit as scary as he looked.

"Yes, Sir," Christina said and quickly rose. She winked at Evie before scurrying off leaving her alone with Marco.

"Are you all right, Evie?" asked Marco, still looming over her.

"Er, yes, Sir. I'm fine, thank you," she whispered, feeling very small. What did he want?

"Good. Then there's no excuse I can think of for your rudeness toward Aaron earlier."

Shame washed over her as she shriveled under Marco's stern gaze. "No, Sir," she muttered. "I'm really sorry, I misunderstood the situation and —"

"It's not me you should be apologizing to," said Marco before she had a chance to explain herself. He gave her a curt nod then turned and walked away.

Evie watched him leave the room and wished the ground would swallow her. God, what must he, and Aaron for that matter, think of her? He was right, there was no excuse for her behavior. She'd been completely out of order jumping to such inaccurate conclusions and behaving as if he'd insulted her when he'd only offered to step in at the last minute to help out.

She looked across the room. Aaron was still there, chatting with a couple at the next table. She picked up her glass and downed the remaining Coke, wishing there was a double shot of rum in it. Then she put the glass firmly back on the table, stood up and braced herself for a large dose of humble pie.

"Er...excuse me."

Aaron sensed Evie's presence before he saw her hovering awkwardly in front of him. Her anger appeared to have been replaced with something else. Fear? Fuck, what the hell had Marco said to her?

He smiled in an attempt to put her at ease. "Yes, Evie?"

"I owe you an apology," she muttered, barely meeting his eyes as she spoke.

What had changed her mind about him? It looked like he was about to find out. "Sit down," he said, nodding at the empty seat on the sofa beside him.

Her startled expression told him she had probably mistaken his invitation to join him for a chat for a Dom's order. Her cheeks flushed as she appeared to struggle with her reaction to him. She ran her hands down her dress then slid into the seat beside him.

"I'm sorry I was so rude to you earlier. You know, when you offered to take Ross' place," she said breathlessly. Her gaze was cast downward and her shoulders were tense.

"Look at me when you address me, please." He could usually read a submissive pretty well, but it helped if he could see the expression in her eyes.

She raised them and blushed. They were beautiful— large pools of soft brown framed with long dark lashes. He glimpsed flashes of warmth, intelligence and humor — all the things he liked in a woman. This was looking up.

"Are you apologizing because Marco told you to or because you really are sorry?" he asked, keeping his voice low. He had already silently accepted her apology, but there was no harm in letting her squirm for a while. He did so enjoy playing with a subbie's mind.

She flushed again, looking even more uncomfortable than she'd done a minute ago. He almost felt sorry for her. Almost.

"Marco did point out that I owed you an apology," she said, keeping her gaze on him this time. "But I would have done so anyway. I jumped to the wrong conclusions and my stupid temper got the better of me."

Aaron laughed and she grinned back, looking a little more at ease.

"Christina put me straight," she explained. "I didn't realize Ross wasn't able to scene with me because the other girl wasn't well. I thought you'd told him to back off because you'd decided that you would top me. I wrongly assumed you used your rock star status to get your own way, regardless of what anyone else wanted."

Aaron frowned. She really didn't have a very high opinion of him.

"I was wrong," she added hurriedly. "It's my fault. I'm so bloody quick to jump to conclusions — especially the wrong ones. I'm an idiot. I'm sorry."

"Apology accepted, but I have to warn you, if you were my sub I'd have to punish such insolence." Aaron grinned wickedly and waited for his words to sink in. He got the reaction he'd been hoping for as her eyes widened and her blush deepened. He'd only been joking, but the fact that she'd reacted with such obvious arousal suggested that he might still get to play with this lovely lady tonight.

"Don't worry," he added, giving her a hint of a smile. "You're not my submissive and we haven't agreed to scene. You're safe. For now."

She giggled and her face reddened even more. "Well, you'd have every right to punish me after the way I behaved," she said, gazing at him through her long eyelashes.

He raised his eyebrows. "Hmm, well, I might just do that then."

He studied her more closely. Had she changed her mind about scening with him or was it just banter? The idea of a lighthearted punishment role-play heated his blood as he imagined Evie draped over a spanking bench, begging for forgiveness as he flogged her. Damn if he wasn't getting hard just thinking about it. He'd better change the subject quick, before he gave his own arousal away.

"Would you like a drink?"

"Oh, that's okay," she said, flushing. "You don't have to —"

"I'm going to have a coffee. Would you join me?" he interrupted before she came out with some stupid excuse for not staying to chat with him.

"Oh, well, okay. Thanks," she said, not looking at all happy at the thought of having a coffee with him. If she didn't want to scene with him for whatever reason that was fine, but her reactions told him otherwise, so what was going on?

He signaled for Drake, the barman, to come over, then turned back to face Evie.

"I get the feeling there's something else bothering you,"

he said, giving her a long, hard look. He knew he could come across as commanding and authoritative, he'd been told so plenty of times. Was it just that she was intimidated by him?

Drake appeared and Aaron ordered two cappuccinos. As the barman hurried away to prepare their coffees, Aaron turned his attention back to Evie and raised his eyebrows to let her know he was still waiting for a response. "I make you uncomfortable," he stated. "Why?"

Evie hesitated then took a deep breath and said, "You're Aaron Holmes—famous, good-looking and probably very rich. You get to tour the world and undoubtedly have beautiful women falling at your feet wherever you go. I'm just Evie, a normal working-class girl from north London."

Aaron remained silent as he thought about what she'd said. She'd assumed he would never be interested in someone like her because she wasn't famous or rich. She was wrong on so many levels.

She looked at him boldly, raised her chin and said, "Well, you wanted to know, so now you do."

He chuckled. "Such honesty should definitely be rewarded," he said with a smile. "But let me tell you right now that if you ever talk such rubbish again the punishment will be for real. And, just for the record, I don't appreciate being judged by what I do for a job. This is the only place where people don't see me as Aaron Holmes, the 'celebrity'. Here I'm just Aaron, a Dominant who happens to like pretty, dark-haired submissives with beautiful eyes and exquisite curves in all the right places."

She stared at him and turned almost puce in color.

"Is that clear enough?" added Aaron, not releasing her from his powerful gaze.

"Yes, Sir," she said softly, and looked down when his surprise broke their eye contact.

*Sir?* She'd called him 'Sir' and they hadn't even agreed to play. His need to dominate this gorgeous woman just grew stronger as his cock grew harder.

"Good," he managed to reply through a tight throat.

He smiled as Drake appeared with their coffees. *Good timing.* When he'd disappeared again, Aaron turned back to Evie.

"So, what do you do for a living?" He picked up his coffee cup, sat back and waited for Evie to open up to him. Although her job wouldn't make any difference to what he thought of her, he found that asking people about their work was usually a good way of starting a conversation and putting them more at ease. And besides, he really was curious to know more about this intriguing woman.

"Well, nothing very exciting really," she said as she emptied a sachet of sugar into her cappuccino. "I own a small shop in Highgate and live in the flat above with my cat, Socks."

"Socks?" said Aaron. "That's an interesting name."

"She's a Birman," explained Evie as she stirred her drink. "Birmans have white paws, which makes it look like they're wearing white socks." Her face softened as she laughed. "I know, it's not a very original name, but it was the first thing I thought of when I saw her."

"Sounds good to me," said Aaron, smiling. "What about your shop?"

Evie shrugged. "It's a dancewear shop, specializing in ballet. I'm a qualified pointe shoe fitter and stock a large range of pointe shoes and other ballet accessories. Nothing fancy," she said modestly.

"Don't put yourself down," scolded Aaron. "It's damned impressive that you've opened your own business. I'd like to hear more about it sometime."

She blushed again and took a sip of her coffee. It appeared she wasn't too keen on blowing her own trumpet. He was well aware of how hard it was opening any kind of business in London—the market was highly competitive and it took real strength of character to succeed in such a ruthless environment. There was more to this cute little sub than met the eye and he hoped he'd get a chance to find out what other hidden delights she had to offer. First, though, there was something he needed to get cleared up.

"Are you still looking for someone to top you?" he asked. He was pretty sure she had been hoping for some kink tonight, but the last thing he wanted was to put any pressure on her. If she didn't want to scene with him, he could arrange for one of the other DMs to help out.

"Well, I…" She looked torn as to whether to admit that she did indeed want a scene or not.

Aaron saw the longing in her eyes as she struggled to decide what to do. To help her out, he ran his finger softly down her cheek then said, "I'd be happy to top you, but if you prefer I could ask Marco if anyone else is free. I won't be at all offended if you'd rather not play with me."

She shook her head. "No. I mean, I'd be happy for you to top me, it's just that…"

"What?" he asked softly.

"It's been a while." She looked thoughtful for a moment, then added, "I guess I'm just a bit nervous, that's all."

Aaron smiled and rested his hand on her arm, hoping the gesture would give her some reassurance. "We'll take it slowly. Tell me about the last time you played. How long ago was it?" He believed it was crucial to understand a submissive's past experiences in order to give her what she needed now.

"Well, it's been nearly two years since I had any sort of kink," she said, fiddling with the empty sugar packet. "My last boyfriend was very straight, *very* vanilla and wanted me to be the 'perfect' girlfriend. I tried really hard to live up to his expectations. I wore the type of clothes I knew he preferred, styled my hair the way he liked it and didn't wear too much makeup." Evie paused and ran her hand through her long, untamed hair. "Then one day it dawned on me that I'd become his puppet. I was constantly trying to please him. It reminded me of a Master/slave relationship, but without the benefits. I finally admitted to myself that I could never be the person he wanted me to be and I didn't want to be either."

"Did you love him?" asked Aaron, pleased that she was opening up to him so easily. He found it hard to believe that this strong, independent woman would allow herself to get drawn into such an oppressive relationship.

Evie shook her head. "At first I thought I did, but I think it was more the idea of living such a 'perfect' lifestyle that appealed to me. I think I confused that with my feelings for him. I gradually came to realize that he didn't love me for who I was either. He wanted the puppet."

"Did he know about your kinky side?"

Evie smiled ruefully. "Not at first. After we'd been together for over a year, though, I asked him to tie me up and spank me, thinking he'd love the idea, but he was really shocked. He said all that stuff was disgusting and wrong. Things were never the same after that and it wasn't long before we went our separate ways. That was nearly a year ago now."

"And you haven't done anything kinky since then?" asked Aaron, understanding now why she appeared so nervous about scening again.

"No," she said, cradling her coffee cup in her hands. "It's not that I'm ashamed of being into BDSM or anything, but I feel as though I'm completely new to it again. I'm not sure I'd know how to submit gracefully anymore, or even what my pain tolerance would be now. It's like re-entering a hidden part of my past with no idea how I'll react to it. That's both exciting and sort of scary."

Aaron reached up and ran his hand through Evie's hair, then he gripped a handful of it and tugged firmly, keeping her head in place. He was testing her reaction to being controlled and was pleased when he saw the obvious surrender in her eyes. His dominant instincts surfaced in response, leaving him with a deep need to bend this beautiful submissive to his will.

"Do you just want a simple flogging tonight?" he asked, not letting go of her hair, "or do you want D/s as well?"

A pink flush rose in her cheeks as her pupils dilated. Yeah, just as he had suspected, she was a submissive all right.

"I'd like to submit, Sir," she whispered, her eyes filling with tears. "I've missed it so much."

"I understand," Aaron said and let go of her hair. "I'd like to be your Dominant for the night, if you agree."

Evie gave him a shy smile. "Thank you, I'd like that very much."

Aaron nodded and tried not to look as pleased as he felt. She needed a stern, controlling Dom right now, not some grinning idiot who was deeply flattered that she was offering him the gift of her submission. He took another handful of her hair and stared into her soft brown eyes, making sure she saw the uncompromising power in his own. Yeah, the night was definitely looking up.

# Chapter Five

Evie almost swayed as she gazed into Aaron's hazel eyes. There was a power in them that told her in no uncertain terms that he was in control. She knew instinctively that he was a Dom who demanded complete compliance from his submissives and the knowledge sent a thrill through her. It had been a long time since she'd experienced the delicious giddiness of being in a submissive headspace and now she welcomed it.

"Are there any hard limits or negative triggers that I need to be aware of?" he asked. His voice had changed from gentle to commanding and was even deeper now. *Sexy.* "Don't worry about edge play," he added. "We won't go there tonight."

Evie smiled shakily. Well, that was good. Edge play had never been her thing and she'd never been tempted to try some of the more risky kinks. Dominance and submission was her main fetish. "Thank you, Sir. Edge play doesn't interest me at all."

He raised his eyebrows. "Have you never had your boundaries pushed just a little?"

Blimey, what was he hinting at? "No, Sir. I've always made anything like that a hard limit."

"So how do you know you don't like it?" he persisted. He didn't look critical at all, but the question still made her uncomfortable.

"I-I don't know," she stammered. "I just don't like the idea of being pushed beyond my comfort zone." He was beginning to scare her now. Was he going to take her further than she wanted to go?

Aaron must have seen the alarm on her face because he smiled and took hold of her hand. "Don't look so worried," he said, giving it a squeeze. "I always respect a submissive's limits and, to be honest, I'm not especially into the more extreme side of kink myself, but sometimes it can be highly rewarding to push the boundaries just a little. It keeps the submissive on their toes and they can always use their safeword if it's too much."

Evie nodded, sort of understanding what he meant. Her anxiety eased as she studied his face. It was open and relaxed. She knew she could trust him not to hurt her more than she wanted to be hurt.

"But," continued Aaron, "we're not going there tonight so don't worry. Answer my question now, please."

*Question? Oh yes, triggers and stuff.* "Well, although I like moderate pain, I'm not really a painslut. Oh, and I don't like ball gags," she added hurriedly. "They hurt my jaw."

"Okay. What's your safeword?" He let go of her hand and caressed her arm with light strokes. She shivered as her skin reacted to his touch.

"Chili, Sir."

Aaron smiled. "Is that because you don't like chili?"

She grinned back and relaxed at the warmth in his eyes. He might be a strict Dom, but there was a good heart in that steely chest. "Yes, Sir."

"Are you aware of the club safewords?"

She nodded. "Green for everything's fine, yellow for slow down and red for stop."

"Good. Use any of them if something becomes too much, including chili. I take the use of safewords very seriously, by the way. I *will* expect you to use it if you need to. I don't know you well enough to be able to confidently read your reactions, so that's important, okay?"

"Yes, Sir." Evie nodded, reassured by his words.

"What about sex?"

Somehow the word 'sex' sent a jolt of electricity through Evie that shocked her. She'd normally restricted sex to regular boyfriends and had always kept casual D/s encounters on the edge of platonic. She'd admitted to Marco earlier that she'd found the idea of coming at Ross' command appealing, but what about Aaron? He exuded a raw sexual energy that would, quite frankly, be hard to resist. She knew she'd succumb to his charms at the slightest hint from him, but her earlier reservations about making a fool of herself now resurfaced. *Damn.*

"I...er...I'd rather not." Bloody hell, had she really just declined the sexual advances of the gorgeous Aaron Holmes? Was she mad?

Aaron just smiled and nodded, apparently not at all put out. "Okay, no problem. As long as I know. Now, are you ready?"

Butterflies swirled through her stomach as she nodded. At that moment, she couldn't separate the apprehension from the anticipation. She'd waited all evening for this and yet, now that it was about to happen, she was suddenly nervous. But she trusted Aaron and knew that he would look after her. She was glad now that Ross hadn't been able to top her earlier.

"Good. I want you to get on your knees for me now," he ordered.

The command in his voice sent a shudder through Evie's bones as she slid off the seat and settled on her knees by his feet. Familiar sensations of gooey happiness flooded her as she acknowledged her position. She was kneeling at the feet of a Dom. Oh, how she'd missed this. She instinctively reached her arms behind her back and lowered her head.

"Do you remember our talk earlier about punishment for your insolence?"

Aaron's words hit Evie in the chest and she fought to control her breathing as excitement exploded inside her. He was going to punish her.

"Yes, Sir," she managed to reply as she caught her breath.

"Good. I do enjoy a little role-play and I think this could be just the right reintroduction to BDSM you need, as it involves submission, light bondage, a little pain and lots of kinkiness. If you have a problem with any of that tell me now," demanded Aaron.

Evie shivered at his dark promises. She loved all that and certainly didn't have a problem with any of it. "No, Sir," she whispered. "I'm fine with that."

"Good. From now on, then, the only control you have is through the use of your safeword. You will obey me without hesitation, do you understand?"

"Yes, Sir." She was still kneeling by those sexy New Rock boots and was easily slipping back into the beautiful headspace she remembered from the past. That delicious floaty feeling she could only get from submission — from kneeling by a Dom's feet to being ordered to obey. The fact that the Dom just happened to be Aaron Holmes made the experience all the more exhilarating.

He gathered her hair into his fist and tugged gently so her head was forced back. She was locked into his uncompromising gaze, unable to escape the power that had complete control over her.

"Follow me through to the dungeon, sub," he ordered, his voice now gravelly.

He helped her to stand, then led her through to the busy dungeon, with a light hold on her arm to keep her steady. He marched her up to a vacant spanking bench in the middle of the large room and stopped in front of it.

"Up you get," he ordered, nodding at the sturdy, leather-covered piece of furniture.

Evie obeyed without question and climbed onto the bench. As cool leather touched the skin not covered by the tiny dress she was wearing, memories of past scenes flooded back. How could she ever have thought she could live without this? The freedom of not having to make decisions, the joy of being commanded so effortlessly and the anticipation of not knowing exactly what was going to happen were things she'd always loved about BDSM. She'd been stupid to think that she could pretend she wasn't kinky when she'd been with Vince, but she knew different now. She *needed* this, the way she needed air to breathe and water to drink.

She stopped thinking as Aaron restrained her to the bench. First her wrists, then her ankles, until she was powerless to escape. The knowledge sent a thrill through her.

"Evie."

She raised her head in response to her name and smiled up at Aaron, who was now standing in front of her. A few people had gathered around and the knowledge that she would have an audience added to her growing excitement.

"You were rude and disrespectful earlier this evening," he growled, his eyes showing the displeasure he must have felt at the time.

Shame washed over her as she recalled her reaction to his generous offer. Yes, she knew this was a game, a role-play designed to heighten their experience, but that didn't stop the deep sense of regret she felt about her behavior. Role-play or not, she deserved to be punished.

"I'm sorry, Sir," she managed to reply as steadily as possible.

Aaron gently pushed her head down so her cheek rested on the bench then he leaned down and put his lips against her ear.

"Are you ready to take your punishment, sub?" he asked, his breath tickling her earlobe.

"Yes, Sir," she whispered through a shiver.

"You will take what I give you and you will thank me for it afterward," he said as he lifted what little PVC covered her ass then caressed the soft skin of her buttocks. She tensed at being exposed, but then remembered that she was wearing a thong, so her private bits wouldn't be on display, and she relaxed again.

Aaron's hands were firm, large, the skin a little rough. He kneaded her flesh then stroked his fingers lightly over the surface of her bottom. He moved down to the backs of her thighs, his strong fingers pinching her unsuspecting skin, making her jump, then he rubbed it better again.

"I'm going to spank you now, Evie. You deserve to be punished, don't you?"

*Oh yes, please punish me, Sir.*

"Answer me, sub." Aaron's deep, gritty voice reminded her she hadn't verbalized her reply. He had positioned himself to the side of the bench with one hand resting on her lower back, a subtle reminder that he was keeping her in place.

"Yes, Sir. I'm sorry." An old familiar warmth started to build between her legs as she acknowledged the impending punishment. Fuck, she needed this.

The first slap wasn't too hard, but the second one made her flinch as its heat burned her skin. Then the blows came harder and faster, sometimes landing on the same spot several times, other times seeking fresh skin to torture. His hand was hard and relentless and when he moved to smacking the backs of her thighs she groaned aloud as the pain became almost too much. In between the harshest smacks, though, he soothed the hurt away by softly rubbing her abused skin before resuming the spanking.

It was funny how her mind played tricks on her. She didn't remember that a spanking had actually hurt so much. But, of course, to get to the good bit she had to endure the pain, and the stark reminder was a bit of a shock. But even as she thought it, the impact of Aaron's scorching blows reached right down to the very core of her being. He continued raining the stinging slaps onto her ass and the heat inside her intensified until she almost came from the spanking alone.

But eventually Aaron slowed until he was stroking her burning skin with a feathery light touch. His hand felt hot and so very good as it soothed the stinging ache. He gathered her hair in a fist and pulled gently, just enough to get her attention.

"Are you sorry, sub?" he murmured in her ear.

"Yes, Sir, very sorry." *Punish me some more. Don't stop.*

*Please make me come.* She nearly begged, but she wasn't so far gone that she'd forgotten that telling a Dom what to do wasn't a smart move.

He let go of her hair and moved away again. Then she got her wish as the tails of a flogger flicked across her warm skin. *Ouch!*

Aaron was clearly a master of the whip, because his rhythm and precision were perfect. The flogger was nice and heavy, landing with a thud instead of a sting. It was more like an intense massage — deep, sensuous and painful. Actually, it was very painful, but that was a good thing because it was incredible.

Sometimes Aaron would whip her across her upper back, briefly taking the torment away from her abused buttocks, but when he returned the blows to her ass and thighs the impacts took her breath away and led her deeper into her world of pleasure.

Then, finally, Evie realized that the pain hurt less than it had a moment ago. He was still hitting her just as hard, but suddenly all she was aware of was the glorious sensation of floating through space. She was lighter than a feather and each kiss of the flogger sent her further away from Earth. The silence of space enveloped her and tears stung her eyes as she marveled at the beauty of the planet from such an unreachable height. Time ceased to exist as her body tingled from the effects of being weightless. She never wanted this to end.

Gradually, though, it dawned on her that the pain that had kept her floating in space had diminished and she started to fall back down to Earth. She landed in strong arms that held onto her and kept her safe. When she opened her eyes she found herself staring up into Aaron's smiling face.

"Welcome back," he said softly.

He'd already released her from the bench and was now carrying her across the room. She smiled, wanting him to know how wonderful she felt, but she wasn't able to move her lips to tell him that. So she closed her eyes again and basked in the warmth of Aaron's embrace.

When she opened them again, they were in the chill-out room. Aaron had found a sofa in a quiet corner and had sat down with her snuggled closely against his body. Without a care in the world she drifted in and out of her dreamlike state until, gradually, the tingling in her veins subsided and the cotton-wool fuzziness in her head cleared. She was safe and cared for, even though her protector was practically a stranger. She trusted this man who, despite her aloofness toward him, had given her everything she'd wanted and more.

She snuggled deeper into him. His body heat kept her warm and his scent was intoxicating...sexy. The muscles of his thighs were like rock to lie on, yet it wasn't uncomfortable. Evie sighed in contentment and looked up into Aaron's face. His expression wasn't as stern as it had been earlier, but he still looked every bit the Dom. The Dom who had made her kneel at his feet and had then punished her for being rude. He'd spanked her hard and flogged her into subspace. He'd given her what she'd so badly needed. She didn't normally reach subspace easily, so the fact that Aaron had taken her there so effortlessly was testament to his skill as a Dom.

As she relived the scene in her mind, she became more aware of a different kind of ache—between her legs. Oh God, was she horny. The whole area down there was hot and most likely very wet. A deep throbbing made her press her legs together, but it didn't ease the need to be touched. Fuck, she needed Aaron to fuck her. Hard!

"Sir?" she asked in a croaky voice.

"Hmm?" He smiled down at her and ran his thumb across her cheek.

"I need... Er... I want you to..." Shit, how could she put this politely?

"What?" he asked. "Do you need a drink?"

She smiled. *Oh no, not a drink. Just your body.* Out loud, though, she sighed and said, "It's okay. I'll go and get one in a minute."

"You're not going anywhere," Aaron said, tightening his grip on her. "No sub of mine fetches her own drink while she's recovering from a scene."

Evie giggled. "I've already recovered. I'm fine."

"Good, and that's how I intend for you to remain. Now, tell me what you were going to ask for just now."

Damn. *Oh to hell with it.* "I was going to ask you to fuck me, Sir."

Aaron chuckled. "Greedy little sub, aren't you?"

"Please, Sir?" Evie was past caring that she might make a fool of herself. She needed him to take her, use her, and that was all that mattered at that moment.

But he shook his head. "No, we agreed. No sex."

"But..."

"I said no. Your judgment is impaired right now due to the endorphins. You said earlier you didn't want sex and I'm not about to cross that line. No means no." Aaron spoke firmly, leaving her in no doubt that he meant it.

*Damn!*

Before she could protest that she really had changed her mind, a commotion from the room next door distracted them both. Aaron kissed the top of Evie's head then gently moved her so he could stand.

Glaring down at her, he growled, "Do not move. I'll be right back."

"Yes, Sir," Evie said and sighed. He'd probably gotten bored with her and was going to find an excuse to leave her. Maybe he'd send one of the house slaves in with a message that she was free to go.

But Aaron returned seconds later with a broad grin stretched across his face. He reached out and took her hand then pulled her up to stand. "Come with me. We're going to watch a little entertainment next door."

Evie frowned. Although she was relieved that Aaron didn't seem to have tired of her, she didn't want to move or share him with anyone else. She wanted more aftercare, although she knew full well that she didn't really need any more. If she was honest, it wasn't so much the aftercare as spending a little more time with him. After tonight she'd probably never see him again. But she remained silent and stood up as he had instructed.

He led her through to the dungeon and straight over to the sofa they'd been sitting on earlier that evening. Aaron sat down then pointed to the floor by his feet. "Kneel here," he commanded.

Evie's legs almost gave way as a rush of pleasure tore through her body. He wanted her to stay with him a while longer and, even better, he still wanted her submission. She smiled happily and sank to the floor. When she was comfortable, she wrapped her arms around his legs and rested her cheek against his solid thighs. When he reached down and stroked her hair, she was so happy she could have cried. This was where she wanted to be.

"Watch," whispered Aaron, and he nodded toward the other end of the room. "This is going to be fun."

# Chapter Six

Aaron chuckled to himself as he watched Marco's face darken at two of the groupies that Jaymz and Jona had brought with them from the concert. How the hell had they found their way to the dungeon? Someone must have left the door open. He knew Marco well enough to know that he would never tolerate anyone gatecrashing his precious play space, but he was also well aware that Marco would very likely turn the situation around to entertain himself and his guests. He never could resist a little harmless intimidation.

He looked down at the sweet sub kneeling by his feet. She looked beautiful, happy. Submission suited her. When Evie had begged him to fuck her earlier his balls had nearly exploded. There was nothing he'd have liked better than to make her come over and over before driving his cock into her sweet, wet cunt. He quickly stomped on the excitement that was rapidly hardening him. No, she had been clear before the scene that she didn't want sex and he respected that but, damn, he wanted her.

To distract himself he focused on Marco, who now had a firm grip on a groupie in each hand. One of them, a tall, statuesque woman with bright pink streaks in her short hair, squealed furiously and tried to wriggle free. The other, a pretty blonde, didn't struggle, but looked horrified at the situation she'd gotten herself into.

"Hey, everyone," called Marco to the already attentive crowd. People had stopped playing when the two girls had loudly stumbled into the dungeon. Apparently, instead of apologizing before making a hasty exit, they'd been disruptive and rude and the Dominion members were now baying for blood. "We have some uninvited guests who seem to think it's acceptable to barge into a private area and then show disrespect toward the people they've disturbed."

The members all murmured their grievances, but Marco kept a good-natured tone that belied the steel hidden beneath it. Aaron admired his friend's ability to use humor to deal with difficult situations. But Marco was no pushover and the girls would without a doubt pay for their bad behavior, although not quite in the same way as they would have if they'd been in the BDSM lifestyle.

"If you'd been respectful when you'd realized you'd taken a wrong turn you wouldn't be in so much trouble now. I would have personally made sure that you were safely returned to your friends in the West Wing," said Marco. Although he was addressing the girls, he made sure everyone in the room could hear.

The blonde hung her head, but the girl with the pink streaks scowled at Marco, although she also remained silent.

"But you weren't and so you will have to be punished according to the house rules. You do realize you're in a dungeon, girls? A dungeon with whips and lots of other delightful weapons of *torture*?" Marco emphasized the word torture, clearly aiming to evoke fear in the girls.

The blonde shuddered, whether from fear or arousal Aaron couldn't tell, while the other one tried again to wriggle out of Marco's grasp.

Marco laughed, his eyes flashing with danger. "You've been very bad," he said, ignoring the tall girl's attempts to free herself. "Do you know what happens to naughty girls who are rude and disrespectful?"

"Fuck off," spat the pink-haired girl while her friend stared at the ground, looking like she might like it to swallow her up.

"They get their bottoms spanked," continued Marco. He was enjoying himself now, judging by the mischievous glint in his eyes.

Aaron couldn't help noticing the blonde's deep flush at Marco's words. Her eyes had widened, revealing something that looked rather like longing. And excitement. Well, well, she appeared to like the idea of being spanked.

"Or I could lock you in the cage over there," continued Marco, nodding toward the far corner. "I think my friends here would rather enjoy seeing your pretty little faces behind bars."

Aaron knew full well that Marco would never lock anyone up without their consent, but the two girls wouldn't know that as they stared with shocked expressions at the cage across the room.

"Or maybe I should tie you, one at a time, to that cross over there and try out my new bullwhip?"

The tall one finally stopped struggling and glared at Marco's face, probably to assess whether he was serious or not. When she saw his expression, she wisely remained quiet.

Aaron grinned. Marco had succeeded in subduing the girls and making them realize just what a precarious situation they were in. He had them scared and that, he knew, was their true punishment.

"But, as you're not familiar with our way of life, at least I presume you're not, I'm going to make this a little easier for you. I'm going to give you a choice. You either get out of my sight right now and never darken my door again or you stay and get your pretty little bottoms spanked." He tugged on the tall girl's arm and spoke directly to her. "What will it be?"

"I'll go," snapped the girl, her face now twisted with fury.

"Okay. When you've apologized you'll be free to leave." Marco retained his grip on her, making it clear she had no choice but to do as he said.

"I'm sorry," she mumbled, looking at the floor.

"Pardon? I'm sure my friends didn't hear you." Marco looked around the room and grinned. "Try again."

"I'm sorry." This time the girl spoke more clearly and

attempted to look at the members.

"What are you sorry for, girl?" growled Marco.

She sucked in her cheeks and scowled at him. "For being disrespectful."

Marco waited in silence, as if trying to decide whether to accept the apology while prolonging the girl's shame. Finally he nodded and loosened his grip. Without even looking at her friend, the girl pulled free and ran out of the dungeon.

"Oh dear," said Marco to the blonde still imprisoned in his other hand. "Your pal seems to have abandoned you. I'd be more selective when choosing your friends in the future. Now, I get the feeling there's more to you than Pinky. Have you ever dabbled in BDSM?"

The girl shook her head. "No." Her voice was barely a whisper.

"But you're interested. Am I right?" asked Marco, not sounding quite as fearsome as he had when he'd spoken to the other girl.

So Marco had also noticed the girl's reaction when he'd talked about punishment and spanking. Despite her discomfort and embarrassment, her eyes and body had betrayed her curiosity.

She nodded. "I hadn't really thought about it before, but when I saw what was going on in here I..." She blushed and looked like she couldn't believe what she was saying. "I'm really sorry about interrupting your...er...party," she added.

"To be fair, Marco," called Andre, one of the dungeon monitors, "she wasn't the one who laughed and caused disruption. She kept quiet the whole time. Too busy watching us."

Marco nodded. "Okay. It seems you're not quite as bad as your friend, so I'll go more lightly on you, but you still need to be punished if you decide to stay, do you understand?"

The girl's eyes widened. "I can stay?"

Marco smiled and released his grip on her arm. "Yes, if

you'd like. You also have a choice," he added. He ran his finger under her chin then tilted her head so she was looking straight up into his face. "You're free to go or you can stay and take your punishment. If you choose the latter you can remain here afterward and find out more about what we get up to. You'll be spanked, but will have a safeword so if it gets to be too much you can stop at any time. Afterward, I'll consider the slate wiped clean. What'll it be?"

"I'll stay," she whispered without hesitation, her eyes wide.

"Good. What's your name, pretty girl?"

"Stephie," she replied.

"My name is Marco Alessi. I'm afraid I have a wayward kitten to discipline so I won't be able to do the honors myself. I'm going to hand you over to your ally and my trusted friend, Andre. He'll take care of you," said Marco. The fearsome tone he'd used earlier was now gone, which seemed to put Stephie at ease as she visibly relaxed.

Marco led Stephie over to the same spanking bench that Evie had been on earlier and was soon joined by Andre. After a few hushed words, Marco marched away, leaving Stephie with the tall Dom. He lifted her onto the bench so she was sitting with her legs dangling over the side then spoke to her quietly. Aaron guessed he was probably reminding her about safewords and emphasizing that she didn't have to do this if she didn't want to.

"I stand by what I said earlier," said Evie. Her gaze followed Marco as he strode over to Christina and ordered her to her knees. "Marco is scary."

Aaron chuckled. "I won't deny that he's a firm Dom, but he's got a good heart. Don't tell anyone I said this, but Christina is right. Marco really is a pussycat."

Evie giggled, a delightful sound that sent a warm glow through his blood. He wondered what she sounded like when she begged to come. His cock sprang to attention. *Fuck!*

He quickly returned his focus to the new girl. Andre had

taken Stephie's hand and was rubbing it as if to warm it. Aaron nodded at them and said, "Andre will be reassuring her right now."

Evie smiled up at him, her eyes still glazed from their scene.

The glow returned and flared through him as he gazed down at his beautiful submissive. Well, at least she was his for now. Until he made sure she was safely deposited in one of the rooms kept for private members. He'd kiss her goodnight before walking away, probably never to see her again. For some reason, that thought took the edge off his contentment.

"Come here," he said and held out a hand. "I want to cuddle you while we watch Stephie get her first spanking. I think we're about to witness the birth of a new submissive."

Evie grinned and took his hand. Once seated on the sofa next him, her body relaxed into his as he pulled her into his arms. She was a perfect fit.

"Do you think she'll stay afterward?" she asked as they watched Andre bend Stephie over the bench.

"Yeah, I do believe she will. Apart from the fact that Marco, and Andre for that matter, would never let her leave until they're sure she's all right, she does seem to be genuinely interested in the kink. When I stuck my head around the door earlier to see what was going on she was rooted to the spot, eyes wide and mouth open. She looked like a kid who had just stumbled upon a hidden sweet shop."

Evie laughed. "I can identify with that. I felt a bit like that when I first saw all this, but at least I knew what to expect."

Aaron nodded and stroked her arm. He loved how his touch left a string of goosebumps in its wake. "Yes, it must have been a real shock, even more so to discover that the depravity she was witnessing actually turned her on."

Evie chuckled and snuggled deeper into his arms. Why did such a simple action feel so damn good?

"Do you want a drink?" he asked, deliberately tickling her ear with his breath.

She shivered. "No thank you, Sir."

Not the answer he wanted to hear. He waved at one of the house slaves and indicated that he wanted two bottles of water. Then he tightened his hold on Evie and growled, "You haven't had a drink since before our scene. You *will* drink some water now. Understood?"

"Yes, Sir," she whispered, looking suddenly very aroused again.

He smiled, pleased. She clearly enjoyed submission as much as he enjoyed domination. Although he liked topping subs without actually dominating them, nothing could ever match the satisfaction he got when a woman truly submitted to him. D/s and all the delicious things that went with it fulfilled his every need and more. He tightened his hold on her and tried to ignore the gnawing ache in his groin as images of Evie, kneeling before him and eager to please, flashed through his head. He could almost feel her lips close around his cock before taking him deep into her mouth. *Damn!*

Luckily, the house slave returned at that moment with their water. By the time she walked away again, Andre had Stephie draped over the spanking bench, ready to begin the punishment. Aaron watched, thankful for the distraction, if only briefly, from his visions of Evie's mouth and what she could do with it.

Evie sighed in contentment and took another sip of the water that Aaron had insisted she drink. He'd been right. As soon as the first drop of cool liquid had touched her tongue the thirst had taken hold and she'd gulped half the bottle down.

The sexy sound of a slap on bare flesh made her look back across at the spanking bench. Stephie's punishment was beginning and Evie watched in awe as Andre tapped and rubbed the young girl's skin lightly before delivering the odd firm slap. She guessed that Andre was testing Stephie's reactions as he gradually increased the intensity of the spanking. She was clearly in good hands.

As Andre found his rhythm, Evie snuggled deeper into the warmth of Aaron's embrace. His arms were wrapped around her, making her feel safe and wanted. Every now and again a hint of musky cologne teased her nostrils and she inhaled deeply, keen to catch as much of it as she could.

Stephie seemed to take the spanking well, considering it was her first time. She did appear to be enjoying it although, to be fair, Andre wasn't being too hard on her. Every now and then, though, he'd deliver a harder slap that made her cry out, but she took it in stride and maintained her position on the bench.

When Andre stopped spanking her and leaned down to whisper in Stephie's ear, presumably to check that she was all right, Evie stifled a yawn. It was late and she had to be at work by ten o'clock the following morning. Saturdays were always busy in the shop and she had three back-to-back pointe shoe fittings booked.

"Tired?"

"I'm fine." She didn't want tonight to end, even though she was exhausted.

Ignoring her reply, Aaron gently nudged her. "Marco has given me the key card to the room that's been allocated to you. Come on, I'll walk you up."

She opened her mouth to insist she wasn't that tired, but was silenced by another yawn that she just couldn't stop. She had to admit defeat—she really did need to get to bed. With a reluctant sigh she stood up and stretched, bursting the submissive bubble as she did so.

"It's okay, you don't have to walk me to my room." Now that the evening was over, her earlier concerns about making a fool of herself were resurfacing. She didn't want to come across as needy or desperate, although Aaron had proved that her initial assumptions about him being arrogant had been wrong. Still, she needed to show a little restraint after having embarrassed herself by begging him to fuck her earlier. Had he really been so honorable, or did he just not think she was attractive or glamorous enough to be worth fucking?

"Don't argue. I'm walking you up whether you like it or not. Anyway, you don't know where it is."

Evie shrugged. "Okay. Thanks."

"Do you need a lift back to London tomorrow morning?"

Evie sighed again. Tonight was well and truly over. "Oh, don't worry about me. I'll probably get a cab back with Christina."

"I'm sure I heard Marco mention that she's staying the whole weekend. Meet me for breakfast at seven-thirty," he ordered, evidently forgetting that she wasn't his sub anymore. "Then you're coming back with me."

"Yes, Sir."

If he'd heard the sarcasm in her response, he wasn't letting on. He took hold of her arm then led her through the dungeon. Evie looked for Christina to say goodnight, but she wasn't anywhere to be seen. She must still be having fun with Marco and Cleo, although Evie wasn't so sure she'd want to be in Christina's place. She'd have to be pretty brave to agree to submit to those two.

They made their way through a series of corridors, up a flight of stairs and through a fire door before reaching what was, presumably, her room. Aaron stopped, unlocked the door then handed her the key card.

"There are toiletries in the room, just help yourself."

"Thank you."

Evie shifted from one foot to the other, not sure what else to say. Aaron's tall frame filled the doorway, so he stepped inside so she could pass him, but she still had to brush his body to get through. The point of contact sent sharp jolts of electricity through her, stunning her momentarily. When she looked up at him, ready to bid farewell, he leaned down and kissed her on the lips.

"Goodnight," he said, his voice gruff.

Then, before she could reply, his lips were on hers again, this time smashing into her as he plunged his tongue into her mouth. Her legs nearly buckled as heat spread through her like wildfire. Never had she been kissed with such ferocious passion and never had she wanted it more. Before she could comprehend what was happening, Aaron kicked the door shut then turned her to face him.

"Fuck," he growled as he pushed her against the door, pinning her to it with such force that she was helpless to move.

Then, as suddenly as he had started, he pulled away again. "I'm sorry. I should leave."

Evie pulled him back. "No, Aaron, please don't go. I want you to stay. Please…"

"Are you sure?" His voice was croaky, his breath hot on her face.

"Yes, Sir. I want you to… Look, I'm completely recovered from our scene and am in full control of my thoughts and decisions, so will you just fuck me?"

With a deep rumble he took her mouth again. His hard body still had her pinned to the door. With one hand, he brought her arms up over her head and gripped her wrists. With the other, he slapped her inner thighs to make her part her legs before thrusting a finger deep into her soaked pussy.

She couldn't move, she was his captive, at his mercy, and the knowledge incinerated all remaining thoughts about not throwing herself at Aaron Holmes.

# Chapter Seven

With her legs wrapped around him, Aaron carried Evie across the room to the large king-sized bed. They both fell onto it, Aaron crushing her as his weight pressed her down into the mattress. He pushed up onto his right elbow, easing the pressure on her chest, then stared down at her with a combination of power and raw primal lust.

"Sir..." She was stunned into silence when Aaron practically ripped down the front zip of her dress before pulling it off her. His eyes burned into her as they devoured her body, now naked except for the tiny scrap of lace covering her pussy. Within seconds he had pulled the thong down and, using his feet, had maneuvered it off. She was naked—he was still fully dressed. Somehow that turned her on even more and reinforced her submission.

He bent his head and licked his way across her left breast until he reached her nipple. He flicked it with his tongue, hardening the nub to a point of almost unbearable tension, then took it into his mouth and sucked hard.

"Oh," she cried as jolts of pleasure surged down to her pussy.

His teeth grazed her aching nipple as he pulled away, making her moan out loud before he moved to her other breast. He sucked and nibbled, taking his time as he consumed her, making her gasp each time he bit ever so lightly down on her tender flesh. He tormented her, causing overwhelming sensations that teetered on pain. Then, just as she thought she couldn't take any more, he pulled away and looked back down at her with blazing eyes.

"Do. Not. Move." He pulled away and quickly stood up

before pulling his T-shirt over his head, revealing his broad chest that had a smattering of dark hairs dusted across it. Not taking his eyes off her, he undid the button on his trousers then pulled them down.

Evie gasped as his cock sprang out—thick, long and very hard. He was every bit as well-endowed as she'd suspected and her pussy spasmed in anticipation of being filled.

When he too was naked, he strode to the bedside table, opened the drawer and took out a condom. Evie grinned. Trust Marco to think of everything. Then her mind blurred as Aaron approached her again, towering over her, his cock sheathed and ready.

"You will not come until I give you permission to. Do you understand?"

"Yes, Sir."

"I want to hear you beg for your orgasms."

"Please, I need you to fuck me now," she grumbled, not in the slightest bit amused by his deliberate teasing.

He chuckled, but remained standing at the foot of the bed, glowering down at her quivering body. Why was he doing this to her? Didn't he realize how badly she needed him inside her?

Finally, just when she thought she was going to scream with frustration, he climbed back on top of her and thrust his cock deep into her pussy. She cried out as she reached up to wrap her arms around his neck. She needed to draw him as close to her as was physically possible. But Aaron grabbed her hands and pushed them up over her head, then pinned them down so she couldn't move them.

He fucked her hard and fast, pounding into her with an urgency that matched her own. All she became aware of was Aaron's strong body on top of her, his hands holding hers in place over her head and his cock as it drove into her with breath-taking force.

All her pent-up passion soared to a plateau so high that her head spun with dizziness as he continued to fuck her. She managed to hold on precariously until, suddenly,

Aaron's cock thickened against her hot walls and she started tumbling.

"Please, Sir, may I come?" she gasped as she tried to hold on to the edge for dear life.

"Yes," he hissed, his voice sounding almost disembodied. "Come for me now."

How she had managed to hold on until he'd uttered those words she'd never know but, on hearing them, she finally let go and fell into the most intense orgasm she'd ever had. With the lusty haze swirling through her body she heard Aaron groan before stiffening as he reached his own peak. Her pussy clamped onto his cock as the thin latex filled with his hot, pulsing cum. He released her hands and she quickly wrapped them around him, clinging to him as she slowly came down from her high. But then Aaron's cock jerked inside her again, setting off a series of aftershocks that sent her back up to the clouds with a high-pitched cry.

Finally, when she was left with only enough energy to breathe, Aaron collapsed onto her then rolled off before he crushed her. He made a couple of small movements, presumably as he removed the condom, then pulled her into his arms and held her close.

The last thing she remembered before drifting off to sleep was the warmth of Aaron's body and the security of his arms keeping her safe.

\* \* \* \*

Aaron opened his eyes and squinted to get them to focus on the clock next to the bed. Nearly five-thirty. He'd slept for just over three hours.

Evie was still asleep. He'd rolled onto his back during the night and was pleased that, even in her sleep, Evie had snuggled into him, her head now resting on his chest and a leg draped over his own legs. He ran his hand along her arm, marveling at how velvety soft her skin was. Such perfect skin on a delectably curvaceous body.

His mind returned to their scene last night. She had submitted with grace, once she'd gotten over her initial distaste for him, and had taken her flogging with the dignity of a true subbie. Beautiful and submissive — and, on top of all that, she was intelligent, warm and funny. Everything he liked in a woman. An overwhelming urge to protect and care for her washed over him as he looked down at her now. She had given herself unreservedly last night and he had used her trust to give them both what they'd needed so badly. She had satisfied his need to dominate, to control a sub's pleasure, on every level. This was one special lady.

He hadn't intended to fuck her last night, but there'd been no mistaking the electrifying chemistry between them and she'd made it clear that she'd been just as aroused as he was. Just thinking about it made his heart beat faster.

He could still hear her begging for permission to come as she'd struggled to control herself. What a good sub to remember under such intense circumstances. His blood heated as he recalled the desperate effort she'd gone to in order to obey his wishes.

And when she'd come… Jesus, he'd exploded when her hot tight pussy had milked him as she'd cried out her ecstasy. Damn, his cock was getting hard again.

He grinned to himself as he weighed out his two options. He could either slip out of bed and sort himself out in the shower or… His cock stirred some more. Or, he could tie his lovely submissive to the bed and fuck her — this time slowly and thoroughly. He didn't need to consider it for more than a split second and so he eased himself away from Evie, who stirred, but didn't wake up.

He padded across the room to the large wardrobe and opened the door, being as quiet as he could. The advantage of being at Dominion was that the special suites had a stash of kinky toys available to their occupants. Marco ensured that each room had a generous supply of rope, floggers and vibrators, among other things, and the bed had discreet hooks embedded all around it. Perfect for tying up sleepy submissives. He took the rope and returned to the bed. Evie was still fast asleep. Good, he'd love it if she didn't wake up until she was bound, spread and helpless. After a chat the night before about her limits, likes and dislikes, he knew how much she enjoyed bondage, although if she appeared alarmed even for a moment when she woke up, he'd untie her immediately.

Slowly he took her right wrist and carefully wound the rope around it before securing it to the hook in the top right-hand corner of the bed. He did the same with the left side then checked her bonds weren't too tight. Her eyes fluttered as she stretched her body out. She was beginning to wake up. He'd have to hurry.

He quickly tied her ankles to the bottom corners of the bed and was just standing back to admire the sight in front of him when she opened her eyes. Fuck, she was beautiful – naked and spread-eagled on the bed, her luscious dark hair tumbling over her shoulders and eyes bleary with sleep.

She tugged at the rope when she couldn't move and instantly awoke properly. He watched her, ready to release her straight away if he needed to. Instead of looking distressed, though, her pupils dilated as she looked up at him and a smile stretched across her sleepy face.

"Good morning," he said, his voice solemn. "Don't say a word, you don't have permission to speak unless you want to use your safeword. You're my captive for now and I intend to use you as I see fit. You may come when you like – oh, and you can scream if you wish."

Her eyes flashed brighter with each word, a pink flush spreading over her face as her nipples hardened into lovely dark peaks. Yeah, she was cool with this.

"Thank you, Sir." Her voice was croaky with sleep.

He nodded, then placed a soft blindfold over her eyes. He stood over her, drinking in the sight of his subbie in her bondage. Something about a woman being helplessly bound and available for him to do as he pleased flipped a switch inside him that forced his heart to pound faster and

71

his cock to ache with the need to fuck. He stomped on the urge to take her right then. No, he was going to have some fun tormenting her first.

She trembled, either with impatience or anticipation of what he was going to do to her. Probably a bit of both. Good, he enjoyed tormenting subs with the unknown. He loved that they couldn't tell if he was going to either kiss a nipple softly or pinch it hard. When they expected something to hurt, it was fun to do the opposite then surprise them with pain when they least expected it. His past subs had often called him devious, but they'd always come back for more.

Now, though, he didn't want to play mind games, he just wanted to explore every inch of this beauty's body. He climbed onto the bed and straddled her. A hint of her musky arousal wafted past his nose and his balls tightened. Leaning over her, he brushed her forehead with his lips, then moved them down her nose until he reached her mouth. She opened it, waiting for his kiss, but he moved away again, forcing her to let out a little sigh. He found her ear, nibbled the lobe then licked it. She giggled and turned her head to try to escape. Ha, she was ticklish. Excellent. He'd make good use of that knowledge.

He continued to explore her with his mouth, now running his tongue down her neck. Another giggle confirmed that she was indeed very ticklish. Then he moved across her chest and down to her left breast. She arched upward to help him locate her nipple, but he deliberately avoided it, circling instead around the dark pink areola until she groaned with frustration. He carried on teasing her until, finally, he took the solid nipple into his mouth and pulled it with his lips. It was so hard, so delicious, and the gasp she elicited made it taste even better. She arched to escape the slight pain then moaned when he released the rigid bud. He tormented her nipple until he was satisfied that it was nice and tender, then turned his attention to the other one. By now she was breathing in short gasps, her chest rising and falling in the most delightful way.

He took his time until, happy that he'd had his fill of her exquisite breasts, he moved to her stomach, licking and kissing his way down and leaving a trail of goosebumps across her silky skin. He explored her belly button then the soft fleshy swell of her tummy before continuing to her smooth, bare mound.

She raised her hips in a cheeky attempt to guide him lower and he lightly slapped her pussy in reprimand. Naughty sub. She groaned then lowered herself back down in acknowledgment of her mistake. One thing Aaron did not tolerate was a sub trying to top from the bottom.

To make her pay, he moved away from the heat between her legs and instead ran his tongue down the inside of her thigh until he reached her knee. She jerked when he tickled it with his lips and he savored the brief torture he inflicted on her. Then he moved down to her feet. If he'd guessed correctly, this could be her first scream.

He took her big toe between his lips and sucked. She gasped as each toe got the same treatment. *Now for some fun, little sub.* He ran his tongue along the bottom of her foot, knowing full well how much that would tickle. She didn't disappoint as she jerked against the rope and screamed.

"Oh no, Sir... Please...don't..."

He stopped for a moment and raised his head to look up at her. "Is there something you want to say?"

She let her head fall back down onto the mattress. "No, Sir."

"Then I don't want to hear another word from you."

A deep sigh was her only response and Aaron smiled to himself as he prepared to torture her some more. As he flicked his tongue over the sole of her foot again he lightly stroked the other one with his fingertips. Her screams were enchanting and the way she desperately fought her bonds made him so hard he almost relented so he could fuck her sooner than he'd planned. But he was enjoying himself too much to stop now.

As he licked his way back up the inside of her other leg,

Evie's body went limp. Her legs were spread so far apart that he felt the heat from her cunt way before he reached it. She was open for him, helpless to stop him doing anything he wanted to her. His cock throbbed as he imagined plunging it deep into those hot juices, but not yet. First he wanted to taste her, eat her.

He ran his tongue along her slit, so wet, so ready. Then he flicked it over her clit, enjoying the way she groaned as it hardened. He loved that she was so responsive. The way she'd reacted to his domination last night, her surrender as he'd flogged her and now her pleasure from his touch. He licked her again, this time inserting his tongue just inside her velvety folds. She tasted sweet, like the purest honey, and he lapped hungrily like a bee gathering its nectar.

When he withdrew from her pussy and returned to licking her clit, he stroked her labia before slipping his finger inside her. Fuck, she was so hot, so wet for him. He circled his finger through the moist heat then shoved it farther up, loving the way her muscles seemed to welcome him. When he added a second finger and started to fuck her with them she groaned as a rush of moisture seeped out of her pussy.

He became lost in his task, mesmerized by the feminine whimpers caused by his touch. The only thing he was aware of was the beautiful creature he was exploring, her reaction, her pleasure. But it wasn't enough, he wanted more of her, and so he slipped his free hand under her buttocks, seeking out the delicate ring of muscle of her asshole. How he'd love to fuck her ass. Maybe one day.

He moved his hand over her pussy, soaking his fingers with her juices, then returned them under her and found what he was looking for. He pushed his finger gently and slowly inside her opening. He waited for any sign of objection from her, but all he got was a moan that sounded a lot like pleasure. Excellent—she liked it.

With one finger in her ass and two fingers in her pussy he licked her clit and gave her everything he had. When he felt her folds begin to swell, his cock twitched and he finger-fucked her harder and faster. He felt the build-up, her muscles clamping onto his fingers, desperate now for release, so he locked his lips onto her clit and squeezed. She screamed as her pussy spasmed in response.

He withdrew his fingers immediately, thrust his tongue in their place and kept it there for the whole time she was climaxing. Her taste seemed to intensify, becoming even sweeter, and her juices became thicker and creamier. How he loved the flavor of a woman as she orgasmed, the feel of her swollen pussy as it fluttered like coral rippling in a giant ocean.

As her muscles relaxed her body seemed to melt into the mattress. He pulled his finger gently out of her ass then ran his tongue one more time along her slit before raising his head to look at her. She was still wearing the blindfold, her hair clung to her damp face and her breathing was raspy and deep.

"Thank you, Sir," she murmured, a smile hovering on her lips.

"You're welcome. I'm going to take the blindfold off now, but I won't release you until I've fucked you. This time I want to hear you beg to come. Do you understand?" He deliberately made his tone harsher, knowing the effect it had on submissives.

Sure enough, as if he'd turned a dial, Evie almost squeaked her reply. "Yes, Sir."

He shifted up along her body and reached out to remove the blindfold. She blinked then focused her eyes on him. They were glazed. Beautiful. She tugged on her bonds as if to check she was still his prisoner and her cheeks flushed pink when she realized that she was still tethered securely.

Reaching across to the bedside table, he grabbed the condom he'd put there before tying her up and quickly sheathed himself. He'd been hard for quite a while now and it almost hurt just to touch his throbbing cock. It wouldn't be able before it became impossible to hold back.

Aaron looked down at her and grinned. Fuck, she looked

cute, all tied up and spread open for him. He guided his cock to her entrance, still swollen and slick from her orgasm, and circled her entrance with it. It was such fun seeing the anticipation on Evie's face as she waited to be taken. Finally, when he couldn't wait any longer, he thrust into her, going as deep as he could in one movement. His cock was a perfect fit inside her, enough for him to fill her completely, but not quite enough to hurt her.

He pulled out then thrust in again, going even deeper as he started to fuck her. She tilted her pelvis up to take more of him and he obliged by grinding into her as hard as he could. Their bodies became one, breathing together in deep, heavy rasps as they sought the ultimate reward.

Evie, who would undoubtedly still be sensitive after her orgasm, gasped each time he drove into her, and Aaron guessed it wouldn't take much to tip her over the edge again. He was close himself, so he reached between her legs and lightly rubbed his finger over her clit as he continued pounding into her.

"Argh…"

God, how he loved her anguished whimpers. He tweaked her clit again and she tried, in vain, to close her legs around him. She shook her head from side to side as if trying to regain some control, but she was helpless to stop the mounting pressure.

"Please, Sir, may I come? Please…"

She sounded desperate. Oh, he did so enjoy hearing her beg. Just one more time.

"What did you say?" Aaron was barely able to contain himself.

"Please… Please, Sir. I need to come, *please*…"

Just as he flicked his finger over her clit again he growled, "Yes, Evie, come for me."

She cried out as her body bucked against his. Her pussy gripped his cock with each spasm as she came in spectacular fashion. Then, after waiting for what seemed like an eternity, he let go of his own control and groaned in ecstasy as he exploded inside her. He rode his orgasm with her, basking in the overpowering release as he shot his load.

His cock continued to jerk with little aftershocks while Evie's pussy seemed reluctant to let him go. Every now and again her muscles would spasm, making her groan each time until, finally, she lay still. He looked down at his lovely subbie and felt an overpowering urge to just hold her.

He pulled carefully out and grinned. "Don't go anywhere."

"Ha ha," she croaked back, her voice hoarse from all that screaming.

He quickly disposed of the condom then untied Evie. He noticed she was shivering now. She needed his warmth as much as he needed hers. Once he'd freed her he climbed back onto the bed, pulled the duvet over them and drew her into his arms. She snuggled into him and he tightened his arm around her protectively. Lying still, he focused on the feel of her heart beating against his chest, gradually slowing as her breathing became regular again. In seconds she was asleep while he just lay and enjoyed the first feeling of peace he'd had in a very long time.

# Chapter Eight

Evie stared absently out of the window of the small room at the back of the shop. Her two o'clock appointment had just canceled and Julia, her assistant, was holding the fort, giving Evie a chance to take a quick coffee break.

Her last customer had had unusually wide feet and had needed to try on over fifteen pairs of pointe shoes before she'd found a pair that fitted properly. Evie was passionate about finding the right shoe for the right dancer and was prepared to give as much time to the customer as they needed, but it was hard work. It had taken twenty minutes to sort through all the discarded shoes after the lady had left, making sure they were all put back in the correct place. It was worth it, though, because she had left with a smile on her face and in possession of a pair of ballet shoes that wouldn't damage her feet. Job done.

Running the shop, providing the best dancewear available and fitting young dancers with their precious pointe shoes was the next best thing to dancing herself. Her own flourishing career had been short-lived. Having trained at one of the top ballet schools in the country, she'd just auditioned for a prestigious ballet company when a devastating injury had torn her dreams to shreds. Ballet had been everything to her. The only thing she'd ever wanted to do in her life was dance and, after snapping her Achilles tendon during rehearsals one day, she'd suddenly found herself facing a bleak future without her beloved ballet. Her family had supported her and helped her establish the shop that was now her life. She loved her customers, loved hearing their excited encounters of auditions and shows.

They'd helped to heal her broken dreams and made her feel like she was still a part of the dance world.

Right now, though, ballet was the last thing on her mind. She smiled as she thought back to the moment she'd woken up that morning. She hadn't felt a thing as Aaron had tied her to the bed until she'd tried to move. She'd never felt more worshipped than when he'd kissed almost her entire body before his mouth had found its way to her pussy. Blushing, she remembered screaming through her spectacular orgasm. And when he'd fucked her afterward... She shivered and reached for her coffee before she got herself aroused just thinking about it.

They'd dozed afterward, savoring the intimacy, until Aaron, in his typical Dom way, had told her to get in the shower while he ordered breakfast to the room. They'd sat by the large window with the sun streaming through, drinking steaming hot coffee and tucking into delicious scrambled eggs and smoked salmon. Never had she enjoyed breakfast more than she'd done that morning.

The ride back to London had been filled with idle chitchat and flirtatious laughter. Aaron had borrowed one of Marco's cars, as he'd hitched a lift with Hunter and Fabiana the night before, leaving him without his own transport. When the speedy red sports car had pulled up outside her shop in Highgate, she'd invited Aaron up to the flat for a coffee, but he'd declined. Her first thought had been that he didn't want to see her again. After all, he was a famous rock star and she was... Well, she was just Evie, and would never be like the glamorous celebrities who always seemed to hang around people like Aaron Holmes. She didn't want to be like them either so it would probably have been for the best if they had said goodbye then.

Before she'd managed to put on her 'I wasn't really bothered anyway' expression though, Aaron had pulled her into his arms and kissed her hard. Then, still holding her, he'd asked if she would go back to Dominion with him that night. At first she'd just looked at him, dumbstruck, before nodding her acceptance.

He'd looked genuinely pleased as he'd brushed her cheek with the back of his hand. "I'll pick you up at six o'clock. That's not too early, is it?"

"Six?" Hell, the shop only closed at five-thirty. How was she going to get ready in half an hour? "Why so early?" she'd asked with a frown.

Aaron had run a finger across the creases in her forehead as if to smooth them away. "I know it's early. I need to be at Dominion at seven because I'm meeting with Marco before the club opens." He threw her an imploring gaze then said, "Please say you'll come. You can get ready there."

Of course, she'd agreed. Luckily, Julia had offered to stay and close up the shop, so Evie could run upstairs and pack a bag before Aaron arrived. Now, with only four hours to go before Aaron returned, a tingle of excitement ran through her as she finished her coffee. She was going back to Dominion *and* she was going with Aaron. *Wow!*

Her phone rang just as she was about to head back into the shop. She glanced at the screen, ready to decline the call, but stopped when she saw it was Christina. She answered it before it went to voicemail.

"Hiya."

"I hear you're coming to Dominion tonight," Christina squealed excitedly.

"Bloody hell, news travels fast. How did you know?"

"Aaron called Marco to get you on the guest list. You know how fussy Marco is about doing things properly."

Evie chuckled. That sounded like the Marco she was beginning to know.

"What time are you arriving?" asked Christina.

"Well, quite early actually. Aaron's meeting Marco at seven so I'm going to bring my laptop and catch up on emails and stuff." She could get quite a lot of work cleared in the hour that Aaron had estimated he'd be with Marco.

"Don't you dare bring your computer. I'm still here so you and I can have a catch-up."

"Sounds good. I'll see you later then."

The rest of the afternoon flew by as the shop became busy again. At half past five, as the last customer left, Julia assured her that she would lock up so Evie could run up to her flat and pack her bag.

Aaron pulled up outside just before six, this time in a sleek black convertible. How on earth she'd managed to get changed, grab a sandwich, feed Socks and pack a bag so quickly she'd never know. She just hoped she'd remembered everything — toothbrush, makeup, kinky outfit for later, jeans and T-shirt for the morning.

Her stomach fluttered in response to the smile he flashed at her as she climbed into his car. She was more pleased to see him than she was comfortable with. *Don't get too attached.* But her warning fell on deaf ears as she grinned back at him.

"How was your day?" he asked as he pulled away.

"Busy. How about you?"

He smiled as he navigated through the traffic. "I've been distracted all day. Couldn't concentrate during a meeting with my manager and restless as fuck. And it's all your fault."

"Oh, really?"

He turned and smiled, melting Evie's little remaining resolve not to get too involved. He looked gorgeous as the sun illuminated his face, his dark sunglasses reflecting the glare away. His hair was tied back and a hint of dark stubble coated his strong jaw. He wore black jeans and a black T-shirt, nothing fancy, yet he still looked like the perfect rock star.

"Fancy some air conditioning?"

Although it was a warm day, the inside of the car actually felt quite cool. She nodded, hoping he wouldn't turn the internal climate to arctic conditions. Then she laughed when he flicked a switch and the roof started opening. Because they were only crawling through the heavy London traffic there was no wild rush of wind, but the warm air was nonetheless refreshing as the early evening sun shone down on them.

"How long have you owned the shop?" asked Aaron as he stopped at a red light.

"Nearly five years," replied Evie, wondering how on earth five years could pass so quickly.

"Is it successful?"

"Yes, because I have a niche market. People come from the whole of the South East to get their ballet shoes fitted, and they always seem to return."

"That's great. It's hard in today's world to start something that sets you apart from others. You clearly have. I'm impressed." He flashed her a quick smile before pulling away from the light.

Evie grinned as she swelled with pride. Yes, she'd done all right, but it was nice hearing someone else acknowledge it. "I'm thinking of renting the office space behind the shop when the current tenants move out. I thought I'd open a small coffee shop where dancers can have a drink and a chat as part of their shopping experience. It's a risk, though, the lease is expensive."

"I admire your spirit. You're not only a successful businesswoman, but a resourceful one too. I'm pretty sure that whatever you decide you'll make it work."

"Thanks." A warm flush spread through her as Aaron's compliment sank in.

"So, who's looking after Socks while you're away?"

Evie drew in a sharp breath and raised her eyebrows. "You remembered I've got a cat. Now I'm impressed."

He grinned. "I love cats. I grew up with them. We had five at one point and I loved them all. My mother has six right now and is officially the local crazy cat lady."

Could this man be any more perfect? "How about you?" she asked. "Have you gone any?"

Aaron shook his head. "It wouldn't be fair on them. I'm away so much, either touring or recording." He looked thoughtful for a moment then added, "But I will have cats again one day. So, what about Socks?"

"Julia, my assistant, is going to look after her."

"I'd like to meet her one day," he said, not taking his eyes off the road.

"Who, Socks or Julia?"

Aaron laughed, a lovely deep rumbling sound. "Socks, of course."

They continued chatting as they wound their way out of London. When they hit the motorway, Evie laughed with delight as the wind raged through her hair. She almost regretted not wearing a long floaty scarf so she could feel like a 1950s movie star.

"Are you warm enough?" asked Aaron, raising his voice to make himself heard.

She nodded. "Yes, thanks. So, how about you?" she shouted. "What's next on the rock star agenda?"

His jaw seemed to tighten as his eyebrows furrowed. His whole profile changed from relaxed to…angry. Had she pissed him off?

"I'd rather not talk about the band if you don't mind," he said, his voice sounding distinctly more chilled than it had a moment earlier. Or was she just imagining it?

She frowned and turned her attention to the road ahead of them. Aaron didn't say much after that. He seemed to withdraw into his own world, allowing autopilot to take over the drive.

Evie didn't know whether to be angry or upset at Aaron's reaction to her innocent inquiry. Bloody hell, she'd only asked him about his job, just like he'd done with her. What was wrong with that? Maybe he thought she was just another nosy fan ready to sell her story to the first tabloid willing to pay. Hah, and to think she'd been thinking he was perfect just a few minutes earlier. Well, screw him. She hated men who ran hot and cold.

By the time they pulled into the long gravel driveway leading up to Morgan Manor, the plush hotel that was home to Dominion, she had convinced herself that Aaron was going to send her straight home in a cab. Well, she didn't want to stay anyway. Aaron hadn't spoken a word for the last part of the journey and must have been punishing her for having the audacity to show an interest in his life. She *knew* she should never have had anything to do with him.

Aaron drove around to a small car park and stopped next to a very expensive-looking sports car. Everything about the place was grand and opulent. *This is not my world. I don't belong here.*

Aaron closed the roof and switched off the engine. "Here we are. We'll get you settled with Christina then I'll come and find you when I've finished with Marco."

Aaron's cheerful voice startled her. She glanced at him and was stunned to see he was smiling as if there was nothing wrong. He got out, walked around and opened the door for her, taking her hand as she climbed out. Then he picked up both their bags with one hand while putting his free arm around her shoulders. She allowed herself to be led up the steps and through the huge doorway, where they were greeted by Cleo.

"Hello, darling," she purred as she gave Aaron a hug. Then she turned to Evie and smiled. "Hello, sweetie. Christina is waiting for you in the bar, third door on your left." She nodded toward the long corridor straight ahead of them.

"Thanks." She turned to Aaron, not sure what to say. "I guess I'll see you later."

"You certainly will." He pulled her close and kissed her hard, letting her know in no uncertain terms that he was going to own her again tonight. When he released her she was more confused than ever. Giving him a brief smile, she turned and went to find Christina.

As she headed down the corridor away from Aaron and Cleo, her mind ran riot. What was going on? Aaron had pretty much ignored her for the last part of the journey and now he was acting as if everything was fine. Was everything fine? She really had no idea.

She found the door to the bar and pushed it open. Christina was lounging in a large leather armchair near the window, reading a book. When she saw Evie she put the book down and ran over to greet her.

"Brilliant, you're here." She gave Evie a hug then walked toward the bar. "Glass of champagne?"

"Ooh, now you're talking. Yes, please."

Evie watched Christina in amazement as she filled two extra-large wine glasses full of sparkling champagne. "Bloody hell, Christina, that's a bit generous, isn't it?"

Christina giggled and handed Evie her glass. "Marco said we could have *one* glass of champagne each. He didn't say which glasses to use, though."

"I see Marco hasn't managed to tame you yet, then," laughed Evie as she took the huge glass.

"He thinks he has, but I'll never be tamed. Remember what I said about him being a pussycat?"

"I'd be careful if I were you. Do you remember what happened last time you called him that?"

Christina giggled again and took a sip of her champagne. "Do you fancy a dip in the Jacuzzi?"

"Jacuzzi? I'd love to, but I haven't brought anything to wear."

Christina rolled her eyes, a long-standing habit of hers, and took Evie's hand. "You're at Dominion now, honey, you don't need to wear anything. Come on."

Evie followed Christina through the house until they reached the plush reception area of a spa. Everything was silent and deserted, with only a few dimmed ceiling lights guiding them through the windowless room. Christina opened a door marked 'private' then went toward another door at the end of a short corridor. As Christina pushed it open Evie caught the smell of chlorine as she stepped into a warm and humid room.

"Wow, this is beautiful." The room was dominated by a large swimming pool, its water glistening as the evening sun shone through a wall of glass. Large ferns and small palm trees made the area feel almost tropical while the reclining chairs scattered around the pool looked comfortable and inviting. The thing that struck Evie the most, though, was the fact that there wasn't a single person there.

"Are we the only ones here?" she whispered.

Christina nodded. "As it's Saturday, the hotel is closed to the business guests and nobody's arrived yet for tonight's Dominion. Tomorrow morning it'll be full of people having a quick swim before breakfast. What's different from a normal spa is that half of them will have sexy marks and bruises on their bodies after a night in the dungeons."

Evie laughed. "Fantastic. I remember being really self-conscious about my marks. I made up the most ridiculous stories to my physiotherapist. I'm sure he didn't believe me."

"Probably not. Now, strip and get in that hot tub."

This time it was Evie who rolled her eyes. Even though they were alone, Evie was surprisingly self-conscious as she stepped into the steaming tub. She might be used to being naked in a dungeon at the orders of a Dom, but she usually wore a bathing suit in a pool or hot tub, so this felt strange. Holding her glass well above the water, she sat down and sighed as the deliciously hot liquid lapped around her bare breasts. When Christina pressed a button that started the bubbles, she relaxed some more as strong jets soothed and massaged her body.

Christina maneuvered her body around one of the jets and when she looked happy with her position she raised her glass.

"Cheers," said Christina, her voice echoing in the large room that, apart from the sound of bubbling water, was otherwise silent. They both took a sip of their champagne then Christina gave her a scrutinizing look. "So, Evie baby, tell me about Aaron. Is he every bit as hot as I imagine him to be?"

Evie shrugged. "Yeah, he's hot, but…"

"What?"

"Oh, I don't know. Sometimes he's a bit weird."

"What do you mean weird? Like, crazy weird?" Christina lifted her foot out of the water as she spoke and wriggled her toes. When she appeared satisfied that they were all still attached to her foot, she lowered it again and looked at Evie for an answer.

"No, not crazy. He's probably the sanest man I've ever met, but one minute he acts as if he really likes me and the next he barely speaks to me."

Christina studied her for a moment then asked, "Do you like him? I mean, *like* him?"

Evie nodded. "Yeah, but I know I'd be stupid to think he'd ever want a relationship with me. I could never be like the women he's used to."

Christina shook her head as if to disagree. "He doesn't actually seem that interested in either the celebrities or the groupies who are always throwing themselves at him, though. I've never seen him with any of them."

Evie shrugged.

"I know I haven't known him for long," continued Christina, "but he seems like a pretty grounded guy to me."

"He is. Mostly. When we're together I forget who he is because he's so normal. But then on the way here I asked him a simple question to do with the band and he went all moody on me. It was as though he was angry with me because I'd asked about his plans for the future. He'd asked about my work, so why shouldn't I ask about his?"

Christina shrugged then nudged Evie's leg with her foot and said, "Drink your champagne before it gets warm. Look, I don't know for sure, but I get the feeling that Aaron's not happy with the band at the moment. Maybe he just wants to forget about it?"

"Yeah, maybe. Anyway, he'll tire of me soon enough so I guess it doesn't really matter."

"Don't be so bloody presumptuous. He seems pretty keen on you, actually. Maybe he's thinking you'll tire of him?"

Evie laughed. "Not a chance, although I think I need to be

careful. I can't risk falling for him."

"Why?"

"Christina, it would never work. We're from different worlds. No, I'll enjoy this for as long as it lasts then, when he gets bored with me, I'll just have to accept it and move on."

"Like I said last night, honey, Aaron's a good guy and I really don't think he'd use you like that. Give him a chance."

Evie shook her head. "The way he changed on the way down here has convinced me not to let him get too close. I could easily fall for him, Christina, but I don't want to get hurt."

Christina nodded her understanding then took another sip of her champagne. "It's funny, but I have a similar problem. I really like Marco, but he doesn't see me as anything other than a trainee house slave."

"I did wonder if you liked him more than you were letting on. He seems fond of you, though. I mean, surely he doesn't let the other house slaves practically live on the premises with him?"

"They're not trainees, though. Marco is protective because I'm still new, that's all."

"So there's no chance of you and Marco getting together then?"

"No, Marco doesn't do relationships."

"What about Cleo?"

Christina smiled fondly. "Cleo is gorgeous. I adore her, but not in *that* way. Yes, we have sex and play together, but it's all lighthearted fun."

"Well, it sounds like we both need to be careful not to get too emotionally involved," said Evie, holding her glass up to Christina's.

Christina clinked her glass and smiled. "Yeah, here's to us."

As they drank their toast, Evie silently reinforced the vow. She was going to do everything in her power to protect herself. She'd submit tonight and would undoubtedly enjoy it. Aaron would fuck her again and she would love that too, but tomorrow morning she was going to walk away with her pride and her heart intact. There was no way she was going to fall for Aaron Holmes. *No way!*

# Chapter Nine

"Any news on the psycho fan?" asked Marco as he chopped an onion with expert precision. They were in Marco's small but high-tech kitchen in his private apartment that was hidden conveniently away at the back of the main house.

Aaron shook his head. "No, it's all gone quiet again. The police are no closer to tracing who sent the letters." He swallowed a surge of anger as Fabiana's worried face flashed before him. Who the hell would do something like that? And why?

"Maybe they'll give up now that the tour's over?"

"Maybe, but what happens when we go on our next tour? Or when we release a new album?" If *there's a new album.*

Marco gave Aaron a sympathetic smile before tossing the onions into a large frying pan. "So, did you want to discuss anything specific or do you just want to sample my cooking?"

Aaron sat down on a stool by the breakfast bar and inhaled as the scents of olive oil, onions and garlic teased his nostrils. Marco was a damn good cook, but that wasn't why he was here. "Look, I don't want to drag up any bad memories for you, but can I ask you a couple of questions about the time you quit your band?"

Marco turned to face Aaron with a look that would have been quite funny if things hadn't been so serious. "Are you thinking of quitting Decadence?"

He gave a noncommittal shrug. "Maybe, but we're contracted to record one more album. Hunter is on the verge of walking out, contract or no contract, and I'm not sure I want to stay if he isn't there to keep me sane."

Marco nodded his understanding before turning back to stir the sizzling onions. "The record company would want to bring in another singer if Hunter left, wouldn't they?"

"Possibly, or they'll try to get me to take over. Either way, I'd want out."

Marco added some chopped tomatoes to the pan then covered it with a lid before turning back to face Aaron. "Yeah, I can understand that."

"You left before you finished recording your new album. Did you get heavily penalized for that?"

"Yeah, it cost a lot, but I had a good lawyer who found a loophole and saved me a fortune. As you know, there were special circumstances around the reason for my leaving and that got taken into account." Marco raised his eyebrows. "Are you seriously thinking of breaking your contract?"

Aaron shrugged. "I haven't decided yet. I just want to check out the options. If Hunter stays I think I can just about stand working on one more album, but if he goes..."

"If both you and Hunter leave it'll destroy the band. There's no way they can survive without their two most popular members."

"I know, that's the problem. What about Levi? And the fans? I'd be letting a lot of people down. That's a massive load on my conscience."

"Maybe Hunter won't quit?"

"I think he will if he gets another letter. He's this fucking close to walking."

"If I get my hands on the little shit who's been sending those letters," growled Marco. He lifted the lid off the pan to give the sauce a stir and the delicious aroma of Italy wafted across the kitchen.

Aaron's mouth watered as he watched his friend chop some fresh herbs to add to the sauce. "So, how long was left on your contract when you quit?"

"Like you, we were contracted to record one more album," replied Marco.

"Any regrets?"

"None at all, but I was a mess for a long time afterward, if you remember. You were touring a lot back then so you didn't see the worst of it." Marco rubbed the stubble on his chin as he seemed to drift back in time for a moment. Then he straightened up and turned back to the simmering pan. "What would you do if you did quit? Start another band?"

Aaron had a vision of getting back together with Marco to form one hell of a rock group that would shake the foundations of the biggest arenas in the world. Grinning, he said, "You up for it?"

Marco laughed. "Now you're talking. We could relive the old days."

Aaron's smile quickly faded. "Seriously, though, I've had it with being in the limelight. I'm sick of the travel and the fact that I can't even go to the supermarket without being hassled by fans." Aaron shook his head as he thought back to an incident last week when he'd been accosted by paparazzi while buying a pint of milk. It was beginning to wear him down.

He'd resolved not think about the whole sorry mess this weekend and he'd almost succeeded until earlier that evening. When he'd picked Evie up he had enjoyed chatting about her shop, her cat and her plans to expand her business, but then she'd asked about the band. Almost instantly he'd sunk back under the gloomy cloud of pessimism that had been hanging over him for a while now. He'd spent the rest of the journey worrying about Hunter and Fabiana's safety and what he'd do if Hunter did quit. Evie hadn't seemed to mind his silent introspection though and had probably assumed he was concentrating on the driving.

Marco tasted the sauce with a teaspoon and nodded in satisfaction. Turning back to Aaron, he said, "Well, whatever you decide, don't do anything rash, but let me know if you need the name of that lawyer."

"Yeah, thanks."

Marco threw some chopped bacon into the sauce then

took a couple of bottles of beer out of the fridge. Grabbing a stool, he sat down opposite Aaron and handed him one of the bottles.

"Thanks." Aaron flicked the lid off and decided to move away from the subject of work. "So, how's it going with your wayward trainee?"

Marco chuckled. "She's a minx. She'd make a terrible house slave."

"Oh? So why are you still training her, then?"

Marco smiled, clearly unable to hide his affection for Christina. "She's fun, sassy and sexy as fuck. She's a natural submissive when it comes to sex, but feisty and bratty at the same time. I like that. I like a challenge."

"Yeah, Evie mentioned that she's very strong-willed." Aaron studied Marco for a moment then added, "You're not going soft, are you?"

"What do you mean?"

"Mate, she's practically living here, you're training her to be a house slave knowing that she'll never make it and you seem to tolerate the fact that she's willful and disobedient. Are you falling for her?"

Marco laughed. "No, but I do enjoy having her around. She knows the score, we've talked about her future here and she's cool with it."

"If you say so."

"Anyway, you can talk. Bringing a girl back here for a second night is very unusual for you. Is there something you're not telling me?"

Aaron smiled. "I must admit I do like Evie a lot, but I don't think she likes me as much."

Marco raised his eyebrows. "Really? She seemed pretty keen last night."

"Well yeah, I'd just flogged her, she was high on endorphins. I mean outside of D/s and sex."

"So what makes you think she's not into you?"

Aaron thought back to Evie's aloofness around him before she'd agreed to submit. Last night she'd made it clear she wasn't impressed by who he was, which he'd actually quite liked. But this evening, when he'd thought he'd cracked her cool exterior, she'd seemed to retreat from him again when they'd arrived at Dominion. What was that about? "She thinks I'm an arrogant, self-obsessed rock star who's only interested in celebrities and groupies."

Marco laughed, his deep voice booming around the kitchen. "What, you?"

Aaron grinned and nodded. "Yep."

"Well I hope you put her straight."

"I'm working on it. But..." Aaron stopped and took a large swig of his beer. Putting the bottle back on the table he added, "Maybe it's just as well she's not that keen. I'm very distracted at the moment, what with worrying about the letters and the future of the band. I wouldn't be able to give her the attention she deserves."

Marco nodded, stood up and strode back over to the stove to check his sauce again. When he seemed happy he put a large pan of water on to boil. "I'm about to cook the pasta so we'll eat in about ten minutes. I'll let Christina know that she and Evie need to start drying off." He picked up his phone and quickly keyed a message to Christina.

"Drying off? Where are they?"

"In the spa." Marco grinned, an evil glint appearing in his eyes as an idea seemed to form in his head. "Maybe I should forbid them to put their clothes back on? I rather fancy watching them eat their dinner naked."

Aaron snorted with laughter. "Shit, man, you're living life a little dangerously, aren't you? Christina would fucking lynch you."

"It would be kind of funny to see what they do. It would be even more fun to punish them later for their disobedience," said Marco with a devious grin.

"Oh, so you don't have much faith in them, then?"

"I know Christina well enough by now to know that she'll be so fucking pissed off that she won't be able to resist defying me."

"You're a brave man, Marco Alessi," laughed Aaron as he finished his beer. He had to admit that the idea of setting the girls up for a punishment was very appealing. Of course it would be a fun punishment aimed at giving maximum pleasure, but the thought of pushing Evie to her knees and making her beg for leniency brought a rush of blood to his cock. Oh yeah, tonight was going to be fun.

* * * *

"What the hell?" Christina's face darkened as she read the message on her phone.

Evie raised her eyebrows at her friend's obvious irritation. "What's up?"

"Marco fucking Alessi," growled Christina. She looked up from her phone, her eyes flashing. "He's just texted that dinner will be ready in ten minutes and we're to go to his apartment as soon as we're dry."

"What's wrong with that?" Dinner in Marco's apartment sounded rather nice, actually.

"He wants us to be naked."

"No way, he's joking." Wasn't he?

"That's the trouble with Marco, you can never tell whether he's joking or not. I wouldn't put it past him to be bloody serious though."

Evie frowned as the first hint of worry seeded itself. Surely Marco didn't expect them to walk through the house then eat their dinner in the nude? Did he? She *hated* being naked. Well, at least when she wasn't in a dungeon. "What do you think we should do? Obey him?"

Christina climbed out of the tub and picked up a couple of towels. She handed one to Evie then started rubbing herself furiously. "No bloody way. If that man thinks we're going walk through the house without our clothes on, then be their fucking entertainment during dinner, he's got another think coming."

"I can see your training is coming along nicely," laughed

Evie.

Christina glared at her and put her hands on her hips, but she didn't quite manage to hide the smile lurking behind her scowl.

Grinning, Evie got out of the tub and toweled herself dry. Christina was the least submissive person she knew, at least outside of the bedroom. How she had ever agreed to be a trainee house slave, Evie would never know. She did seem happy, but it was very apparent that the role didn't come without its challenges.

She finished drying herself then hesitated before picking up her underwear. "So clothes it is, right?"

Christina threw her a mutinous smile. "Yeah, we'll show those Doms they can't tell us what to do."

Evie thought about that for a second. "But isn't that why they're Doms? Because they *can* tell us what to do?"

"Don't be so bloody logical."

"They might punish us for disobeying them," mused Evie.

Christina raised her chin in defiance. "They can punish us all they like, but I'm *not* walking through this house without my clothes on."

"We can always take them off again just before we get to Marco's apartment. They'd never know."

"Yes they would, there are security cameras everywhere. And anyway, even if they did believe it I'm still not going to eat my dinner whilst sitting naked on the floor like a fucking animal."

Evie's eyes widened. "On the floor?"

"Oh yeah, trust me, once Marco gets going he won't stop at just making us get naked. He might even insist that we kneel by their feet and wait for them to feed us titbits." Christina's face was a picture of indignant protest as she threw the towel on a chair.

"So we defy them and risk punishment?" reiterated Evie, needing to be completely clear on their plan of action.

"Hell, yeah. Are you up for it?"

"Absolutely. We'll take our punishment with stoic pride and stand our ground whatever the consequences," cried Evie, holding up her empty glass in a mock salute.

Christina laughed and wriggled into her jeans. "Let's do this."

As soon as they were dressed they made their way to Marco's apartment, Christina leading the way. By the time they reached what looked like the entrance to a private area, though, their bravado had faded a little.

"You do realize that we're going to pay for this, don't you," whispered Christina, looking a little worried now.

"Shall we quickly take our clothes off before we go in?" Now that the buzz of the Jacuzzi and champagne was wearing off, so was Evie's fighting spirit. She swallowed and hoped Christina would relent.

"Nah, too late. Come on, let's go to battle."

When Christina pushed open the door, Evie found herself in what looked like a perfectly normal apartment. They were in a large airy hallway with several doors leading off it. Christina headed straight for the door directly opposite and Evie followed, now overcome with nervous butterflies. Were the men going to be angry with them for such deliberate defiance? Would they order them to strip in front of them? More to the point, would she do it if they did? Probably not, given her issues with her body. This didn't bode well.

As soon as Christina pushed the door open, Evie was greeted by the most incredible smell of Italian food. Her stomach growled with hunger, but then it flipped with nerves as she and Christina were met with stern glares. Evie's legs weakened as she did her best to look unruffled by the two imposing men leaning against a breakfast bar with their arms crossed in disapproval. She'd never known any Dom to be so commanding without needing to say a word and now she was faced with two of them. *Shit.*

"Hi," said Christina, her voice sounding almost squeaky. She flashed the men a smile obviously designed to melt hearts then sashayed over to Marco. When she reached him she stood on tiptoes and planted a kiss on his lips, clearly trying her hardest to soften him with her feminine charms.

"You're late," Marco said, his eyebrows drawn together in disapproval.

"Are we? Oh, sorry," said Christina, looking confused.

Evie frowned. She and Christina had been so taken up with worrying about the clothes issue that they hadn't even considered the time. She braced herself for a lecture on timekeeping and obedience, but Marco just nodded and indicated for the girls to sit down at the table on the other side of the breakfast bar. He made no mention of their clothes. She threw a puzzled look at Christina, who looked just as mystified. Why didn't they mention the fact that they were fully dressed? Somehow, that made her far more nervous than she would have been if Marco had confronted them about it. She knew the men wouldn't let it go though – she and Christina would pay at some point.

Aaron showed Evie to her seat, pulling out the chair for her. As she sat down he casually placed his hand on the back of her shoulder. The subtle contact was enough to send little shivers of pleasure through her veins. She looked up at him and was stunned by the combination of power and warmth looking back at her. Such an unusual and compelling contrast. She shivered again and looked away before she fell completely under his spell.

Evie's attention was diverted when Marco placed a large bowl of steaming fusilli, covered with what looked like a rich tomato sauce and fresh basil, on the table. Her mouth watered as the delicious smell reminded her of how hungry she was.

When they were all seated, Marco filled their glasses with white wine straight from the fridge. He then raised his glass and fixed his eyes on herself and Christina. "Here's to naughty subs and the Doms who get to punish them."

Evie's stomach flipped while Christina giggled and took a large sip of her wine. It appeared that her friend was not in the slightest bit bothered by Marco's threat.

The meal turned out to be one of the most enjoyable ones she'd had in a very long time. Not only was the food delicious, the conversation was relaxed and jovial. Marco and Aaron had the same sense of humor and had the girls howling with laughter at their hilarious banter.

When she had finished eating, Evie sat back and sipped her wine as Marco and Aaron debated whether acoustic or electric guitars were better. They were just like big kids comparing their boy's toys, which was really quite sweet. Seeing them like this, regular guys talking about normal stuff, made them more human and so much less intimidating. She forgot Aaron was a famous rock star who she had been convinced wouldn't be interested in her. Even Marco seemed less scary, and Evie was glad of the chance to see them both in this new light.

Later, Marco cleared the empty plates away, refilled their wine glasses then sat back down and looked straight at Evie. The relaxed, carefree man of a few minutes ago was gone and had been replaced with the scary Dom she'd met only yesterday. Her belly fluttered as his dark gaze seemed to penetrate her. God, the man was intense.

"So, Evie, are you looking forward to tonight?" Coming from Marco that almost sounded like a threat.

She glanced at Aaron and tried her best to keep the warm flush from her face as she imagined what he might do to her later. "Er, yes, thanks. Very much." *I think.*

"You will have to be punished for your disobedience, of course," he said smoothly, returning his attention to Christina as she spoke.

Evie gulped the last of her wine down. Except for Marco's toast, not a word about the fact that they had ignored his order had been uttered and Evie had almost forgotten about it. She glanced back at Aaron to try to gauge whether Marco's words had included her. He nodded darkly, just a hint of a smile stopping him from looking outright scary.

"Talking of punishment," quipped Christina, still not

looking in the least bit worried, "What happened to that girl last night? What was her name, Stephie?"

Marco grinned knowingly back at Christina. "Nice avoidance tactic, sub."

Christina had the grace to blush, but remained silent in an obvious attempt to get Marco to answer her question and thereby divert the focus away from herself. Evie had a feeling her friend's attempt at manipulating Marco would be futile. When Marco took a handful of Christina's hair and growled something in her ear, Evie knew he'd made it perfectly clear who was in control. She grinned as Christina's face paled as whatever Marco had said sank in.

Apparently satisfied that he'd made his point, Marco let go of Christina's hair, sat back in his seat and smiled. "I thought Stephie took her punishment well," he said with a hint of admiration in his voice. "She ended up staying right until the end. Andre looked after her and found her a room away from the musicians and the other groupies. Apparently she didn't want to be anywhere near them."

"At least she's got some sense, then," muttered Christina. "What a bunch of tossers."

"Yeah, I can vouch for that," said Aaron, his face darkening.

Evie's mind drifted back to Stephie's reaction to being caught snooping the night before. Her embarrassment had seemed genuine and she had looked quite upset about what had happened, unlike her friend. "It's odd," she said with a frown, "because she didn't seem like she belonged with them. She appeared almost grateful that she didn't have to go back with that other girl."

"There's clearly no love lost there. She sure as hell got more than she bargained for last night," said Marco, grinning.

"Well, at least now she's had her eyes opened to a lifestyle that could potentially make her very happy. She did seem keen on staying, didn't she?" Evie smiled as she recalled the girl's obvious battle with herself as she'd agreed to stay and take her punishment. She could identify with that.

Marco nodded. "Andre said she was a natural. I've invited her back in the future so she can explore the idea a bit further."

"I knew you were a softie," giggled Christina, looking at Marco with adoring eyes.

"Don't you dare repeat that to anyone outside of this room," Marco said, smiling. "But, for your information, there won't be any soft side to me tonight." He looked across at Evie then back at Christina. "Aaron and I will be expecting you both to surrender without any questions or smart remarks. We expect your complete obedience, understood?"

"Yes, Sir," said Christina, visibly melting at Marco's words.

Evie shivered. What was it about a Dom demanding a sub's compliance? It was damn hot. She shifted in her seat as little waves of excitement slowly built somewhere deep inside her. When she looked at Aaron she was stunned by the fire smoldering in his eyes. Her heartbeat skyrocketed as she found herself unable to look away. Somehow she felt connected to him by some sort of invisible force, bound to him by imaginary rope. She couldn't escape even if she wanted to.

"Evie, the same goes for you," said Aaron, his dark gaze engulfing her. "If we play again tonight, I'll expect the same beautiful submission you gave me last night. You will hand over all your control. Do you agree to that?"

"Yes, Sir," she said, her voice trembling. At that moment she would happily have stripped naked if he'd demanded it. Somehow, all her earlier reservations and defiance drained out of her and left her with the old, familiar need that clenched her insides. But this time it was different. This time it wasn't just the need to submit that overpowered her, it was the fact that she'd be submitting to Aaron that left her practically breathless. Despite the fact that she'd sworn that she wasn't going to allow herself to get too close to Aaron

Holmes, she knew she would give him everything she had tonight, and more if he demanded it. *Oh crap, I'm doomed.*

# Chapter Ten

"Marco is going to do *what?*"

Christina grinned at Evie's shocked expression. "He's doing a violet wand demo tonight. Don't you like electro play?"

Evie shuddered. "No. I hate everything about it — the feel, the sound, the smell. Everything." She'd only tried it once, but she'd been so scared of being electrocuted or burned that she'd used her safeword after just five minutes. *Never again.*

"I quite like it," said Christina as they watched Marco laying out a selection of nasty-looking glass attachments. "But he's using Mimi tonight because she's really into electro, which means he can push her a lot further than he can me."

"That must be a relief," said Evie, her eyes darting everywhere except for the stage.

"Sort of, but..." Christina frowned and ran her hand through her long golden hair. "He usually uses me for the demos."

"You're not jealous, are you?"

"No. Well, not really, but..."

Evie watched her friend bite her lip and felt a pang of sympathy for her. She put her arms around Christina and hugged her. "Remember, don't get too attached, sweetie."

"I know," whispered Christina, tightening her arms around her.

"Don't forget what you just said, Mimi can take more from the violet wand than you can so it makes sense that he uses her."

She felt Christina straighten herself up before she pulled away. She flicked her hair back then grinned at Evie. "Yeah, it's cool."

Evie squeezed her hand as Aaron approached carrying three bottles of water. "No more wine?" she whispered, frowning.

Christina shook her head. "Marco and Aaron are really fussy about alcohol when we play. I'm surprised they let us drink wine at dinner, to be honest."

Aaron reached them before Evie could reply, so she swallowed her sarcastic retort and took the bottle Aaron held out to her. She knew alcohol and kink didn't mix, but still... It was going to take a while before she got used to having to do as she was told again. Ironically, obeying a Dom had been one of the things she had always loved about D/s, yet it had been so long since she'd had anything to do with BDSM that she'd forgotten that it didn't come easily. Outside of the D/s dynamic she didn't appreciate being bossed around.

"Are you looking forward to the demo?" asked Aaron as he slipped his arm around her waist. "Marco's pre-club night scenes are legendary."

"So I hear," laughed Evie, glancing around the dungeon. It was already packed full of eager kinksters, even though the club had only just opened. The atmosphere was already charged with excited anticipation as the guests watched Marco prepare for the demo.

When Marco appeared satisfied he had everything he needed, he had Mimi, who was naked, sit down on a wooden chair, then he started binding her with rope. Evie swallowed nervously as Mimi lost the freedom of movement — and the possibility of escape. Being the subject of electro play was bad enough, but being restrained so you couldn't get away was downright terrifying. She shuddered as Marco secured the girl to the chair, her arms tied to the armrests and her legs spread and bound to the chair legs. He wound the rope mercilessly around her torso, above and below her breasts and across her stomach, making her completely immobile and helpless. Finally, he stepped back and inspected the bound girl. He turned to the audience and smiled, revealing a lethal flash of danger that reinforced his dark reputation. Anyone who didn't know him would be seriously intimidated now, but Evie knew that Mimi was in safe hands.

Then the lights dimmed and the crowd fell silent. Marco started by massaging Mimi's neck and shoulders until she visibly relaxed. Then he whispered something in her ear and she looked up at him and nodded. Her wide eyes betrayed the outward appearance of calm—she was nervous. But the tiny hint of apprehension that Evie had just seen was overshadowed by absolute trust. She kept her eyes on him as he took a fistful of her hair and firmly pulled, forcing her head back while he glared down at her. It was a sight of pure power and domination and Evie's legs trembled as if she herself were in Mimi's place.

Then Marco picked up the wand and switched it on. The glass bulb emitted a soft purple light and, despite her fear, Evie found she couldn't take her eyes off the ethereal glow. When the low humming sound reached her ears though, she jumped as if it had touched her.

Aaron's arm tightened around her. "You okay?"

"Uh-huh." She smiled up at him, not wanting him to know about her fear of electro. *Never tell a Dom your weaknesses.*

Marco started by running the wand along the rope that bound Mimi to the chair. The darkened space around the stage lit up in purple bursts as the wand crackled on contact. Evie clenched her fists and braced herself for Mimi's screams as the torture began. But Mimi sat quietly with her eyes closed, looking surprisingly calm under the circumstances.

As Marco had insisted that Christina, Aaron and herself were to stand at the front, so close to the stage that Evie could hear Mimi's shallow breaths, the metallic smell of ozone didn't take long to reach them. Evie screwed up her nose — she *hated* that smell. She soon forgot about it, though, when she noticed something incredible — the rope around Mimi's body lit up with little sparks of light. She gasped as the light moved along the rope, following Marco's trail.

"It's conductive rope," whispered Aaron.

"Wow." She'd never seen anything like it. It was really rather beautiful.

Marco upped the intensity of the power, making the crackling electrodes sound even scarier, but Mimi remained relaxed. In fact, she looked as if she was actually enjoying it. Evie shook her head in amazement as the girl barely flinched when sparks flew off her left breast. But then Marco changed the attachment to one with a much smaller surface area and this time Mimi did jump as Marco continued to fry the poor girl.

Evie was mesmerized as she watched the scene. At one point, Marco attached what looked like a glass comb onto the wand and ran it through Mimi's hair. Evie was so entranced that she almost felt the tingling current run across her own scalp, as if it had been done to her. She rubbed her head subconsciously, not taking her eyes off Mimi or the wand.

Marco changed the attachments several times and, judging by Mimi's reactions, they obviously felt very different. Some of them had Mimi moaning in obvious pleasure while others had her writhing in her bonds. It was extremely erotic and, despite her own apprehension about the scene, Evie was drawn deeper into the heady atmosphere.

Just when Evie thought things couldn't get much more intense, Marco signaled to Christina and had her join him on the stage. He whispered something to her and she nodded her understanding. Then Christina stood behind the chair Mimi was sitting on and in front of Marco. When the humming started again Marco used the wand on Christina's back, but when she started running her fingers along Mimi's arm it was there that the sparks flew. Wow,

Marco was using Christina as an electrical conductor.

Evie became more and more intoxicated by the sight in front of her as Christina moved around and ran her nails down Mimi's legs, sending tiny sparks flying as she did so. Marco followed, keeping the wand buzzing against Christina's skin the whole time. The light and smell had somehow become an intrinsic part of the charged air surrounding the stage as Marco, Christina and Mimi were simultaneously connected by the power of the wand. Marco's expression was one of pure concentration as he regulated the intensity while Christina had a look of complete serenity about her as she continued to touch Mimi's body. Mimi's head had dropped as if she was asleep, a sure sign that she was in subspace. *Wow, is it really possible to reach subspace from electro play?*

When Marco slowed things down and the scene ended the audience sighed collectively for a second before erupting into loud applause. Leaving the equipment to be put away later, Marco untied Mimi then led both the girls to a nearby sofa. He sat down first then pulled the girls down, one on either side of him, and cuddled them both. Evie smiled as she watched him softly kiss the heads of both girls in turn, their bodies melting into his as they recovered from the scene.

"Did you enjoy that?"

Evie looked up into Aaron's face and smiled. "Yes, Sir." Incredibly, despite her dislike of the violet wand, she had enjoyed it. As she studied him she was stunned by the arousal that shone from his eyes. Oh crap, it looked like Aaron was a fan of electro play. She crossed her fingers and hoped that Aaron wouldn't get any ideas about trying it on her. Much as she had enjoyed watching it, there was no way she wanted to try it herself. *No way!*

Aaron grinned to himself and made a mental note to remember Evie's reaction to tonight's demo. Although she had clearly enjoyed the scene, her tense posture, clenched fists and jumpiness had told him that Evie wasn't a fan of electro. He'd love to show her the beauty of the wand one day, to change her mind about it and even have her begging for more. Oh yes, if ever he wanted to push her boundaries a little, he now knew how to do it.

Not tonight, though. Tonight he had other plans for this pretty subbie. The joint punishment with Christina that he and Marco had planned would make them both scream and giggle at the same time. As soon as Mimi and Christina had recovered from the demo, he and Marco would tie their subs together and give them a flogging they wouldn't forget in a hurry. Christina wasn't very spaced out and was probably okay to play now, but Mimi needed Marco's attention for a while longer and he knew that Marco would stay with her until she was fully recovered. That gave him a bit of time to get Evie into the right headspace.

"Follow me," he said, his voice gruff, narrowing his eyes at Evie and leaving her in no doubt that the game was beginning. He strode toward the chill-out bar, confident that Evie would follow. He loved the fact that this strong, feisty lady was so naturally submissive when it came to D/s. It was a combination he found addictive and thrilling, especially in the early stages of play when her dominant side still struggled with giving up control. Fuck, it was sexy to watch her battle with herself as she slowly melted under his command. She was beautiful and graceful in her submission and he was going to nurture it so she could reach the euphoric heights that total surrender could take her to.

He stopped at a sofa in a discreet corner of the room then turned to find Evie behind him, watching a group of people chatting about the electro scene at the bar. He took her chin firmly in his hand and turned her head so she was forced to look at him. "Eyes on me," he growled. Oh yeah, the first sign of surrender flickered through her eyes as she absorbed the dominant energy he was emanating. His blood warmed in response, feeding his natural urge to control this gorgeous woman.

He let go of her chin then grabbed a handful of her hair and tugged it toward him, capturing her gaze with a fire that raged deep inside him. Her pupils grew bigger as her eyes watered – he could almost see the reflection of the flames from within his soul.

"Do you agree to submit to me again tonight?" Although he'd already asked her earlier, he wanted to be absolutely sure that she really wanted this and hadn't agreed just because Marco and Christina had been listening. Now he made his voice stern, wanting her to know that she'd be consenting to being dominated in the most primal way.

"Yes, Sir," she gasped, her voice raspy as she struggled to keep her emotions in check.

"The only control you will have will be by using your safeword. Your purpose will be to serve me, to obey me and to please me. Do you understand?" He wanted his words to dispel any remaining control and internal resistance that might still be lingering.

"Oh, yes, Sir."

Yeah, she was getting there very nicely. "Good girl. Kneel."

With her face flushed, she sank to the floor at his feet. Without appearing to think about it she put her arms behind her back and looked down at the floor. *Nice.* As his eyes roamed over Evie's body he noticed her shiver, hopefully in anticipation of what was to come. *Fuck, she's beautiful.* She was wearing the shortest leather miniskirt, so short that the lower part of her ass peeped sexily out beneath the hem. Sheer black stockings, high-heeled shoes and a shiny PVC bra were the only other items adorning her body. She just needed one more thing. He pulled a leather collar from his pocket and held it up for Evie to see.

"Lift your hair for me."

She quickly complied and reached up to scoop her hair off her neck. Such a beautiful neck, perfect for kissing and biting. He fastened the collar then sat back and studied her.

*Gorgeous.* The sight of Evie wearing his collar reinforced his need to control her. How fucking lucky was he that the wrap party had been moved to Dominion? Christina had said that Evie had only agreed to come after the venue had been changed. The thought that he might never have met her chilled him. He didn't know why, but he knew she was special. He was going to make the most of every moment he had with her and give her every ounce of his dominance to satisfy both their kinky cravings. Starting right now. "Evie, look at me."

She raised her eyes and gazed up at him. The hint of worry that had shadowed her face earlier was gone. The corners of her luscious mouth were ever so slightly turned up, baring just a hint of a smile. She looked happy, content even. Good, because now he was going to take her further into the headspace she needed to be in.

"Remove your bra and present your breasts to me."

Aaron was delighted to see the pink blush that swept over Evie's face, but her hesitation told him that she still wasn't completely there yet.

"Evie, I won't tell you again. Remove. Your. Bra. *Now!*"

Oh, how he loved to see her in such a quandary, battling with her spirited and more reserved side while the submissive inside her screamed to get out. Aaron waited, sure in the knowledge that she would obey. She wanted this, and when she surrendered she would finally be in the headspace that both of them needed her to be in. When she let out a little sigh and reached for the clasp at the front of her bra, he smiled to let her know that he was pleased. She flushed as the straps slid down her arms and the bra fell to the ground, exposing her gorgeous full breasts. Still looking at him, she reached down and lifted her tits from beneath as if offering them to him on a silver platter. Her dark pink nipples were bunched into hard peaks and he couldn't resist the temptation to run his thumb over one of them then pinch it hard enough to elicit a sweet little gasp.

"Good girl."

He watched her melt a little more and knew that she was there. Her whole posture was different now — her back was straighter and shoulders relaxed. Beautiful. Submissive.

"You can let go of your breasts now. Rest your head on my lap."

She smiled up at him, clearly happy with his command. He had yet to meet a subbie who didn't love laying her head on her Dom's lap while kneeling by his or her feet. What they didn't know was that the feeling was reciprocated. Having a submissive willingly show such trust and subservience brought a sense of such utter wellbeing and satisfaction to a Dom that the balance was evened. The desire to dominate and control the submissive merged with the instinctive need to protect and care for them.

As she rested her cheek on his thigh, she sighed, and when he stroked her hair she almost purred like a kitten. *My kitten.*

They remained like that for a while, until Marco strode over with Christina, who was now naked. He smiled as he looked down at Evie, who seemed oblivious to their arrival. Then he sat down next to Aaron and nodded at Christina, who dutifully sank to her knees. Evie raised her head and sat back on her haunches. The sight of the two gorgeous submissives kneeling by his and Marco's feet sent blood gushing to his cock, and an image of Evie wrapping her lips around it made it throb painfully. He glanced at Marco, who grinned back at him, clearly thinking the same thing. What better way was there for the subs to thank their Doms for their joint punishment than with a bit of cock worship?

"Christina. Evie." Marco's deep voice had both girls looking up at him, their eyes wide. "Earlier this evening I gave you an order. I asked you to be in my apartment in ten minutes *and* I wanted you naked. Apart from the fact that you were late, you were also both fully clothed. You disobeyed me. Bad subs."

Christina and Evie quickly glanced at each other then looked back up at Marco, their faces making it clear that they knew they were in trouble. Aaron had to smother a smile as he watched them struggle with their composure. Evie gazed at him and he hardened his eyes as he glared back at her. This was going to be fun.

"You will, of course, be punished. Aaron and I are going to flog you hard and will end the punishment with ten strikes each of the cane."

The mixture of apprehension and enthusiasm in the girls' eyes was fuel to Aaron's growing excitement. When Marco handed him a leash and a pair of leather cuffs, he nodded his thanks and stood up, towering over Evie to make her feel as small as possible. They both attached the leashes to the girls' collars, then fastened the cuffs securely around their wrists. Giving Evie's leash a quick tug, Aaron said, "You will both crawl on your hands and knees. Follow us."

He and Marco led the girls into the main dungeon and stopped in the middle of the room, right below a mechanical hoist. Marco had the girls stand up, facing each other, then he clipped their wrist cuffs together before getting them to raise their arms so he could attach the cuffs to a ring on the lowered hoist. When they were securely hooked up Marco flashed the girls a wicked smile as he pressed a button, raising their hands upward. The hoist rose higher and higher, stretching the girls, and only stopped when they were standing on tiptoe.

Aaron grinned. Fuck, they looked sexy. They were cheek to cheek, their bodies pressed together, tits pushing into tits and groin rubbing against groin. They were restrained, helpless and forced to endure their punishment together. His cock strained against the tight leather of his trousers as he helped Marco check that the cuffs weren't cutting into their skin. When they were both satisfied that the girls were safe in their bonds they stepped back and crossed their arms, making sure the girls could see their stern faces.

Aaron stood behind Christina so that Evie could see him over Christina's shoulder. She looked so damn cute. He leaned over Christina's shoulder and kissed Evie lightly on the lips then whispered in her ear, "Enjoy your punishment, naughty sub."

He pulled away so he could see her face and was pleased when her eyes blazed with excitement at her predicament. Marco was whispering something into Christina's ear that had her whimpering. Aaron knew he liked to play with a sub's mind and was probably making her think that he was about to do all sorts of horrible things to her. Marco had a talent for convincing a submissive that he going to inflict far more pain and torture than he actually was. Poor Christina was beginning to look seriously worried, unlike Evie, who was glowing in anticipation. He preferred it that way — if a scene, whether role play or not, was meant to be fun, he wanted his subbie to know that. On the other hand, if a punishment was real he made damn sure she was left in no doubt about the ordeal ahead of her. The only reprieve she would have would be through the use of her safeword. He took discipline very seriously.

As Aaron drank in the sight of the two helpless women he realized that something wasn't quite right. Christina was naked, but Evie still had her leather skirt on. That wouldn't do. He strode up to her, undid the zip at the back and slid the skirt down her lovely legs. "Step out of it," he ordered as it pooled on the floor by her feet. When she obeyed he flipped the skirt away and stood back to look at her again. Better. But she was still wearing a thong. He approached her again.

"Is being completely naked a hard limit?" he whispered in her ear.

She shivered. "I... Well... No, I guess not, Sir."

"Good." He wasted no time pulling down the tiny scrap of material covering her pussy and having her step out of it. That was much better. Now the girls' bare pussies were touching and would be far more accessible to their Doms. To make the point, he pushed her thighs apart from behind then ran his finger along her slit. She was so wet that his finger slipped against her clit. She groaned and tried to grind herself against him as he circled the little nub with a light touch. "Stay still," he growled and slapped her pussy — not too hard, but enough to make his point. She shuddered and let out a little cry of pleasure. He withdrew his finger and brought it up to Evie's lips, which she automatically parted for him. When she licked her juices from his finger he was overwhelmed by how natural and instinctive she was in her response. She had known what he'd wanted. The connection between them seemed to strengthen, like some sort of invisible force pulling them together.

Finally, Marco stepped away from Christina and nodded at Aaron. They picked up a flogger each and positioned themselves behind the girls — Aaron behind Evie and Marco behind Christina.

"Are you ready, girls?" Marco swung the flogger through the air. As it hit the back of Christina's legs he said, "Let the punishment begin."

# Chapter Eleven

Evie shivered as Christina's gasp tickled her ear. Her friend's mouth was so close that Evie could feel her rapidly quickening breaths as Marco's first stroke landed. Their bodies were stretched taut, their hands secured by cuffs attached to a hook — they were helpless and would be forced to endure the punishment together, each experiencing the other's pain — and pleasure. Desire flared somewhere deep inside Evie as the reality of their predicament hit home. Was there something wrong with her for liking this? *Who cares? I belong here – with Aaron.*

"You okay?" she whispered, so quietly that only Christina would hear.

"Yeah. You?"

"I'm…argh…" Evie cried out as heavy strands of suede struck across her bottom.

"Jesus, I felt that," groaned Christina.

Evie opened her mouth to reply, but her words froze as she felt Christina's body jerk from the impact of Marco's flogger. She closed it again and braced for Aaron to strike again. When he did, she let out a groan as the blow warmed her skin. Then they started in earnest, both Doms alternating the lashes until it became difficult to tell who was being hit by who. The tips of Marco's flogger occasionally flew past Christina's thigh and wrapped around her own, leaving a burning sting in their wake. *Ouch!* Aaron expertly wielded the flogger with just the right force, making the impacts hover between pleasure and pain.

But, as Evie relaxed into the flogging, Aaron stopped, then moved around to her right and kissed her cheek.

"Such a naughty girl," he whispered before continuing around to stand behind Christina.

Evie frowned. Why the hell had Aaron moved over to Christina? And where was Marco? She got her answer when Marco's whip lashed across her ass, making her scream in surprise. Bloody hell, they'd swapped places. Marco's flogger was so very different from Aaron's. It bloody hurt! The fronds must have been thinner leather because they left a sharp painful bite rather than the heavy thud of Aaron's more forgiving suede one. Another lash across the backs of her thighs quite literally took her breath way. She'd overheard Marco whispering to Christina that he would start gently and work his way up to a hard whipping. If this was Marco's idea of gentle she pitied Christina. She whimpered as he struck her again. She wasn't sure how much of this she could take. She squeezed her eyes shut and vowed not to use her safeword so early on in the scene.

Then, thankfully, he stopped and murmured in her ear, "Naughty subs who defy their Doms deserve to get punished, don't you agree?"

A rush of hot moisture pooled between her legs as she managed a very pathetic, "Yes, Sir." *Damn.* Despite the pain, she was becoming more and more aroused.

She didn't open her eyes, not wanting to know what was next, but when Aaron's flogger kissed her burning ass again, she released the breath she'd been holding in relief. Christina's body flinched against her own as Marco resumed his whipping on her and Evie realized that she was now even more mindful of her friend's pain than she had been before.

"Relax." Aaron's soothing voice made her aware of just how much she'd tensed up her muscles. But now that Aaron was back behind her she let go of the tension keeping her rigid and allowed her body to soften against Christina's again.

"Good girl."

Aaron resumed the flogging, this time focusing on her

upper back and shoulders, and Evie sighed in contentment as she absorbed the thuds that were just the right side of painful. *Nice*. She let go of the last remaining control and allowed herself to drift off to that dreamy place she loved going to during a scene.

But then Christina's cry shook her out of it with a jolt. Bloody hell, what was that brute doing to her? She was about to ask her friend if she was all right when Christina snarled, "You'll pay for that, you bastard."

To hear Christina threaten Marco while she was completely at his mercy was so funny that Evie had trouble suppressing a giggle. Despite the fact that they were in the middle of a scene, Evie couldn't stop the bubbles of laughter that rushed up inside her from bursting out. A split second later, Christina's loud guffaw sent her over the edge and she quickly buried her face in Christina's hair to stop the shriek of laughter that just wouldn't go away. She tried so hard to control herself, but the more she attempted to quash it, the more her body racked with massive, deep belly laughs. Christina's body heaved against her own as her infectious giggles reverberated in her ears and when Evie felt damp tears of laughter on her cheek she had no idea whether they were her own or Christina's.

Eventually, though, as the worst of the hysterics died down, Evie became aware of the stern glares of the two bemused-looking Doms. *Oh crap*. Silently, Marco lowered the hook and released them, the solemn expression on his face sending a little quiver of worry through her. Without a word, Aaron took hold of Evie's arm and led her across to a leather-covered sawhorse-style bench. He pushed her upper back to make her bend over it then clipped her wrist cuffs to a hook in the legs of the bench. A moment later Christina was also bent over next to her and secured. They were side by side, bodies pressed close together, asses in the air and unable to escape whatever was to come next. Judging by her and Christina's behavior just now, she didn't expect it to be a nice gentle massage.

But that was exactly what she got as a pair of strong hands rubbed and soothed the sting on her warm skin. *Mmm, don't stop.* A sharp smack on her right buttock reminded her that this wasn't meant to be a reward. He spanked her hard several times, Aaron, she presumed, until her skin burned again. Only when she wriggled her bottom to try and escape the blows did he stop. Her relief was short-lived though, as Marco's voice confirmed her worst fears.

"Now for the ten strikes of the cane."

Evie cried out with genuine fear. She wasn't a painslut, not the way a lot of the submissives she knew were. She wasn't sure she could take the bite of the cane on top of her already abused bottom.

"It's okay," whispered Aaron in her ear. He'd moved around so that he was standing in front of her, his strong hands resting on her shoulders, giving her some much-needed reassurance. "I won't hurt you more than you can take, I promise. Do you want to continue?"

Aaron's words calmed her. So far he hadn't pushed her further than she could take. She needed to trust him to push her boundaries without going over them. Despite her reservations about getting too involved with him, she did believe in him as a Dom. She might not trust him with her heart, but she was in safe hands when it came to kink.

She raised her head and met his eyes. Warmth and passion radiated out of them. Yes, she trusted him. "Yes, Sir, I want to continue."

"Good girl." He kissed her on the lips before stepping back. When he'd disappeared out of her sight again Christina whispered, "Are you really all right?"

Evie smiled. "Yeah, I'm the one who should be asking you that."

"Oh, don't worry about me. I may scream and curse at him, but I love it really."

Evie shuddered. "Rather you than me."

As Evie waited for the men to start the torture, she became aware that her right breast was pressed against Christina's left breast, their nipples squashed against the leather as their weight flattened them. She was aware that Christina's rapid breathing matched her own and the warmth of her skin was comforting. Christina must also be feeling the same from her. That was nice — sexy.

"Are you ready, subs?" Marco's deep growl reminded Evie that this was real. The earlier hint of fear fluttered in her belly, but when she recalled Aaron's words the fear became muted.

"Yes, Sir." She and Christina replied in unison and Evie was tempted to giggle again, more from nerves this time than humor. But no, now was definitely not the time.

"You will take the strikes in turn and will count each one. Christina, you go first."

"Yes, Sir," whimpered Christina, her bravado gone.

The *woosh* of the cane, the *thwack* as it hit Christina's skin and the cry of pain that followed did strange things to Evie. On the one hand it reignited more of the fear, but on the other it stoked a different kind of fire. One that had been smoldering deep inside her all evening.

"One, Sir," cried Christina.

The heat between them became more intense as the pain and arousal in Christina's voice reached Evie's own core. She was next. She braced herself, expecting unbearable agony to assault her, but the firm tap across her buttocks was nothing like she had been expecting. It stung, but it was okay.

"One, Sir." She could do this.

Christina took her next strike with another shriek, then it was Evie's turn again. As before, Aaron didn't hit her anywhere near as hard as Marco was hitting Christina. It was just hard enough for the impact to make her body flinch, leaving the lingering heat to hurt in a nice kind of way. She remembered to count then waited for Christina to receive her next strike. She screamed when the cane hit her again. The bastards were teasing them, changing the turns so they wouldn't know who was next. But Aaron was keeping to his word and didn't hit her harder than she could bear. In fact, she almost wished he would until she heard another anguished cry from Christina.

The next few strikes were similar in that they were firm but bearable. So far she'd taken eight and was bracing herself for the last two. She was aware that Aaron had gradually increased the force of the impacts and that he was hitting her quite a bit harder than before, but she was okay with it – until he whispered in her ear.

"These last two will hurt, Evie. Can you take them for me?"

*Oh, crap.* She whimpered as she fought the urge to beg him to be gentle with her, but she didn't actually want that. Despite her fear of the pain she also wanted it, so she managed to reply, "Yes, Sir," and prayed that she really could take it.

Marco had given Christina some evil-sounding whacks that had left her friend's body shuddering next to her. Feeling Christina's reactions had heightened her own experience of the scene – the flinch of Christina's body as the cane made contact with her skin, the damp film of sweat as she responded and the thundering echo of her heartbeat as she became more aroused. Christina's cries had now changed into mewling sounds and Evie guessed she was probably in or very near subspace. Lucky girl.

"Are you ready, Evie?"

She'd been so absorbed with Christina's reactions that she'd almost forgotten about the assault she was about to get herself. "Yes, Sir," she cried, her body trembling with expectation.

At first the line that struck her ass didn't seem too bad, but it rapidly spread inward, sending scorching pain all the way through to the core of her body. Her cry caught in her throat as she tried to lift herself to stand on her toes. *Oh God, it hurts.* But somehow, eventually, the agony morphed into dreamy clouds of pleasure that blunted the edge of the pain.

"Nine, Sir," she gasped when she was able to breathe again.

Christina should have been next, but Evie guessed she was too far gone to count and Marco was clearly happy to leave her in her world of bliss.

"Last one, Evie," growled Aaron.

Could she take one more? Her legs trembled as she braced herself for the hardest strike yet, but, when it came, the impact that kissed her skin was nowhere near as hard as the last one had been. In fact, it seemed almost gentle in comparison. Warm currents of pleasure rippled through her blood as the residual heat on her bottom throbbed softly. She'd done it. And, incredibly, she'd enjoyed it.

"Well done, beautiful. I'm so proud of you."

Aaron's words warmed her even more as the knowledge that she had pleased him rewarded the natural submissive in her. She smiled as Aaron released her from the bench and helped her to stand, his hand steadying her as she swayed a little. Then he lifted her effortlessly so she was sitting on the bench with her legs dangling over the side. She flinched as her sore buttocks took her weight.

"Thank you, Sir," she whispered as tears pooled in her eyes. It was odd, really, that she wanted to cry, because she certainly wasn't sad. In fact, she felt wonderful.

Aaron grinned and handed her a bottle of water. "Here, drink this. We're not finished yet."

Really? She took the water and drank while wondering what on earth he was going to do to her next.

"Where's Christina?" Christina and Marco were nowhere in sight. She hadn't even noticed her friend being released from the bench.

"Marco has taken her away for some aftercare. She's deep in subspace and needs some quiet time away from the crowds."

"He hit her very hard," she said, frowning as she recalled the sound of the cane *whooshing* through the air before making Christina cry out in agony.

Aaron pulled her to him and held her in a tight embrace. "Yes, he did, but remember she likes it. Marco is a very good judge of what a sub likes and how much they can take. That's why he didn't continue to whip you, he could tell you wouldn't have been able to cope with any more of that particular whip, which is why we swapped back so quickly."

"Oh, right." She sighed, feeling a bit envious of Christina, who could surrender so completely to the pain that she was able to float into the empyrean paradise of subspace with ease. Although Evie had experienced subspace, it had never been from extreme pain.

As if reading her mind, Aaron said, "I could also tell that you would have struggled with the tenth strike of the cane if it had been as hard as the ninth. You were nearing your limit." He pulled away and tucked a stray lock of hair behind her ear. "That's why I let you get away with not counting the final stroke."

"Thank you, Sir." She sighed happily and snuggled her face into his broad shoulder.

"You might not want to thank me when you find out what's in store for you next," he said as he chuckled into her ear.

That sounded ominous. But she trusted him. Despite the implied threat, she knew he wouldn't go too far. Aaron seemed to know what she wanted and how much she could take without her even voicing it. It was as if they had known each other in a previous life. He understood her crazy need to be controlled and, in return, the desire to please him overrode her own urge for gratification.

She finished her water and barely had time to put the bottle down before Aaron pulled her off the bench, onto her feet, then gripped her firmly at the back of her neck and marched her across the room. His controlling grip sent shivers of excitement through her that intensified when she saw they were heading toward a St. Andrew's cross.

Without a word, Aaron turned her so she was facing

away from the cross then pushed her gently until her back was pressed against the center of the wooden X. He secured her wrist and ankle cuffs to the four arms of the cross so she was, once again, helpless and unable to escape. Her heart pounded frantically in her chest as a rush of hot liquid leaked out of her pussy and trickled down one of her legs. Then Aaron placed a soft blindfold over her eyes, throwing her world into darkness.

"You can come when you want," he whispered in her left ear. "I'm now going to take you into your own world of subspace. Enjoy."

She swallowed hard. What exactly did that mean? More pain? She pulled on the restraints to test them but, of course, they held her captive. The giddy feeling she'd experienced during the flogging and caning returned in an instant as she tried to anticipate what Aaron was about to do to her.

She jumped when he took her right nipple between his lips and sucked hard. She knew without the use of sight that it had bunched into a hard peak, and when his teeth grazed it, her little cry was rewarded with fresh arousal. When he pulled away she moaned in disappointment until he did the same to her other nipple. She stopped thinking then, but her mind was soon snapped back to reality when cold metal pressed against the first nipple he'd played with. Searing hot pain shot through her breast, weakening her knees. When he clamped the other nipple she couldn't help the scream that escaped her. *Fuck, oh fuck, it hurts.*

"Go with the pain, Evie." Aaron's voice distracted her momentarily from the hurt, and by the time she refocused on it the pain did seem to have numbed a bit.

"Good girl."

The remaining throb was soon forgotten when she heard a buzzing sound. A moment later a large smooth object was placed against her clit and the buzzing increased. *Oh God, a wand.* Thank goodness he'd said she could come when she wanted, because there was no way she could resist the insistent vibrations of a wand for long.

It took no time at all for the delicious sensations of hot pleasure to tingle through her pussy as Aaron pressed the wand firmly against her clit. Already aroused from the previous scene, Evie found herself succumbing so fast that she barely had time to think about what was happening. Tension built up deep inside her until her legs trembled with the need for release and, when it came, she screamed as wave after glorious wave washed over her.

When the orgasm had faded she waited for Aaron to remove the wand so she could recover. But he kept it pressed against her now sensitive clit, apparently not aware that she needed a break. She tried to close her legs, forgetting they were tethered to the cross, and when she realized there was no escape she tried to wriggle out of the toy's range.

"Stay still," commanded Aaron. "I want another two orgasms from you."

"But...I can't," she cried, now desperate to get away from the torturous weapon.

"You can and you will."

Evie growled. "Yes, Sir." And so the torture continued and Evie shuddered helplessly in her bonds as she battled with the lethal combination of pleasure and pain.

*Fuck. Oh God, oh God, I can't stand this.* The sensations were close to unbearable until, finally, the tension started building again toward another explosion of pleasure. This time the powerful waves seemed to carry on forever as her body devoured the delicious surge crashing over her until, finally, she quivered as the last billowing wave died away.

But the vibrations still didn't stop. She wanted to swipe the damn thing away from her, but she was powerless to move. Ironically, despite her desperate predicament, the knowledge that there was nothing she could do to stop Aaron's torture sent her arousal soaring higher still.

"One more, beautiful."

"No, please. No more. Please," she begged. She couldn't bear that thing near her any longer.

"Is there something you want to say?"

"Nooo, damn you," she screamed as her clitoris felt like it was going to explode. The pleasure had turned to pain again, unbearable, agonizing pain, and yet she didn't want him to stop. Well, she did, but she didn't... *Shit!* This was unbearable. She could make it stop by using just one word, yet she refused to say it. What the hell was wrong with her?

When the vibrations started to feel as though they had possessed her entire body she danced on her toes to escape them. But Aaron kept the wand firmly in place and there was nothing she could do about it. Then, *finally*, the pain bordered on bearable again as new seeds sprouted countless buds of pleasure that rippled through her body. The tension mounted again, but she was so oversensitized now that she couldn't quite reach the edge as fresh pain intercepted the pleasure.

"*No, no, no,*" she cried as it became too much. She screamed when her body finally rolled over the crest of a massive new wave, bigger and deeper than the two before. Then, at the height of her climax, excruciating pain tore through her nipples as blood rushed back after Aaron removed the clamps. Reality blurred as she rode her orgasm like a surfer. Her body felt disconnected from her mind as it buzzed with sensation overload. Eventually, when the swell of the tidal wave started to calm, she slumped on the cross, exhausted and spent. Only then did the vibrations stop, although the whole area still felt like it was on fire. Evie was vaguely aware of Aaron kissing her aching nipples, but that was her last memory before her legs buckled and she fell into a deep pool of euphoria.

# Chapter Twelve

Evie's eyelids fluttered as Aaron carried her across the room to a vacant sofa. He grinned down at her as she tried to focus her eyes on him.

"Hello, beautiful." He laid her carefully onto the sofa then sat down next to her and pulled her close until her head was resting on his lap.

"Mmm."

An enormous sense of wellbeing washed over him as he stroked Evie's head, his fingers running through her hair as he moved a stray strand away from her damp face. The intimate moments of aftercare were as special as the scene itself, that precious time when a submissive recovered from his dominant touch. The fact that this particular submissive was Evie made the swirling satisfaction in his belly spread through to the rest of his body, leaving him feeling more alive than he had in a very long time.

This had been a spectacular punishment. Well, it had been more of a funishment really, as the girls had been set up from the beginning. Dishing out real punishments was something he tended to avoid, although he had no problem disciplining a wayward sub if she needed it. But staging a scene like the one they'd just had was so much fun. He loved mind games almost as much as Marco did. The worry on Evie's and Christina's faces when they couldn't quite work out if they really were in trouble or not had been priceless.

He grinned as he recalled the delightful sound of Evie's uncontrollable giggles while she and Christina had been unable to stop laughing during the scene. That was what he wanted kink to be like—fun. Although he took being a Dom seriously—after all, it was an integral part of his psyche—it had to be enjoyable for everyone involved. In his opinion, some kinksters took it a little too seriously, which was fine if that was what worked for them, but that wasn't what he wanted. The fact that Evie could laugh like that while restrained and being whipped was fantastic, but that she could then refocus on the scene and fall into subspace the way she had just now made everything perfect. *She* was perfect.

She had taken quite a lot of pain for someone who claimed she wasn't a painslut. That a submissive was prepared to suffer for him like that satisfied a hunger inside him that could only be satiated with the sort of scene they'd just shared. He didn't actually want her to suffer, of course, but the knowledge that she was prepared to do so if he desired it humbled him deeply. Warm joy swam through his blood as he gazed at this incredible lady.

"You okay?"

She smiled up at him and nodded. "Yes, Sir, although I don't know whether to throttle you or kiss you for that."

He chuckled and tugged playfully on a handful of her hair. "Oh, don't worry, you'll get to show your appreciation when you've recovered. I'm not done with you yet."

Her eyes widened and her cheeks reddened when his promise hit home. He loved the way she was so open with her responses. She didn't need to say anything for him to know that she was excited by the prospect of playing some more later on.

After a few more minutes of lying on his lap, Evie raised her head and looked around the large room. The atmosphere had heated up nicely, the erotic sounds of BDSM replacing the need for loud, thumping music. The alternative beat of the electro-dark wave music playing through hidden speakers was just loud enough to complement the sounds of impact play, groans and hushed chatter without drowning them out. There was no dance floor here and no crowds of poseurs who just wanted a chance to show off their latest fetish outfits. This wasn't a trendy club where people came to socialize and dance, where the little bit of kink going on was pushed to the background. No, Marco had always intended Dominion to be a place where serious players in the BDSM community could unleash their erotic fantasies in a decadent and discreet environment. There was a social side, people were friendly and chatty, but the kink always came first.

Evie stretched and started to sit up. Even in the dimmed lights he could see the flush on her cheeks. He instinctively ran his fingers across the warmth that gave her face the rosy glow. Her nipples were still hard and looked tender after the clamps. They were calling out to him to kiss them better, so he bent down and took one of them into his mouth then massaged it with his tongue. Evie suddenly tensed, pulling away.

"What's up?" He frowned. Something was bothering his sub and it wasn't her sore nipples.

She looked down at herself and blushed. "Well...I...I just realized that I'm naked."

"And?"

"And I'm not comfortable with that."

"You said earlier that being naked wasn't a hard limit. What's changed?"

"We were doing a scene then. This is different. I don't want people looking at me." As if to make her point, she wrapped her arms protectively around her torso.

"Why? You're beautiful."

"No, I'm not. Please can I have my clothes?"

Aaron raised a questioning eyebrow at her.

"Sir."

He laughed. That wasn't what he'd meant, but the way she'd assumed he was reminding her that he was the Dom satisfied something deep inside him. He could tell that she was uncomfortable though so he fished her skirt and tiny bra out of his toy bag and handed them to her. It was a shame she was so insecure about her figure. He'd have loved for her to remain naked all night, but he didn't want to spoil her time here. He couldn't think why she'd be so negative about her body image — in his eyes she was perfect. "Go and put them on, but no underwear. That's non-negotiable."

"That's okay, as long as my wobbly bits are covered up I'm fine." She giggled shyly before disappearing to the Ladies'.

So it wasn't modesty that was her problem. He shook his head. Why the hell did so many women aspire to be like the airbrushed beansprouts in the public eye? He was constantly surrounded with skinny celebrities in his day-to-day life and he hated the whole plastic image. Evie was everything he liked in a woman, it was just a shame she didn't see herself in the same positive light that he did. *Well, I'll just have to change her mind, then.* That would mean seeing her again. He couldn't help the smile that spread across his face at the thought of getting to know Evie better. Despite his resolve not to get too involved because of his hectic career and all the problems that came with it, Aaron's pulse soared as he wondered how he was going to capture the little submissive's heart.

* * * *

Evie closed her eyes as she took a sip from the steaming cup of hot chocolate. *Mmm.* Never before had a warm drink tasted so good. The freshly made bacon roll she'd just eaten had been delicious and had fed the growling hunger that had been gnawing away in her stomach for the last half an hour. She put her cup down and glanced at Christina, who was stuffing her face with a Danish.

Christina met her gaze and grinned. "Good, huh?"

She nodded and picked her cup up again, reveling in the surreal atmosphere. Was she really wedged between the gorgeous Aaron Holmes and the formidable Marco Alessi? She was in one of the best BDSM dungeons in the country, surrounded by friendly kinksters who chatted away as they munched on the food and drink the club had provided. And the best thing of all was the sense of belonging all this gave her. To an outsider these people might seem strange, scary even, but to her they were normal men and women who were lucky enough to embrace their kinky sexualities by living out their fantasies. Just like her.

Aaron put his hand on her leg as he chatted to Cleo, who looked even more stunning and dangerous than she had the night before. When he squeezed Evie's thigh she was in no doubt that he was letting her know he hadn't forgotten about her.

"Did Aaron tell you that he and Marco are taking us down to the dungeon in a minute?" Christina, who was sitting on the floor by Marco's feet, appeared to have recovered from their scene and was now grinning happily as she reminded Evie that the night was far from over.

"He did say something about not being done with me yet. I wonder what they're going to do to us?" Somehow the fact that both Aaron and Marco had planned something more sent little shivers of excitement through Evie's contented body. Was it possible to feel better than this?

"Whatever it is, I think we're going to enjoy it." Christina winked at her, suggesting that she had an inkling as to what it might be.

"Well, as long as they don't get within a hundred feet of me with a vibrating wand I'll be fine." Evie's clit still ached from the earlier torture. There was no way she wanted any more attention down there tonight. With or without a bloody wand.

Christina giggled. "You never know with Marco."

"That's what I'm worried about," said Evie with a nervous laugh.

She hadn't forgotten what Christina had said the day before about the dungeons downstairs and couldn't help the little niggle of anxiety at the prospect of going down there. Apparently, where the upstairs play space was comfortable and relaxed, the dungeons below the vast building were downright terrifying. She was sure Christina had said something about real prison cells where they used to torture people in the old days. She had a feeling the night was about to get way more intense and couldn't quite work out if the fluttering in her belly was from excitement or fear.

As if sensing her trepidation, Aaron turned around and fixed his eyes on her. They were dark again with occasional flecks of danger flashing from them as they held her prisoner. Little hairs on her arms tingled as they rose in response to his scrutiny and the goose bumps that danced across her skin reinforced her inability to escape from his burning stare. She was powerless to do anything except obey any command he was about to give, and the knowledge turned her bones to trembling jelly.

His gaze continued to bore into the center of her soul as he took her chin in his large hand. "Evie, I'm going to take you downstairs now. We're going to intensify your submission a bit so I'd like you to observe a little protocol. All right?"

She wasn't normally that keen on the restricting protocol more serious D/s called for but, right now, she would do anything he asked of her. In fact, the idea of a little protocol was oddly arousing, so she nodded and replied, "Yes, Sir."

"Good girl. Don't worry, it's nothing too intense, but when Marco and I take you girls downstairs neither of you will have permission to speak unless you're answering a direct question. Is that understood?" His tone was deep, the echo of his words vibrating seductively through her skin.

"Yes, Sir." This time her voice came out as a tiny squeak. She was falling fast into the familiar headspace she loved so much. What would she be like when he got her down to the dungeon and took complete control of her mind and body? She shivered and bowed her head forward as she basked in the beautiful sensations floating through her.

Somehow she managed to find her feet when he ordered her to stand. She had no idea how she arrived at the heavy-looking oak door that Aaron was pulling open. Stepping through it as if in a trance, she followed Marco and Christina down steep stone steps that seemed to go on forever. The farther down she went the darker and cooler it became until they were in a long, dark, cobbled tunnel. The only light was from candles in iron sconces on the wall, the flickering glow adding to the austere and spooky surroundings.

Their footsteps echoed as she and Christina followed the men to the end of the tunnel, and when they reached another door, she jumped when the click of the latch bounced around the stone walls.

"Bloody hell," she whispered to Christina as Marco pushed the door open. "It's creepy down here."

"I know. Apparently it's haunted. Cleo told me that she was down here on her own clearing up after a scene once when she heard someone scream."

"Maybe it was someone from the club upstairs?" Evie frowned. This place was scary enough without the prospect of ghosts.

Christina shook her head. "Nope, the club was shut and there was nobody else around."

Evie's skin prickled with unease as she followed Christina into a large room that could only be described as having been built for the purpose of torture and imprisonment. A real bona fide dungeon with chains hanging from the walls and a prison cell at the back.

"Shit!"

Everything that had been added to the room had been done to accentuate the authentic and intimidating atmosphere. A wall of mirrors at one end of the room drew her eyes to a vast array of whips, floggers and other implements hanging from hooks on another wall. The only thing that gave her some much-needed reassurance was the fact that the dungeon furniture and sofa were the same as upstairs. Modern, sturdy and clean — a reminder that this wasn't real. Still, it looked bloody creepy, not helped by the fact that the only light appeared to be from red bulbs hidden discreetly in the ceiling and a few candles flickering around the room.

"Marco put me in those stocks over there last week," whispered Christina, pointing to some old wooden stocks in a dark corner. "The bastard left me while he sat on the sofa there and read the fucking newspaper."

"Remind me never to piss him off." Although the idea of being locked in the stocks made her seriously uneasy, she couldn't help smiling as she imagined Christina cursing at Marco as she watched him chilling out in front of her.

"Who gave you two permission to talk?" Marco's deep voice made Evie's stomach jump.

*Oh, crap.*

"Sorry, Sir," mumbled Christina, while Evie remained silent in case she somehow said something she shouldn't. Damn protocol.

"Evie, remove your clothes at once." Aaron's commanding voice echoed through the room. "Then kneel in front of me."

Evie's stomach flipped as Aaron's voice reached deep inside her. Without a word she took off the bra and skirt that she'd been allowed to put back on earlier, this time not even remotely worried about her body image. She was far too focused on obeying the Dom who seemed to have grown even taller and more powerful since coming down here. Once naked she sank to her knees, thankful for the cushion Aaron had placed by his feet. She lowered her head and reached behind her back, linking her fingers together to keep them in place.

A cushion was placed directly next to her then Christina lowered herself onto her knees. She was so close to Evie that their arms were touching.

"Close your eyes, both of you."

She didn't hesitate in obeying Marco's order and a split second later a soft blindfold was placed over her eyes.

"The only word that is permitted is your safeword. Use it if you need to, although I doubt you'll find it necessary." Aaron chuckled and stroked the top of her head.

As she waited for whatever was coming next she was aware of the sound of Christina's rapid breaths next to her.

Ha, her friend wasn't quite as nonchalant as she tried to make out.

Evie tried to calm the thundering beat of her heart as she strained her ears for a clue as to what might happen. What was Aaron going to do? Was he going to whip her, hurt her? Would she enjoy it or would she be forced to use her safeword? She swallowed, mentally pushing down the prickle of fear teetering on her nerves.

She jumped when something sharp prickled across the back of her right shoulder. The tiny pinpricks rolled across her skin, sending shivers shimmying in their wake. A pinwheel. Aaron rolled it across her back, over her other shoulder then down until it reached the bottom of her spine. Although the sharp metal pressed quite hard against her skin she knew it wasn't puncturing it, but still the sensation bordered between tingling pleasure and just the tiniest hint of pain. She sighed and allowed her body to relax, luxuriating in the glorious sensations.

Then Aaron moved it around to her front and ran it over her breasts, circling each nipple before running it directly over one of them. She gasped. Although Aaron had eased up on the pressure before going over her nipple it still stung. But it hurt in a nice way. Her body was beginning to feel like a pincushion, which was, oddly enough, very sexy. He rolled it down her belly and she couldn't stop the cry that escaped from her as she became more sensitive to its touch.

Then, suddenly, the pinwheel was removed and she was left missing its sharp kiss. Until something colder and even sharper clawed its way down her back. *Oh my God! What's that?* A metal claw? It scraped its way back up then over her shoulder and down her left arm. Logically, she knew it wasn't breaking her skin, but she was also aware that it would be leaving long red scratch marks. This was more intense than the pinwheel, but, fuck, it was good. A little more pain, but with that came more pleasure.

She swayed as her mind emptied itself of everything

except for the sensations over her skin. A delicious feeling of absolute contentment wafted into her mind and body as she devoured the sensuous touch of whatever Aaron was using. She'd stopped trying to guess and now just allowed herself to enjoy whatever he was doing to her. *Don't ever stop.* Incredibly, she was beginning to enter the floaty consciousness that she got from subspace. Was it really possible to reach subspace from sensation play alone? There was no pain, well, not real pain anyway, and yet she could almost feel the endorphins surging through her blood. Whatever it was, she loved it.

Eventually, though, the sharp scratch of the claw thing subsided and she sighed as she missed its thorny touch. Then strong hands rubbed over the tender skin, soothing away the lingering sting. *Mmm, nice.* She had somehow traveled to a universe where only she and Aaron existed. The unknown no longer worried her. Now she embraced whatever was to come next because she knew, whatever it was, it was what Aaron wanted, and that meant she wanted it too.

In her dreamy state she'd forgotten about Christina being next to her, but suddenly she became aware of her friend again as her steady, deep breathing told her that Christina had also reached the same beautiful place that she had. The Velcro at the back of her head was undone then the blindfold removed, allowing her to look up into Aaron's gorgeous face. His eyes glowed in the dark room, radiating power and lust. He smiled down at her and when she smiled back he reached down and gently stroked her cheek.

"Are you okay, beautiful?"

"Yes, Sir," she managed to whisper back as she leaned her face into his hand.

"Good. Now, keep your hands behind your back and use only your mouth to make me come on your lovely face."

His words sent a shock of lust through her body, like a bolt of lightning striking directly at the center of her soul. Without warning an almost painful wave of heat throbbed through her pussy as she licked her lips in anticipation of what she was about to do. She made eye-contact with Aaron, something that D/s protocol normally forbade, but to hell with protocol. He wasn't that bothered either, by the look of it, because the mixture of control and warmth swimming in his eyes was still there, glowing seductively down at her.

She remained silent as he unzipped and allowed his huge dick to spring out of the tight leather. *Mmm, long, thick and very hard.*

Leaning forward, she flicked her tongue over the tip of his cock, tasting the pre-cum that had gathered there. Her blood buzzed as it mixed with the adrenaline shooting through her veins, leaving her a little lightheaded. Her vision of kneeling at Aaron Holmes' feet with his cock in her mouth was quite literally coming true. His pleasure was down to her, she had control of how much she would give him and she was damn well going to give him everything she had. With that thought, she sucked his whole length into her mouth until it touched the back of her throat.

His low groan gave her the confidence to take him even deeper. When she couldn't hold her breath any longer she pulled away until she could take a lungful of air then took him all the way in again, massaging his cock with her tongue as she did so. She wanted to give him everything she had, to let him use her any way he wished. Her own reward would be his groan of satisfaction as he exploded on her face. A shudder rocked her body at the mere thought.

She continued drawing his cock as far inside her as she could then rolling her tongue around it until she needed air again. He was now so hard that she could have sworn he'd grown even bigger than a minute ago. She had to stretch her lips around him to accommodate his expanding size, which was now so thick that he filled her throat completely.

All her focus was on Aaron at that moment, so it was quite a shock when a deep growl reminded her that Marco and Christina were still there.

"Watch your teeth, sub."

Christina's giggle made Evie want to laugh, but all she could manage was a muffled rumble. Aaron shuddered in response, probably due to the vibrations of her voice, and she soon lost herself in her task again. When Aaron took hold of her head and held it still the knowledge that he was going to fuck her face almost made her come there and then. He fucked her mouth hard and deep, only holding back long enough for her to take a breath in between the thrusts. The more he used her, the more the burning between her legs intensified, until, despite her earlier protestation that her clit had retired for the night, the insistent throb became almost unbearable.

"Make yourself come, Evie. I want you squirming as I come on your face."

Whether Aaron was a mind reader or not, she could have cried with relief at his command. As soon as she touched her soaked pussy and sought her little hard nub a coil started winding up inside her, tighter and tighter until, when she couldn't bear it any longer, the spiral of pleasure snapped. Her body bucked as her world exploded and Aaron slid his cock out of her mouth. Even through the throes of her almighty climax she remembered to raise her face up toward Aaron and just managed to catch the first shots of his cum. Most of his hot juice landed on her face but she swallowed what went in her mouth then, when the flow slowed, she urgently took him back in to catch the last few drops.

Finally, when she'd licked him clean, she collapsed in a heap at Aaron's feet just as Marco's deep growl reminded her again of his and Christina's presence. Unable to stand on her own, she allowed Aaron to help her up. Before she was able to grip onto his arm for support he'd swept her into his arms, where she fell into a dreamy world of ecstasy.

"Thank you, my beautiful sub girl."

Over the deafening sound of her thundering heart she just about caught Aaron's whispered words before her mind finally shut down and returned to the paradise of dreamland.

# Chapter Thirteen

Evie took a sip of her coffee and smiled. What a lovely way to enjoy a late breakfast. They were relaxing on the patio looking out across Morgan Manor's vast gardens after having eaten a delicious meal of bacon, poached eggs, sausage and hash browns in the early afternoon sunshine.

Aaron had woken her up at half past eleven, informing her that he'd already been for a five-mile run. He'd then ordered her into the shower, where he'd fucked her slowly and thoroughly under the hot pulsing jets of water. After a cup of steaming-hot coffee, he had suggested going for a swim before breakfast. Just as Christina had predicted last night, the pool had been busy with Dominion members, many now proudly sporting the marks of their kinky fun. Despite the fact that dawn had broken before she and Aaron had collapsed into bed, spent and exhausted, Evie had swum thirty lengths with more energy than she'd had in a very long time.

Now, with a full belly and a satiated body, Evie turned her face toward the sun and closed her eyes as she absorbed its warm rays.

"I'm just going to make a phone call, then we should go back to our room and pack."

Evie's heart sank as Aaron's words reminded her that this wonderful dream was about to end. She opened her eyes and smiled, careful not to let him see her disappointment. As soon as he'd disappeared inside she closed them again in the hope that time would somehow slow down and allow her a little longer here.

"Morning."

Evie squinted up to see Christina flop into the chair next to her. As soon as her pert bottom touched the cushioned seat Christina winced, jumped up and sat back down more carefully.

"Sore?" asked Evie, grinning.

A broad smile spread across Christina's face as she nodded. "Do you know, when I first met Marco I told him I wasn't into a lot of pain and he said that he believed there was a painslut in me desperate to get out."

"You did take quite a beating. Way more than I did, and even I've got a couple of marks." Evie had almost squealed with joy when she'd seen the two small bruises on her buttocks this morning.

Christina giggled and stood up. "I guess he was right," she said and flipped the short skirt of her dress up to reveal several dark red stripes welted across her ass.

"Wow, that must've hurt." No matter how much Evie had enjoyed her flogging and even the caning last night, she could never imagine getting off on the level of pain it would take to leave marks like that. She suppressed a shiver at the mere thought.

Christina just shrugged as if it was no big deal then sat carefully back down. "So how about you? Did you have a good night?"

Evie smiled as memories of her night with Aaron warmed her blood. "The best. You were right when you said that Aaron is a shit-hot Dom. He's a good lover too. I honestly can't remember how many times he's made me come this weekend." She giggled as Christina gave her a subtle wink and pursed her lips ever so slightly. It wasn't very often she could shock Christina so she added, "I'm not sure which is more sore, my cunt or my ass."

"Well, it's good to know that Aaron hasn't lost his touch."

Evie jumped. The deep male voice that had just spoken definitely didn't belong to Christina. So that was why Christina had given her *that* look. She turned slowly and looked up into Marco's amused face.

"I tried to warn you," said Christina, not looking in the least bit sorry that Marco had overheard her.

Evie tried her hardest not to look bothered, even though her burning cheeks would undoubtedly be giving away her embarrassment. Would she ever get over this stupid shyness? Marco was as kinky, even more so, than she was, so it really shouldn't matter what he, or anyone else in the BDSM lifestyle, thought about her own escapades.

"Are you ready, Christina?" asked Marco, diverting his attention away from Evie thank goodness. "Cleo is waiting for you in reception."

"Okay." As Christina rose from her seat she blew Evie a kiss. "Cleo is taking me to an alternative market in London today. Apparently there's a lady there who makes the most amazing corsets. I'll call you tomorrow."

Evie laughed as Marco swatted Christina's ass to make her hurry. She was still smiling when Aaron strode across the patio, looking very pleased with himself.

"Are you in a hurry to get back to London?"

"No, not really. Why?" *Uh-oh, now what does he have in mind?* Her aching clit quivered at the thought of any more stimulation. She really didn't think she could cope with any more pain or orgasms any time soon.

"Do you fancy a walk along the beach followed by fish and chips for dinner?"

He cocked his head to one side and waited for her reply with a boyish grin. How could she resist such an endearing look?

"I'd love to. But what about your meeting back in London?" Apparently he had needed to be in town for a meeting with his manager that afternoon. It seemed that even rock stars didn't get Sundays off.

"I told Bill that something more important has come up. Come on, let's get packed and be on our way. Hastings is less than an hour from here and I don't want to waste a second of what's left of the day." He grabbed her hand and pulled her up into his arms.

"So I'm more important than a meeting with your manager, am I?" she teased, not believing for a second that he'd canceled because of her.

"Too right you are." He kissed her hard, as if to affirm the fact and, just for a second, Evie allowed herself to believe it. But it didn't take long for reality to remind her that she was just a convenient distraction in this rock star's busy schedule. *Don't get attached. He'll only hurt you.* But she pushed the subconscious words of warning to the back of her mind where they belonged. She'd had a fantastic couple of days with Aaron and would damn well enjoy the rest of the weekend with him. Then tomorrow, when it was all over, she'd forget about him and get on with her life as if nothing had ever happened. *Easy.*

* * * *

Aaron nearly choked with laughter as a seagull flew away with a piece of Evie's battered fish. The bird had been lingering near them ever since they'd sat down on the pebbly beach with their cod and chips and must have been plotting the theft for some time. Without warning it had swooped in from behind and literally grabbed the food from Evie's hand just as she'd been about to pop it into her mouth. Her face was a picture. First disbelief, followed quickly by amusement, despite the fact that she'd just lost a portion of her dinner to the cheeky bandit.

He held a piece of his own fish to her lips and she took it eagerly into her mouth.

"Mmm, it tastes even better coming from you," she murmured, closing her eyes as she swallowed the food.

A vision of Evie kneeling naked at his feet as he fed her popped into his head. *Hmm, that's definitely something I want to try with her.*

Today had been fun. He had no regrets about canceling his meeting with Bill. This was way better than sitting in a stuffy office listening to his manager waffling on about the damn interview they were due to attend tomorrow. Even though the band was supposed to be on holiday now that the tour was over, Bill was still intent on booking them for endless interviews and TV appearances. Like the music awards next week. Aaron knew they had to go, after all, they had been nominated for two awards, but the last thing he wanted to do now was to jet off to Los Angeles and make small talk with a bunch of arrogant rock stars and wannabe celebrities.

Especially now that he'd found Evie. Today had shown him what he'd been missing for so long. They'd had a lovely carefree day strolling along the water's edge hand in hand like a real couple. That had felt fucking good. Little things had delighted him, like when he'd tried to teach her how to skim pebbles along the surface of the water. Her frustration every time the stone she threw landed with a plop and sank had been hilarious. It had felt good to laugh again.

Before hunger had reminded them of the time, she'd convinced him to go for a ride on the small railway, much to the amusement of some kids who had recognized him. They'd then raced each other in the go-karts. Evie had beaten him, but only just. It had been the most enjoyable and normal afternoon he'd had for months, maybe even years, and it was beginning to dawn on him that it was times like these, not the endless slog of touring and promos, that he wanted more of.

He stuffed the last couple of chips into his mouth then scrunched up the empty paper and turned to Evie. She was licking salt from her fingers—a completely innocent action that somehow sent little shockwaves down to his cock. Trying his best to ignore the pulsing need down below, he watched Evie as she finished her food. When she caught him staring at her though she frowned and self-consciously wiped her mouth.

"What?"

"I was just thinking how lovely you are."

He just caught a glimpse of the deep flush staining her

cheeks before she looked away. "Oh… Thanks." She had picked up another chip, but now, instead of putting it into her mouth, she dropped it back into the greasy paper. When she noticed the puzzled frown furrowing his brows she threw him an odd look and said, "I don't like people watching me eat, okay?"

Aaron laughed, assuming she was joking. "Why on earth not?"

"I just don't." She carefully folded the paper around the remaining food, making it clear that she was finished. "I don't mind eating around people, I just don't like being stared at while I'm making a pig of myself."

Not wanting to spoil the afternoon by pushing too hard on what was obviously a sensitive subject, Aaron decided to let it drop. *For now.* But he had a sneaky suspicion that this might somehow be related to the insecurity about her body that she'd hinted at last night.

Taking the paper from her, he stood up then took her hand and pulled her up. "Come on, let's go for a walk," he said softly. A stroll, hand in hand, along the stony rim of white foam as it crept in to claim the beach would be the perfect end to a perfect day.

As they made their way along the water's edge, Aaron's senses seemed to come alive in a way they hadn't done in a very long time. He closed his eyes, letting Evie guide them both, and thought of nothing except the sounds of his surroundings. The *swoosh* of the swell as it rolled over the pebbles and the crackling shushing sound when the stones settled into their new positions as the water receded. It was like two finely tuned musical instruments playing harmoniously together—soothing and beautiful. He squeezed Evie's hand and when she squeezed back a current of warm electricity shot up his arm straight to his chest. Reveling in this newfound contentment, he took in a big lungful of the fresh, salty air and could almost taste the tang of seaweed as he exhaled. It reminded him of his childhood. Happy memories.

He opened his eyes again and looked down at Evie. She was staring out to sea as they walked. Every now and again her hair blew across her face as the breeze whistled softly past her. She didn't seem to notice. One look at her face told him that she had also drifted into the hypnotic trance that he'd just been in. She looked at peace as she gazed out at the little white crests dancing on the surface of the water, mesmerized by the pure perfection of the stunning scenery.

It was at that moment that everything fell into place. Stunned, Aaron stopped then turned toward the vast ocean and took a deep breath to steady himself. He hadn't expected this, hadn't bargained on the overwhelming emotions flooding him as he walked with this woman that he barely knew. Suddenly everything that had been plaguing him for the last few months faded away and all that mattered was being with Evie. He'd written songs about love at first sight, but he'd never really believed in it. Was it possible that the fluttery swirls in his belly that surged to his brain and left him so lightheaded could be the first seeds of love? *Love?* Fuck, where the hell had that come from?

Evie had stopped walking when he had and was now looking at him questioningly. He stared back, not trusting himself to speak. Her eyes were glowing, drawing him in like beacons. Little specks of amber danced in the deep brown pools, making them come alive with energy that matched the gentle force blowing in from the sea. Could she be feeling the same thing?

He mentally shook himself back to reality. Of course she wasn't. Who was he kidding? They barely knew each other, for God's sake. The harsh reminder broke the spell, leaving him feeling strangely empty and dazed. What the hell had gotten into him?

In an effort to regain his composure, he took hold of Evie's hand again and started walking. "Let's go," he said, his voice sounding oddly distant as the wind carried it away.

They continued walking, mostly in amiable silence, until they reached the old pier. The Victorian structure was now a burnt-out shell with no hint of its past grandeur. Thankfully it was going to be rebuilt after the fire that had destroyed it a few years ago and Aaron hoped that he might one day walk along its restored decks, maybe with Evie.

"I guess we should start heading back," he said regretfully. He'd love to stay longer, but he knew that Evie had to be up early to open her shop and he had a trip to get ready for.

Evie nodded, looking as reluctant to leave as he was.

He was going to be away for a whole week. Damn, that was too long. He needed to see her again before he left. Tomorrow morning, he had to attend an interview, then he was meant to be packing, but to hell with that. "Look, I'm flying out to the States on Tuesday, but I want to see you before I leave. Are you free tomorrow night?"

She shook her head and his heart sank. "No, sorry. I have a two-hour ballet class at eight o'clock."

He tried his hardest to hide his disappointment but just couldn't help asking, "Do you have to go?"

He regretted the words as soon as her face clouded over. "Yes, I do actually. Dancing means everything to me and now that I can't dance professionally my lessons are all I have left. I'm not about to start missing class to fit in with your schedule." She straightened her shoulders and glared at him, as if daring him to persist. Was she angry?

"Sorry," he said, taken aback. "I didn't mean that you should drop everything because of me. I'd just hoped to see you before I leave."

Her face softened then, and she reached up and ran her fingers along his stubble. "No, I'm sorry. I didn't mean to jump down your throat. How long will you be away?"

"Bill has crammed a month's worth of interviews and appearances into a week, including the music awards on Sunday. I think we're due to return a week on Wednesday."

Evie smiled, although it was obvious from the slight crease in her brow that her guard was still up. "That sounds exciting."

Exciting? There was a time when Aaron would have

agreed, but now it was just something that had to be done. The sooner he was back home again the better. "Can I see you when I get back?" he asked.

Instead of looking pleased, though, Evie frowned. Fuck, had he read her wrong? He'd been so sure that she'd been feeling the same as he had. Her hesitation now had him seriously worried.

After what felt like an age, she gave him a tentative smile and said, "Yes, if you'd like."

"I'd like," he said firmly.

"Okay."

Just to make sure that she fully understood how much he really did want to see her again, he kissed her. Hard and possessing, just the way he knew she liked. Sure enough, her body soon melted as she responded with the same passion she'd had over the weekend. Her reaction told him what he needed to know. Despite the fact that she didn't fully trust him yet, she did want him. As he deepened the kiss, he resolved to change her mind about him when he got back. When he was finished with her, she'd be in no doubt about his feelings for her.

As they strolled back to his car a thought suddenly occurred to him. "Is your shop busy on Monday mornings?" he asked.

"Not especially. Why?"

"Have lunch with me. In fact, meet me earlier and come along to an interview we're doing, then we can sneak off afterward."

Evie's face told him what he already knew she would say. As her mouth started to form the negative word he refused to hear he put his finger over it to silence her.

"Please?" He gave her his best puppy dog look and threw in a lopsided grin for good measure.

He held his breath as she let hers out. Then she smiled. "All right. But I have to check my diary to make sure I don't have any appointments."

"When can you do that?" He didn't want to wait for an

answer. He needed to know now.

She laughed. "As soon as I have a signal on my phone."

When they reached his car she took her phone out again. "That's better. It'll just take a minute while I log onto my diary."

The minute felt more like ten. Suddenly her answer became more important than anything else. He *needed* to spend more time with her before he went away. He had to make sure she understood how he felt so she wouldn't convince herself that he didn't want her because of who he or she was.

"Well?" he asked, trying to hide his impatience.

"Okay," she said, as she scanned the screen on her phone. "Tomorrow is quiet, Mondays usually are. I have a fitting booked in at three o'clock, so as long as Julia doesn't mind being on her own until then I don't see why not."

Relief flooded him as he flashed her a happy smile. The interview would be over in an hour, then he'd have a good couple of hours with her afterward. That should be enough time to convince her that he wanted her. He just hoped that, after all that, she wanted him just as much.

# Chapter Fourteen

As soon as Evie spotted Aaron striding toward her from the other side of the plush hotel lobby her jittery nerves calmed. The busy flow of beautiful people faded to the background as his smile reassured her that she was the one that mattered.

"Hello, beautiful." He pulled her into his arms and hugged her. "I'm so glad you came."

She nearly hadn't come. The thought of being around the likes of Jaymz and Jona hadn't exactly filled her with joy as she had made her way across London to Park Lane. She didn't want to be reminded that Aaron's life revolved around the types of people she hated — arrogant celebrities, intrusive journalists and fanatical groupies. But Aaron had seemed genuine when he'd almost begged her to come along today. She'd spent the whole bus journey wondering why he was so keen to see her. She had finally conceded that maybe he really did want to just spend more time with her.

Something had changed yesterday as they'd walked along the beach. There had been a connection between them that couldn't be measured by anything specific, but she had been sure it hadn't just been her imagination. He had seemed to pick up on it too. Like that moment when he'd stopped walking and turned to stare at her. His eyes had been alive with something she couldn't put her finger on. Enlightenment? Thankfully, she had managed to shake off the stupid delusion that he liked her as much as she did him. It would have been so easy to embarrass herself by saying something stupid.

"Come on, let's get away from the crowds," he said as the clicking of cameras reminded her of where they were.

He ushered her through a doorway guarded by a mean-looking security guy, into a quieter side room. Evie's relief to be away from the crowds and cameras was short-lived when Jaymz wandered toward them with a sly grin on his haggard face. Sex, drugs and rock 'n' roll were clearly taking its toll on him. He had the bloated look that drunks get after too many binges and the skin around his nose was red and flaky, hinting at a possible drug habit.

Her skin prickled as he looked her up and down with bleary eyes, his insolent gaze settling on her breasts. She gritted her teeth and glared at him. She was damned if she was going to let a little weasel like that unsettle her.

Luckily he continued past them with just a curt nod to Aaron, but not without leaving behind a stench of alcohol hanging in the air. She sighed and looked away, careful not to inhale too deeply while Jaymz's odious fumes lingered.

Aaron gave her a reassuring smile before taking her hand and leading her across the room to join Hunter and Fabiana. They were sitting near the back chatting to two men, one whom she recognized as Levi. As they approached, Fabiana turned and gave Evie a warm smile.

"Hello, how lovely to see you again. It's Evie, isn't it?" Her voice was soft with the tiniest hint of a Latin accent.

Impressed that Fabiana had remembered her name, Evie smiled back. "Yes, it's nice to see you too."

"Hello again, Evie," said Hunter and gave her a quick hug.

*Wow, I've just been hugged by Hunter from Decadence.*

"This is Levi and our manager, Bill," said Aaron, nodding at the two men who were now standing up to greet her. "Guys, this gorgeous lady is Evie Lloyd."

"It's a pleasure to meet you," purred Levi, reaching out to shake her hand. His deep brown eyes radiated warmth and charisma. He looked far too smooth and well-polished to play in a rock band. His smart suit looked out of place next to Hunter's and Aaron's black jeans, biker boots and leather jackets. His long dreadlocks were the only thing that set him apart from a stylish businessman.

Bill smiled at her, but was clearly preoccupied with the sort of stuff managers are supposed to stress about. He glanced at his watch and frowned. "Okay, boys, let's get this shit over with," he snapped, looking at Aaron, Hunter and Levi.

"No rest for the wicked," grinned Levi before heading over to join a small team setting up microphones, lights and cameras.

"I'm going to leave you with Fabiana during the interview. It shouldn't take too long," said Aaron. He handed her a security pass then pulled her into his arms. "And then you and I are going to have lunch—just the two of us."

Evie sat down next to Fabiana and watched the members of Decadence take their seats in front of the interviewer. Jaymz stumbled as he reached his bandmates then let out a loud belch as he slumped onto his chair. Jona, who sat down next to him, snorted with laughter, as if that was the funniest thing he'd ever heard.

As they sat in the neat row that had been arranged for them the differences between them all were very clear to see. Jaymz and Jona looked like a couple of life's rejects who had just been plucked from the street, whereas Levi looked far too cool to be associated with them. Hunter looked handsome in his carefully styled rock outfit that must have cost a fortune. Then there was Aaron. His untamed long hair hung down his back and the dark stubble on his chin made the tiny amount of eyeliner he wore look masculine. His tattoos and leather wristbands blended perfectly with the whole image to make him the most striking and sexy member of the band. Evie's stomach flipped as she reminded herself that this God-like superstar was her lover and Dom. At least for now.

"They're a real mismatch of characters, aren't they?" mused Evie.

Fabiana laughed. "Oh yes. But that's what the fans like. They're all different enough for people to have their favorites." She lowered her voice and leaned closer to Evie. "Except Jaymz and Jona don't seem to have a lot of fans."

"I wonder why." Evie grinned, glad she wasn't the only one who disliked the terrible twins so much.

"They're starting," whispered Fabiana as the sounds in the room became hushed.

Evie watched, fascinated, as the interviewer introduced herself to the band as Emma. She was the epitome of a rock chick with her long black hair, heavily applied black eye makeup and skin-tight black clothes.

"Congratulations on the completion of your tour. I understand it was a complete sell-out?"

"Yeah," boasted Jona. When he didn't elaborate any further, Emma glanced hurriedly at her notes, then directed her next question at Hunter.

"Right, er… Hunter, your lyrics have become a lot darker over the last couple of years. Are they from personal experience?"

Hunter laughed. "If I wrote from personal experience nobody would listen to the songs. They'd be too boring." A polite ripple of laughter broke a little of the tension in the room.

"What inspires you?" Emma looked at Aaron for this one and Evie's focus sprang to attention. Emma smiled sweetly at him, her false eyelashes fluttering just enough to look cute. Was she flirting with him?

"Anything and everything," replied Aaron with a shrug. "I once wrote a song about a woman who rescued stray dogs. I get inspiration from the strangest of places."

Emma nodded and looked down at her notes again. "Do you all get along?"

After a brief moment of silence Levi came to the rescue. "It would be very hard to work so closely with people you didn't get along with."

"Nice save," mumbled Fabiana.

"There has been a bit of negative press recently, particularly involving Jaymz and Jona," said Emma, moving the microphone over to Jaymz. "Do you have any comments for your critics?"

"Yeah, fuck 'em," he sneered. "They're fucking twats who don't know nothing."

"Like you, then," muttered Evie under her breath. Fabiana must have heard her because she tried to stifle a giggle.

As Emma continued the interrogation, Evie's mind began to wander. She wasn't a journalist, but even she could see that the questions weren't loaded to get the best out of the opportunity. Apart from Emma's not-too-subtle flirting with Aaron and Hunter, she didn't seem very interested in probing any deeper into their lives and work.

As Hunter explained their song-writing process, memories of Aaron's discipline at Dominion kept her deliciously distracted. She was just reliving the joint scene with Marco and Christina when a noise snapped her out of her reverie.

A woman had gotten into the room and was running toward the band members. She must have barged past the security guard because he came charging after her, his outraged face glowing deep red. But he wasn't a match for her youthful adoration and before anyone was fully aware of what was happening the woman had skipped behind the seats and flung her arms around Hunter. The skin on Evie's neck tingled as the hysterical woman wailed, "Hunter, I love you so much." This was creepy.

The burly bouncer finally caught up with her and dragged her off Hunter, who seemed frozen with shock. "Hunter," she cried. "I love you. I love you."

As the door closed behind the woman an eerie silence hung in the air. The band members all looked shaken, even Jaymz. Aaron was the first to snap out of the temporary paralysis. Standing up, he announced, "I think now would be a good time to take a break."

Everyone mumbled their agreement and rose from their seats. Bill cornered Hunter before he could get away so Evie turned to Fabiana, who had gone deathly pale.

"Are you okay, Fabiana?"

Fabiana gave Evie a feeble nod then shook her head.

"I thought this sort of thing happens all the time?" asked Evie. Something didn't seem right. From what she'd heard about rock stars it would have been unusual if a woman *hadn't* gotten in and thrown herself at one of them.

"Yes, but…" Fabiana shook her head again then said, "I guess you never get used to it."

Fabiana's words rang in Evie's ears. *I guess you never get used to it.* Was that how it would be for her and Aaron if they continued to see each other?

Aaron strode over, followed by Hunter, who had managed to extricate himself from Bill. Both had worried concern etched onto their faces. "Are you all right, Fabi?" asked Hunter, pulling his wife into his arms.

"Yes, really. What about you?" she cried, gripping his hand.

"Yeah, of course." Hunter's face finally seemed to regain some of its color.

"This raises new security questions," said Aaron gravely. "How the hell did she manage to get through?"

"Do you think it's her?" asked Fabiana, her face still ashen.

"Probably not," said Hunter as Emma approached them. "We'll talk later."

"Are you guys ready to continue?" Emma looked at her watch, letting them all know that the unscheduled break was a big inconvenience.

"Give us a minute, please," said Aaron.

As Emma made her way back to the interview area Aaron turned to Evie. "Are you all right?"

"Yes, of course." Why wouldn't she be? They did seem to be making a drama out of something that must happen all the time.

"Good." He kissed her on the lips, then he and Hunter headed back to join the others.

As the men took their seats again Evie stole a quick glance

at Fabiana. The poor woman still looked shaken so she smiled at her, took her chilled hand and gave it a squeeze. There was more to this than they were telling her. Maybe Fabiana was insecure and resented the attention Hunter got from the female fans? But Fabiana always came across as very confident, so that didn't make sense.

She stopped speculating about it when Emma resumed the interview. The questions didn't get any better, though, and after another twenty minutes Evie noticed Aaron fiddling impatiently with a pen.

"So are you playing at Download this year?"

"Nah, but we'll probably headline there next year," quipped Jona. He blew a bubble with his gum and leered at Emma.

Evie didn't miss the look between Aaron and Hunter. It was a look that said that it was highly unlikely the band would be appearing at the popular rock festival in the foreseeable future.

"So, what does the future hold for Decadence?" asked Emma. She had stopped flirting now and seemed more interested in admiring her fingernails than she was in what the band actually had to say.

"When we get back from America we're going to take a break for a few weeks, then Hunter and I are going to get together to write songs for a new album," said Aaron, sitting back in his seat and folding his arms. Even Evie could tell that the interview was over as far as he was concerned.

"Oh yes, good luck with the awards next week," said Emma as if it was an afterthought.

"Thanks." Hunter stood up and stretched. "Are we done?"

"Er, yeah. Thank you for your time," mumbled Emma as she gathered her papers.

As Emma and her entourage packed away their equipment, Aaron, Hunter and Bill joined Evie and Fabiana. Levi waved across the room. "See you tomorrow at the airport," he called then disappeared through the door.

Jaymz and Jona slouched near Emma as she checked her phone. *Oh God, they're going to hit on her. Poor woman.*

As Bill answered a call Hunter took Fabiana to one side, leaving Evie and Aaron alone. "Come on," he said, taking her hand. "Let's get out of here. Take a deep breath and don't say a word."

Then he led her across the room and out of the door. Evie was still wondering what he meant when they were ambushed by a sea of excited faces. Aaron gripped her hand tighter and followed a bouncer away from the densest part of the crush. "Aaron. Aaron. Aaron," the crowd chanted and seemed to close in on them as the cries got louder. Girls' screams pierced Evie's ears as she was pushed and shoved by the fans desperate to get closer to their heartthrob. A knot of fear formed in her stomach. This was really rather scary. Even though the crowd probably didn't mean any harm, her and Aaron's vulnerability was obvious. Finally, the bouncer managed to get them through and out of the doors to a waiting car. They were quickly ushered in then the car sped off before they'd had a chance to fasten their seatbelts.

"If you thought that was bad, you should see the reaction when Hunter leaves," laughed Aaron as the hotel disappeared behind them. Unlike herself, he seemed unfazed by what had just happened.

"That was scary," she said, shaking her head to get rid of the ringing of screaming teens in her ears.

"Part of the job, I'm afraid." Aaron took her hand and squeezed it. "Thanks for coming today."

"That's okay. Thanks for asking me. So, where are we going?" she asked as they approached Edgware Road.

"The only place where I blend in unnoticed and that's relatively close to your shop. Camden."

"I love Camden."

"Me too."

They both smiled and Evie's heart did a little somersault in her chest. She sat back in her seat and mentally hugged herself. Despite the unnerving experience with the fans just now, she was surprised at how comfortable she felt with Aaron. The cautious part of her that wanted to protect her heart tried to ring inner alarm bells, but she didn't want anything to spoil today, so she pushed the warning to the back of her mind. She was bloody well going to enjoy herself — and to hell with the consequences.

* * * *

"Wow," gasped Evie as they stepped through the door to Aaron's favorite haunt.

He grinned as she scanned her surroundings with wide eyes. He had considered taking her to one of the many smart restaurants dotted all over Camden Town, but he would have been hassled by fans. Normally he would deal with them with a smile and an autograph, but today he didn't want anything to interrupt his precious time with Evie.

Nick, the burly biker in faded jeans and a Motorhead T-shirt, showed them to a discreet table near the back. The quirky backstreet eatery looked more like a bikers' den than a restaurant, but its eccentric decor and friendly welcome, combined with the best pasta this side of Italy, made it one of London's secret gems that the tourists hadn't yet discovered.

"It's good to see ya, buddy," said Nick as he handed them both a menu. "Where've ya bin?"

"On tour," replied Aaron, putting his menu down without glancing at it. "Nick, this is Evie, a very good friend of mine."

Nick turned to Evie and beamed. "*Ciao, bellissima.*"

"Hi, Nick. It's nice to meet you," she replied, blushing at Nick's appreciative smile.

Nick used to be the toughest, most feared biker in London, although Aaron knew him as a fun-loving and loyal friend who loved animals. He had mellowed a lot since meeting his wife Angie, and the two of them now ran this unique venue that was just as well known for its excellent food as it was for the live gigs at weekends.

After Nick had left with their drinks order Aaron said, "The pasta here is as good as Marco's. I keep telling him that if he ever gets bored with running Dominion he should get a job here."

Evie laughed, her eyes sparkling and catching the light from the candle stuck in an old Mateus wine bottle on the table. "I can't imagine Marco ever getting tired of Dominion."

"Nah, me neither. So, what did you think of the interview?"

"Honestly?"

"Of course."

"It wasn't what I was expecting," she replied, smiling at Nick as he brought their drinks. "Emma didn't seem very experienced, did she?"

"She was a last-minute replacement, apparently. I got the feeling that this might have been her first professional job," said Aaron, trying to quash his irritation. It wasn't just the girl's amateurish questions that had annoyed him, her whole attitude had been perfunctory.

"Aaron, that woman who ran in during the interview, does that happen often?" she asked. She took a sip of her cola, looking at him over the top of her glass as she waited for an answer. Fuck, she was cute.

"Oh yeah, like the crowd thing in the foyer, it happens all the time."

"That's what I thought. So why did you all react as if the woman was about to murder you all? And why was Fabiana so upset?"

Aaron shrugged. "Wouldn't you be if some madwoman threw herself at your husband?"

"Yes, but..."

"Don't worry about it, Evie. It's one of the drawbacks of success. She was harmless." When Evie didn't look convinced he added, "Perhaps we need to find a new security company."

Aaron picked up his beer and took a large swig. Unlike Evie, he didn't have to work anymore today, so he could enjoy a beer or two. He felt bad that he hadn't been honest with her about the threatening letters Hunter had been getting. Right now it was Hunter being targeted, but it could very well be any of them in the firing line. In truth, he was scared that it might put her off him if she knew. He didn't want to take that risk—after all, he was well aware that she already had reservations about him and his career.

Evie seemed happy with his answer and picked up the menu. He didn't need to look at it—he knew every delicious dish by heart.

"What do you recommend?"

"The cannelloni is good. So is the seafood linguine. And the lasagne is exceptional. Oh, and…"

Evie laughed. "Okay, thanks. I'll have the cannelloni."

Aaron called Nick over and ordered the food.

"Hunter and Fabiana are nice," said Evie as Nick walked away.

"Yeah, they've been together over fifteen years and are still totally in love. Hunter has become a good friend since joining Decadence."

"How long you have known him?" She picked up an olive and popped it in her mouth.

"We'd never met until he joined the band. We knew of each other. The music industry is quite small." He grinned as Evie licked the juice from the olive off her lips. *Sexy.* "Our previous singer left unexpectedly the day before a gig, leaving us in the lurch. Levi knew Hunter and asked him to stand in for one night. He was so good that we hired him on the spot."

"Didn't you want to have a go at singing?"

Aaron shook his head. "Nah, I'm not a natural frontman, unlike Hunter. It's thanks to him that Decadence is as big as we are."

"I said to Fabiana earlier that you're a real mixed bunch. There's you and Hunter, the cool rockers, then there's Levi, the smooth one. And then there's Jaymz and Jona. Have they always been so obnoxious?"

"No, believe it or not," laughed Aaron. He loved how direct Evie could be. "The success has gone to their heads and then drugs got involved."

"Do you do drugs?"

"Nope, drugs are for losers. You just have to look at Jaymz and Jona to see that."

Evie nodded in agreement as Nick brought their food over. He watched as she took a bite of the steaming cannelloni and was pleased when her eyelids fluttered as she swallowed the mouthful. *Good, she likes it.*

"So, how do you and Christina know each other?" he asked.

"We went to school together. It's funny, at school we were total opposites. She was the rebellious outgoing one and I was the studious one who always missed out on all the fun because I had a ballet class to attend. We weren't best friends then. It was only after my accident that we grew closer. She supported me through an incredibly difficult time." Evie's eyes glazed over a little as she spoke and Aaron's heart went out to her.

"What happened?" he asked gently.

"My left Achilles snapped as I was preparing for a major audition. If I'd been successful I would have joined one of the biggest ballet companies in the world. But there's no point in dwelling on that now. It's a risk all dancers have to face." She shrugged and tried to look brave, but he could see right through her. He now had a newfound admiration for her. She was one plucky woman for getting through that and rebuilding a successful career.

"That's something else we have in common," he grinned, keen to move the subject away from something that was clearly still very painful for her to talk about.

She raised her eyebrows "What's that?"

"Well, apart from being kinky, we've both lived through the horror of auditions."

"That's true," she chuckled. "So what time are you flying out tomorrow?"

In a flash, his smile vanished. He didn't want to think about the damn trip. He wanted to stay here with Evie. He wanted to get to know her more, to dominate her, whip her before fucking her senseless. "About eleven in the morning, I think. I need to check my schedule when I get home."

"Have you packed yet?"

"Nope. I'll do that later."

Evie chuckled. "If it were me jetting off across the Atlantic to be worshipped by millions of adoring fans I'd have packed a week ago. You must be chuffed to be nominated for an award."

"Yes, but I have to admit the novelty is wearing off. I'd rather not go."

"You're kidding?" She put her knife and fork down, tilted her head to one side and fixed her eyes on him.

"No, seriously. I'd much rather be getting to know you better. I want to take you home, tie you to my bed and never let you go." Just the thought made his cock twitch.

Evie giggled, probably not sure if he was serious or not.

"Promise you'll wait for me?" he asked, looking her straight in the eyes. He was pleased when faint goosebumps on her arms gave away her answer before she spoke.

"Aaron, you're only gone for just over a week," she said, blushing now.

"That's a week too long. Well?"

"Yes, I'll wait for you."

"Good." He reached out and took her hand. "Evie, I know we've only just met, but I mean it when I say that you're special. I'll call you every day unless I'm traveling, okay?"

"You don't have to do that," argued Evie.

"Yes, I do." And he would. Hearing her voice on the end of the phone every day would be the one thing that would get him through this trip. He would be counting the days, and nights, until he could return, and when he did he would do everything in his power to convince her that she

161

was perfect for him.

# Chapter Fifteen

Evie slung her bag on the sofa and flopped down next to it. Tonight's ballet class had been tough, with half an hour's pointe work after a particularly challenging series of *allegro* exercises. She always enjoyed the *jetés*, *assemblés* and other jumps that made up this energetic part of the class, but they usually took their toll on her weakened ankle. She'd loved it nevertheless and had left the studio on the high she always got after a grueling class.

With an exhausted sigh she dragged herself off the sofa and managed to hobble out to the kitchen to retrieve the salad she'd prepared before leaving for class. As she hunted in the fridge for some dressing something soft and fluffy rubbed against her aching legs. She looked down to find Socks looking pleadingly up at her with her beautiful blue eyes. Butter wouldn't melt.

"Hello, gorgeous. You can look as cute as you like, but I won't fall for it again. I've already fed you so stop trying to con me out of another pouch of Sheba."

Socks gave her a cheeky little meow and rubbed her head against Evie's foot. Laughing Evie picked her up and cuddled her. "You're incorrigible," she murmured into her soft fur, "All right, you can have a few cat treats, then we can watch the music awards together."

That seemed good enough for Socks so, when Evie had eaten her salad and Socks had polished off a handful of cheesy treats, she settled down in front of the TV with Socks curled up on her lap, purring loudly. Even though the awards had taken place the day before, the program wasn't aired in the UK until seven o'clock that evening, so she'd set the Sky box to record it while she was out even though she already knew that Decadence had won two awards. Aaron had called as soon as the ceremony had finished last night and had given her all the gossip. Normally she didn't give two hoots about what celebrities got up to, but she couldn't help laughing when Aaron had described Jaymz's disgruntled face when Hunter had won most fanciable male singer.

It was a week since they'd had lunch together in Camden. Aaron had kept his promise and had called every day since, except for when he was traveling, which had surprised her. She'd assumed he'd forget all about her once he was back among the glittering world of showbiz. Sure, he'd said that he wanted to see her when he returned home, but she'd been under no illusions that he'd actually meant it. Why would he be interested in her when he could have practically any woman he wanted?

But the protective barrier she had put up around herself had slowly been broken down as Aaron had kept his word and called her every time he'd said he would. She'd even started believing him when he said that he missed her. Well, it was most likely the sex that he missed rather than her. Even she couldn't deny that the sexual chemistry between them was scorching hot. Unfortunately for her, though, she missed more than just the sex. She missed *him*. That hadn't been a part of the plan. She was only too aware that if she allowed herself to hope for more than no-strings-attached sex she'd get her heart broken. She *knew* that, but that hadn't stopped her from constantly thinking about him and dreaming about his dominant touch. *Damn!*

Shaking her head to rid herself of the erotic lust that always seemed to invade her body when she thought about Aaron Holmes, Evie fast-forwarded through the program until the award for Best Group was due to be announced. The camera panned around the large room to focus on each band as the nominations were shown on the big screen behind the presenters. Decadence was the third band to be

164

nominated, and as soon as their name was called a loud roar filled the auditorium.

The camera focused in on their table and there he was. Evie's stomach did a little flip as a close-up showed Aaron laughing and waving to the crowd. He looked gorgeous. His long dark hair hung loosely down his back and, with his rough stubble and striking tattoos, he looked every bit the successful rock star. Then the camera moved to include the person sitting next to him and Evie's heart sank. The blonde woman, barely out of her twenties by the look of her, was super-skinny and ultra-sexy. And she had her hand on Aaron's arm as if making a statement to the world that he was hers. Someone said something and the blonde laughed, throwing her head back and pushing out her ample bosom. Her nipples were hard and poked provocatively through the material of her sparkly and probably very expensive dress. This woman was everything Evie wasn't. Evie hated her.

As she watched with growing dismay it became more and more apparent that Aaron and Blonde Bitch made the perfect couple. Evie could never live up to that image and she didn't want to either. But Aaron was an international rock star and people would expect him to be with someone who fitted the image of a superstar's girlfriend. Someone like Blonde Bitch.

Thankfully the camera moved away from them to focus on Hunter and Fabiana. Fabiana looked stunning and, as usual, seemed completely comfortable surrounded by so many rich, famous and beautiful people. She looked like one of them. In fact, she *was* one of them. Unlike Evie.

*I don't belong with any of them and I never will.* In a sudden moment of clarity, the cruel truth dawned on her, leaving her with a growing ache somewhere deep inside her. *Aaron will never see me as anything more than a bit of kinky fun. I've got to end this now before I get hurt.*

With tears blurring her vision, she watched as Decadence was announced as the winner. Blonde Bitch jumped up, threw her arms around Aaron and kissed him on the mouth. As the band strode up to the stage to collect the award, Evie had had enough. She picked up the remote and turned the program off, then she buried her face in Socks' fur and cried like she hadn't done in years.

* * * *

Aaron frowned at his phone as the line went dead. *What the hell?* There had been no mistaking Evie's aloofness just now. She'd sounded cool, distant and had been quick to end the call. What had happened to make her act so differently? And just when he'd thought he was finally cracking her armor.

His calls to Evie had been the only thing keeping him sane during this trip. Where once the screaming fans and constant attention had been fun, now it irritated him. Just that afternoon, during another tedious interview with another faceless journalist, his mind had wandered back to the weekend he'd spent with Evie. Had he really only spent two nights with her? He felt as if he'd known her for so much longer. The afternoon he'd spent with her in Hastings had been one of the most enjoyable days he'd had in years. He'd had a sort of epiphany as they'd walked along the water's edge that Sunday afternoon and he hadn't been able to stop thinking about it since. Could he really be in love with a woman he barely knew?

His phone rang, snapping him out of his thoughts. He glanced hopefully at the screen, but it wasn't Evie. He didn't recognize the number and nearly didn't answer it, but Bill had arranged so many interviews that he'd lost track of who was who so he reluctantly accepted the call in case it was important.

"Aaron?" purred a smooth female voice.

"Yeah." He wasn't in the mood to speak with any more journalists and nearly ended the call there and then.

"Hey, sweetie, it's Roxy."

"Who?" He didn't know anyone called Roxy.

The woman laughed, a saccharin-sweet cackle that sounded as fake as the inference that they knew each other. "You know, from the awards. We spent the night together."

What the fuck? "Hey, I can assure you that I did not spend the night with you or anyone else after the awards."

"No, baby, I didn't mean *literally*. I was the model sitting next to you at the table during the ceremony."

Oh yeah. He had a vague memory of a blonde woman sitting next to him. Hunter had said something about the 'models' that had been seated at the table being high-class prostitutes. This particular woman had been shrill and damn annoying.

"How did you get my number?"

"Jaymz gave it to me. He said that you might want a bit of company."

"Did he now?" He was going to fucking kill Jaymz next time he saw him.

"I can be at your hotel in ten minutes," said Roxy in a voice that Aaron assumed was supposed to be seductive.

"No thanks. Look, I don't know what Jaymz said to you, but I can assure you that I do not want any company tonight or any other night. Goodnight." He prodded the screen hard to end the call then threw the phone angrily onto the bed. What the hell was Jaymz playing at? He picked up his phone again and searched through the list of contacts. Enough was enough, he was going to have it out with the prick once and for all.

Before he found Jaymz's number, though, a soft knock on his door halted the search. *For fuck's sake.* If that was Foxy or Roxy or whatever her name was he was going to fucking explode. With an irritated growl he flung the door open and snapped, "I said I don't want any company... Oh, it's you."

"Yeah, mate. Why, who were you expecting?"

"Never mind. You okay?"

Hunter held up a bottle of whiskey and grinned. "Thought you might want a bit of company."

All Aaron's annoyance drained away as he smiled back at his friend and stood to one side to let him into his room. "Sorry about that. Jaymz has been up to his old tricks again. I thought you were the blonde from the awards."

"Nah, blonde doesn't suit me. Got any ice?"

"You bet." As Aaron headed for the small kitchenette that housed a fancy fridge with a built-in ice machine, he said, "Where's Fabiana?"

"Resting because she's exhausted. She went shopping with a couple of the backing singers while we were working today." He laughed as if he found that amusing. "Isn't it funny how we used to find back-to-back interviews and TV appearances fun? Now we just think of it as work."

"Yeah." Aaron watched as Hunter scooped ice into two crystal tumblers then poured a generous amount of whiskey into both of them. As Hunter handed him a glass Aaron sighed. "What happened? Where did the fun go?"

They made their way to the sofas in the plush suite and sat down. "I don't know, mate, but it sure as hell isn't what it used to be," said Hunter, frowning. "Is it the success? I mean, have we just got used to it and the novelty has worn off?"

"Probably. But the atmosphere in the band stinks. That doesn't help." Aaron took a sip of the golden liquid and relaxed as it burned smoothly down his throat. *Mmm, that's a fucking good whiskey.*

"Why? What's changed?"

As Aaron studied his friend he noticed for the first time that Hunter had lost some of the sparkle that had always made him stand out from the crowd. Now he looked tired and pale. He shrugged in response to Hunter's question and shook his head. "I don't know, mate, but Jaymz and Jona have become more obnoxious. That's what Evie called them and she's right. They're becoming intolerable."

"Fucking drugs," muttered Hunter.

"I know for a fact that they're doing coke. I saw them both snort some last night, but it wasn't the time or place to say anything."

"So much for making a no-drugs pact. Fat lot of fucking use that was. They're going to drag us down with them, Aaron."

"Yeah, I know. So what do we do?" Aaron tipped the remaining whiskey into his mouth and shook his head as it blazed its way down to his stomach.

Hunter picked up the bottle and refilled both glasses. "I don't know, mate. But with that and those letters I'm at breaking point." He took a sip then looked at Aaron, his expression solemn. "Look, I wanted to chat with you tonight because I've decided that I'm going to quit the band after the next album. I wanted to let you know first."

Aaron nodded. "I'm not surprised to hear that. I've had similar thoughts myself. What will you do?"

"Go solo, I think. But I need you to know that this has nothing to do with you. You're the only one in this band who's keeping me here. Levi is cool but he keeps himself to himself — you're the only person in the band I actually talk to. It's fucking crazy."

"Yeah, same here. And don't worry about me, I can look after myself."

Hunter stared into his glass as he swirled the drink around in it. "What'll you do?"

Shrugging, Aaron thought about the question for a moment then replied, "I've had enough of being in the limelight, that's for sure. Fame doesn't sit well with me anymore. I'm far more suited to working behind the scenes, so I might try my hand at producing. Are you going to wait until after the next album, then?"

Hunter nodded. "Yeah, I've had my lawyer look into the consequences of breaking our contract and it could get messy. I don't think we've got much choice, we need to do this last album. With any luck, we can go our separate ways in about eighteen months or so."

Aaron's heart sank. Eighteen months. That was a long time, but Hunter was right. Marco might have gotten away with it, but the record companies had learned a harsh lesson from what had happened with Marco and had tightened the clauses binding them to the band.

"What about the letters? Have the police made any progress?"

Hunter shook his head. "Nope, but there haven't been any more since the London gig so maybe whoever's behind it has become bored."

"What if they haven't?"

Hunter sat up straighter and tightened his grip on his glass. "Well, I'll tell you one thing, mate, while they're just targeting me I can deal with it, but if there's any way it could affect Fabiana..." He trailed off and ran his hand through his hair. "I'll do whatever it takes to keep her safe. If that means breaking the contract, then that's what I'll do. If we get any more threats that'll be it."

"Yeah, I don't blame you. I'd do the same." Aaron imagined how he'd feel if Evie had been threatened and his blood ran cold. No way could he ever risk anything happening to her because of his crazy career. No, Hunter had to put his and Fabiana's safety first.

They sat in silence for a while, each in deep thought as they drank more of the whiskey.

"Hey, why the hell were you turning down the advances of that blonde, anyway?" said Hunter suddenly.

Aaron grinned as the heavy atmosphere lifted in an instant. "I've never been into groupies, but I've met someone and she's the only woman I'm interested in."

Hunter raised his eyebrows. "Evie?"

"Yeah." Aaron grinned, his heartbeat speeding up at hearing her name.

"She's cute. I did wonder if there was something going on when you brought her to the interview. Is she...you know, is she into the same kinky stuff that you're into?"

Laughing, Aaron downed the rest of his whiskey and said, "Oh yeah, she's a true submissive and very kinky. And she's funny, warm, intelligent..."

"Mate, you've got it bad. How come you didn't tell me?"

"It's early days yet." Growing serious again, Aaron thought back to Evie's cool manner with him during their earlier phone call. "I'm not sure she likes me as much as I like her, though. I don't mean sexually — the sex is fucking awesome. I want more than that, but I don't think she does."

"So she's using you for kinky sex? You poor man."

Aaron shrugged. "Seriously, mate, something is holding her back and I need to find out what it is. I'm sure it's not just the sex that's special — we have a connection, you know? Yeah, yeah, I know it sounds corny, stop fucking laughing."

"Look, mate, if you like her that much and you think there might be something there, then just tell her and ask that she be straight with you in return."

Nodding, Aaron thought about what Hunter was saying. Yeah, he needed to be honest with Evie, tell her how he felt. But what if he'd read her wrong and he frightened her off? Did he want to risk losing her before they had a chance to explore the relationship further?

"I'm not saying you should declare your undying love to her," continued Hunter as he poured more whiskey into their glasses. "But you do need to get her to open up to you. I thought that's what you kinky people prided yourselves on? You know, total honesty and open communication and all that."

Hunter was right. As soon as he arrived back home he was going to go straight around to Evie's and have it out with her. If she told him to get lost, then at least he'd know where he stood. And if she didn't he'd put her over his knee and give her a good, hard spanking for worrying him. Then he'd fuck her hard until she screamed his name over and over again as she begged to come. Grinning, he put down his glass and said, "Do you think the guys would mind if I got an earlier flight back tomorrow?"

# Chapter Sixteen

"Congratulations, I'm so happy for you." Evie meant it, Tiff deserved this break.

"Thank you. I'm still going to get all my shoes from you, though. I'll just have to make sure I buy in bulk before I leave." Tiff grinned, her pretty face glowing with excitement and happiness.

"When do you leave?" asked Evie, running her fingers along the side of the shoe Tiff was trying on to check the fit.

"Two weeks. I still can't believe it."

"Go up on pointe for me," said Evie, sitting back so she could study the shoes as Tiff rose effortlessly onto the tips of her toes. "These are perfect."

Tiff spent the next twenty minutes trying on leotards, flowing wraparound skirts and scraps of material that were meant to make a dancer look fashionably professional. The whole time Evie listened to Tiff's detailed account of the auditions she'd had to attend before being offered a place with a prestigious ballet company that was about to embark on a world tour. Tiff deserved her success. They'd both attended the same ballet school from the age of eleven and had been friends from day one.

Tiff had been a loyal customer since Evie had opened her shop. She only ever bought her ballet shoes from her and Evie always enjoyed hearing her friend's stories every time she came in. But although she was genuinely pleased for her friend's success, it didn't stop the pain from piercing through her soul at her own loss. As she watched Tiff pick up a packet of convertible tights she swallowed the lump in her throat and forced back the tears lingering just behind her eyes as she made every effort to keep her mask of professional efficiency in place. But Tiff knew her well and her smile faded when she must have seen the pain in Evie's eyes.

"Oh, honey, I'm sorry." Dropping the tights, Tiff wrapped her arms around her and hugged her.

"Don't be," whispered Evie, enjoying the comfort from Tiff's hug. "It's one of the hazards of being a dancer. I really am happy for you."

"Thank you. When I get back, how about you and me go for a night out?"

Evie pulled away and grinned. "Now you're talking."

As Evie cleared away after Tiff had left, Julia popped her head round the door of the stockroom. "Evie, your three o'clock just called and canceled."

"Okay, thanks. Do I have anyone else booked in today?"

"No, that's it."

Evie nodded her thanks and glanced at her watch. Two-thirty. She was quite glad that her next appointment wasn't coming now. It would give her a chance to catch up on some overdue accounts. But first, a well-earned break.

"Fancy a coffee?"

Julia grinned. "Yes please."

"I'll be back in a jiffy." Evie grabbed her purse then headed off to the little café down the road that made the best cappuccinos this side of the river.

Despite her jovial tone a moment ago, Evie queued in the café with a heavy heart. Seeing Tiff was lovely, but it had left her with the same old question that had been haunting her ever since she'd been forced to stop dancing. Why her? Who knew where she could be now? Her ultimate goal had been to audition for the Royal Ballet, and she knew she would have stood a good chance of getting in. The distinctions she'd been awarded for every exam she'd ever taken had promised a glittering career. But now she was an overweight shopkeeper. Okay, she wasn't exactly fat, but next to Tiff she certainly felt like it.

She sighed, the sound of her breath merging with the hiss of the busy espresso machine. Was there some sort of curse on her? It was beginning to feel like everything she wanted was dangled in front of her like the finest chocolate then snatched away before she could taste it. First her career and now Aaron. She'd been a fool to let her guard down where he was concerned. Just when she'd started to believe that it might work she'd watched those bloody awards and reality had kicked back in. An image of Blonde Bitch flashed in front of her eyes, reminding Evie why she'd made the decision to finish with Aaron. No, it was for the best. Better to get it over with now than risk a broken heart a few months down the line.

"Here you are, beautiful." Tony, the flirty barista, interrupted her lament. As he handed her the two takeaway cups of coffee he gave her one of his special smiles that, according to him, was reserved for his favorite customers.

"Thanks, Tony."

Walking back to the shop, she gave herself a pep talk. She was wallowing in self-pity and that had to stop. *For God's sake, Evie, get a grip.* She had so much more than a lot of people did — a business that she loved, plenty of friends and her family who were always there for her, including her precious Socks. *From now on I'm going to focus all my attention on my business and forget about Aaron Holmes.* With her affirmation made, she squared her shoulders and pushed open the door to the shop while trying not to spill any coffee. And very nearly dropped the cups as she stepped into the shop and came face to face with Aaron.

"Hello, Evie." Aaron beamed, looking very pleased to see her.

Evie clutched the cups tightly with numb fingers. Her whole body seemed to be buzzing. Aaron was here. "Hi." Her voice sounded odd. She cleared her throat. "What are you doing here?"

Aaron, who looked like he'd been about to embrace her, stepped back. Still smiling, he said, "I got an earlier flight."

174

"Oh." Every instinct inside her told her to fall into his arms, to kiss him and tell him how happy she was to see him. But that would give him the wrong message so she forced herself to remain rooted to the spot, the coffees balancing precariously in her shaking hands.

Aaron's expression changed from happy to concerned. A worried frown now cast a shadow across his handsome features and Evie ached to reach out to him. But she mustn't. *I must stand my ground.*

"You don't look very pleased to see me. Is there a problem?" Although his voice was calm, Evie picked up the slight edge behind his words and her heart splintered.

"I..." She looked helplessly across at Julia, who looked just as uncomfortable. Although her assistant didn't know what was going on with Aaron, it was blindingly obvious that something wasn't right.

Julia walked across the shop and took the cups from Evie's hands. "Why don't I mind the shop while you two go out for a coffee and a chat?"

Still speechless, Evie looked at the cooling coffees that Julia was setting down on a table. "I'll drink both of them," added Julia. "Go on, *go.*"

Evie turned back to Aaron, who nodded. They could go up to her flat, but there was no way she was going to risk that. Being on her own with Aaron might weaken her resolve. No, it had to be the coffee shop. Safety in numbers and all that. "There's a café down the road where we can talk," she said, desperately fighting the urge to run into his arms. It would be so easy. She could blame her reaction on the shock of his unexpected arrival, then he'd kiss her and everything would be all right. Except that it wouldn't. It would just prolong the inevitable and allow her to become even more attached to him.

"Okay," he said and opened the shop door.

Like the gentleman that he was, he held it open for her to go through first, but as she did, her arm brushed against his. The spark from the contact burned into her skin and

175

her uncertainty grew. Maybe she was being too hasty? *No, it's got to be now.*

It was surreal, retracing her steps from a few minutes ago, this time with Aaron walking silently next to her. As they stepped back into the café, Tony looked at them in surprise. "Hello again," he said, giving her a dazzling smile. "It must be my lucky day. What'll it be this time?" He gave Aaron a puzzled look, as if he thought he recognized him but couldn't remember where he knew him from.

"Just two cappuccinos please, Tony." It occurred to Evie that she hadn't asked Aaron what he wanted, but he didn't say anything so she assumed he was okay with that. "To drink here."

"Okay, beautiful. Take a seat and I'll bring them over."

They sat down opposite each other at a small table by the window and waited for Tony to bring the coffees. She tried to ignore the curious stares but it was bloody hard when almost everyone in the café was looking in their direction. "Oh my God, is that Aaron Holmes?" cried a teenage girl, gawping at them with her mouth hanging open.

"I've missed you," said Aaron, seemingly oblivious to the attention he was attracting.

*Oh, I've missed you too. More than you will ever know.* "Aaron, please don't." This was going to be harder than she'd feared. She locked her fingers together so tightly that her knuckles were white.

It was a relief when Tony brought the coffees over, providing a brief distraction. He was gone all too soon though, leaving her alone again with Aaron. She took a deep breath. Might as well get it over with. "Aaron, I've had some time to think while you've been away and I don't think we should continue to see each other."

"Why not? I thought we were pretty good together. Have I done something to upset you?" He didn't look angry, just hurt, which made her feel even worse.

Evie ran her hand through her hair as she gathered as much strength as she could muster. "No, Aaron. You're lovely, please don't think this is anything you've done. It's me."

"Right, I'm getting the 'it's not you, it's me' brush off. I get it."

"No! Sorry, I didn't mean to say that. It's just..." How the hell could she tell him that she was terrified that she might fall in love with him only to be cast aside when he tired of her and moved on to someone more glamorous? He'd deny it, of course, which was why she had to be ruthless. "I don't want any kind of relationship right now," she managed to say. "I want to focus on my business. You're a great guy and a wonderful Dom and I've really enjoyed playing with you, but I've got other priorities right now." *Like trying to protect myself from a broken heart.*

Aaron stared at her in silence for what seemed like forever. Neither of them had drunk any of their coffee, but Evie found that clutching the hot cup was easier than crunching the bones in her fingers. She couldn't bring herself to look at him so she stared blindly down at the chocolaty froth.

Finally, Aaron broke the silence. "Evie, I'm not sure what's prompted this, but if you can promise me that this is what you truly want I'll respect that and leave you alone. But be in no doubt it's not what I want."

"I'm sorry, Aaron. I really am." The words hurt as if they were cutting her throat as she spoke them.

"Tell me again. Is this *really* what you want?"

*No, no, no.* "Yes, Aaron. I don't want to see you anymore."

Evie held her breath. For the tiniest moment she thought he was going to argue, to demand that she rethink, but when he nodded then stood up she knew he'd gotten the message loud and clear.

He put enough coins to pay for the coffees on the table then turned and left without another word, leaving her staring after him through the blur of her tears.

\* \* \* \*

177

"She did what?"

The look on Christina's face would almost have been funny if Aaron hadn't been hurting so much.

"She finished with me." He tried looking casual, as if it was no big deal, but he knew Christina would see straight through him. He had arranged to meet Marco for a drink tonight, but his friend was held up in traffic. Christina had popped in to join them for a quick drink, but wasn't staying long. Apparently she was shopping nearby and that was far more important. Aaron would never understand how shops could be preferable to a bar.

Christina was shaking her head, as if she had difficulty processing the information. "Why?" she finally asked.

Aaron swirled the rich golden whiskey around in his glass as he tried to make sense of Evie's decision. "Apparently she wants to focus on her business."

"Bullshit."

"I know."

"Aaron, the shop is really successful and she has Julia to help now. I don't believe that for a second." Her wide eyes mirrored the shock that had stunned him since yesterday.

"She did say something when I first met her about expanding the shop," he muttered, rubbing his chin.

"But that's no reason for finishing with you. Look, she really liked you, Aaron. I mean, *really* liked you."

"Did she?" He'd thought so too. He'd spent the most of last night thinking back over their time together, trying to work out where he'd gone wrong. She had submitted so beautifully to him and appeared to have enjoyed their scenes, and the sex that followed, as much as he had. And what about that day at the beach? He'd been so sure that she had also felt the spark that had stunned him as they'd walked along the shore. And she had promised to wait for him to return from his trip. But on the other hand, she had declined him that first night when he'd offered to stand in for Ross. And there were the times when she'd seemed to withdraw from him without any apparent reason.

"I don't get it," said Christina.

He shrugged and took a large sip of his whiskey. No, he didn't get it either. Damn, he'd felt so sure that there was a special connection between them. Surely he hadn't imagined it?

"So what did you do?" asked Christina, her voice a little calmer now that she'd gotten over the initial shock of his news.

"Nothing. What could I do, Christina? I have to respect her wishes and I could tell she was struggling…" He trailed off. Should he have given her a harder time and demanded more of an explanation? But that wasn't his style. The last thing he'd wanted to do was make her feel worse. But maybe that was exactly what he should have done?

"Aaron, you donut, don't take no for an answer. I told you, she's bloody crazy about you." She frowned for a moment as if something had occurred to her then said, "I've just remembered something she said last week. She told me that she doesn't believe that someone as rich and famous as you would be interested in someone like her and that you'll eventually dump her for someone more glamorous. I think she believes that she's not good enough for you, Aaron."

"Don't be stupid, of course she is," he retorted angrily. "She's the most amazing woman I've ever met."

"And did you tell her that?"

"I didn't know that's how she felt." Fuck, had he really gotten it so wrong? And he'd walked away without a fight thinking that that was what she wanted. And now she was going to be thinking that she'd been right all along and that he didn't really care. *Fuck!*

Christina reached across the table and took his hand. For a submissive she sure as hell didn't hold back with her opinions or gestures. Giving it a squeeze she said, "Don't give up on her so easily, Aaron. Call her, insist on seeing her and tell her how you feel. Then punish the fuck out of her for dumping you."

Aaron nearly spat out the mouthful of whiskey he'd just

taken as laughter bubbled up inside him. There was nothing he'd like more than to put Evie over his knee and give her a damn good hiding, followed by a good hard fuck, of course. Christina was right, he'd believed what she'd said and given in far too easily. He sat up straighter, feeling as if a heavy weight had been lifted from his shoulders.

"Thanks," he said, holding his glass up to salute her. "You subs sure as hell know how to make a point. Thank goodness."

"No problem. It's our job to keep you Doms from acting like complete halfwits," she said with a cheeky grin.

"Watch it or I'll tell Marco you've been misbehaving." He smiled back. Marco was a lucky bloke, he'd struck gold with this one.

"So are you going to call her?" she asked, clearly not content with leaving the subject unfinished.

"Yeah, but she won't agree to see me. I wouldn't if I were in her shoes."

Christina laughed and picked up her phone. "No, but she'll see me."

Signaling to the barman for another drink, he held his breath as Christina keyed a text message on her phone.

"There." She looked pretty pleased with herself as she put her phone back down on the table.

"What did you say?"

"I told her that I need to talk to her and that I'll pop round to hers tomorrow at seven p.m. She'll think I'll want to moan about Marco."

Aaron raised his eyebrows and put on his sternest expression. "You moan about your Dom behind his back?" He had to try really hard not to ruin the effect by laughing.

Christina giggled. "Of course I do. It's a sub's prerogative." Her phone bleeped with an incoming text and Christina picked it up and read the message. "There, it's sorted. The rest is up to you. Don't blow it."

Aaron chuckled. "In the last few minutes you've called me a donut and a halfwit, you've admitted that you complain about your Dom and you've just told me not to blow it with Evie as if I'm completely useless. I must have a word with Marco about your training. You really are quite impudent. But thanks, I appreciate it."

"You can always tell Marco that I need a good spanking as punishment," she said coyly.

"And now you're topping from the bottom, you little brat."

Laughing, she stuck her tongue out at him. "Seriously, Aaron, I'm so pleased that Evie has met you. She's been through a lot and deserves a chance to be happy. Don't hurt her, will you?"

Aaron smiled. "You have my word, Christina."

"Good. Because if you do you'll have me to deal with."

Despite the warmth in her smile, Aaron suspected that she might only have been half joking. Evie had a good friend in Christina. By the time Marco turned up the need to drown his sorrows with his mate had vanished. It was time to celebrate.

"What are you looking so pleased about?" asked Marco, giving Christina a kiss.

"Oh, nothing." She winked at Aaron and stood up. "Just putting the world to rights."

"Aren't you staying?" asked Marco as Christina picked up her jacket.

"Hey, it's Thursday, which means late-night shopping. I'm out of here. See ya."

As Christina left the bar, Marco studied Aaron. "You all right? I got the feeling from the tone of your message that something was wrong."

"Wrong?" replied Aaron, laughing, "Whatever gave you that idea?"

At that moment a couple of giggling girls approached their table and asked for Aaron's autograph. As he posed for a photograph with them, his thoughts were filled with hope and determination that he would win Evie back. One way or another.

# Chapter Seventeen

The doorbell rang just as Evie put a bowl of food down for Socks. She really wasn't in the mood for company, but Christina had sounded pretty insistent in her message so she hadn't had the heart to say no. As she passed the mirror in the hall she caught a glimpse of herself and thanked God it was only Christina at the door. Her hair was scraped back in a ponytail, she'd removed her makeup and had changed into old leggings and a baggy T-shirt. Tonight was about girly comfort and gossip. It might do her good to voice her doubts about finishing with Aaron to Christina. Her friend would soon reassure her that she'd done the right thing and that he would only have hurt her in the end. She pressed the door release for the external door without bothering to pick up the entry phone. Christina knew her way up.

"Hi." She swung the door open, expecting to see Christina waving a bottle of wine at her, but nearly slammed it shut again when she saw Aaron, grinning sheepishly. He was holding two takeaway pizza boxes in one hand and a bottle of champagne in the other.

She quickly stomped on the urge to run into his arms. Doing her best to stand tall and unyielding, she folded her arms and glared at him. *Why won't he leave me alone?* "I'm expecting company," she said.

"Yes I know, *me*." He smiled and looked down at the pizza boxes. "Are you going to let me in before these get cold?" Without waiting for an answer, he pushed past her and strode into her flat.

Speechless at his sheer cheek, Evie put her hands on her hips and scowled.

"Where's the kitchen?" asked Aaron and headed toward the bathroom. "Not here, obviously. How about this one?" This time he found the room he was looking for and walked brazenly in. Socks looked up from her bowl to check out the new human. Aaron put the pizza boxes on the table and smiled down at the curious cat. "Hello there." He kneeled down and gently scratched her behind the ear. The little traitor then looked up at him with adoring eyes before head-butting his hand for more attention.

When Socks had had enough fuss she resumed her dinner and Aaron stood back up and faced Evie. "Where do you keep your glasses?"

"Aaron. What are you doing here? Didn't I make myself clear yesterday?"

"Oh yes, perfectly." After opening a couple of wall-mounted cupboards Aaron finally found what he was looking for and picked up two long-stemmed champagne flutes. "Now let me get this champagne open. I don't know about you, but I could do with a drink." He popped the cork then poured the sparkly liquid into the two flutes. Handing her a glass he said, "Cheers."

Evie took a large sip of the champagne in an effort to control her outrage. How dare he barge into her flat like this? *Mmm, nice champagne.* "Aaron—" she started, but stopped when he held his hand up to silence her.

"You made yourself clear yesterday, Evie, but I didn't. I was so shocked that I didn't say any of the things I needed to say. I honestly thought you meant it when you said you didn't want to see me again. I even believed your story about needing to focus on your business. By the way, you're due a punishment for lying to me."

*What the hell?* But she couldn't deny the rush of adrenaline the word 'punishment' sent soaring through her veins. *Damn him.* Anyway, what was he talking about? She raised her eyebrows and hoped she looked as fierce as she felt.

"You promised me that this was what you wanted. I don't believe you were telling the truth." He leaned against the doorframe, looking impossibly gorgeous, and studied her.

"You arrogant bastard," she spat as fury swept over her. She'd been right in her assumption that celebrities had egos the size of Greater London.

Aaron, who seemed infuriatingly oblivious to her exasperation, picked up the pizza boxes. "Come on, let's eat," he said and strode out of the kitchen. "And talk."

She sighed as she followed him into the living room. "Aaron, there's nothing to talk about. I can't believe you've taken this so badly. It's not even as if we had a relationship, we've only known each other just over a week."

"Two weeks, actually."

"Whatever."

Aaron sat down in the armchair and nodded toward the sofa. "Sit down."

"Don't tell me what to do," she snapped.

Aaron shrugged. "Okay, if you're comfortable eating your dinner standing up."

"Oh for God's sake," she muttered under her breath as she slumped onto the sofa.

"Here, it's pepperoni," said Aaron, handing her one of the pizza boxes.

"Thanks." She took the box with reluctance. As she opened it the delicious smell of cheese and pepperoni wafted up to her nostrils and sent her stomach into overdrive. She hadn't eaten since breakfast. She took a bite of the triangle she'd picked up and closed her eyes as the melted cheese and spicy meat partied on her tongue. *Heaven.*

When she'd swallowed the mouthful, she tried again. "Aaron, I appreciate the effort you've gone to, but this doesn't change anything." She wished it would, but there was no way she could allow herself to reconsider. It was her heart on the line, not his.

"Okay, all I'm asking is that you listen to what I've got to say. Then, if you still want me to leave I will. Deal?"

Seeing as he'd brought dinner and champagne, that seemed reasonable enough. "Okay."

"Good. I'm going to be completely honest with you. I didn't tell you this before because I appreciate that it's early days and I didn't want to scare you off."

Evie ate in silence as she waited for him to continue, but she didn't take her eyes off him. She couldn't. When he ran his hand along his stubble her stomach tightened. For the first time Evie saw a different person, not the confident rock star, but a man struggling to open his heart. That little bit of vulnerability struck a chord with her because it made him seem more real.

"Evie, I won't beat around the bush. I like you a lot. In fact, I'd go as far as saying that I can see myself falling in love with you. Yeah, I know we've only just met and I'm not about to declare my undying love just yet, but I believe there's something special between us and I think you feel it too. Am I right?"

Whoa! Where the hell had that come from? Evie had stopped chewing the piece of pizza in her mouth as Aaron had said the word 'love'. Now she tried to force it down as it stuck in her throat. *Love?* Was he joking? But his eyes were warm with sincerity and his focus on her was unwavering. Yes, she had felt it, but that didn't change the fact that she would never fit into his life.

"Please say something." He rubbed his chin again and held her eyes with a beseeching gaze.

"Yes," she managed to say, "I did feel it, but it scares me. Aaron, you can't begin to compare our lives, we're as different as the sun and the moon. 'Never the twain shall meet' springs to mind."

Aaron rose and crossed the room to where she was sitting on the sofa. He sat down next to her and took her shaking hand. "What exactly are you scared of?"

"Being hurt. I'm scared you're going to break my heart because sooner or later you'll tire of me and move on to someone more befitting your lifestyle." There, she'd said it. Those words conveyed everything she'd been feeling since last weekend.

Aaron laughed. "Evie, you don't get it, do you? I don't want the glitz and glamor. I hate the life I'm leading right now — in fact, I'm thinking of quitting the band. But forget that for a minute. If you think I'll hurt you because you're not a celebrity then you cannot be more wrong. You are everything I like in a woman. You're beautiful, intelligent, warm, funny, sexy — need I go on?"

Evie smiled. "No, you're embarrassing me."

Aaron grinned and reached up to wipe a crumb or something from her lips. "We're not as different as you think. We both have successful careers, we have similar interests, the same taste in music and you're as kinky as I am. I know it's early days yet, but I know we're right for each other. Once we've ironed out the kinks we'll be the perfect couple."

"Ironed out the kinks?" said Evie, unable to hide a smile. "Nice choice of words."

Aaron chuckled. "Just believe me when I say that you are everything I want in a woman, kinks and all."

This was everything Evie wanted to hear, but it was too good to be true. Something wasn't right. "Are you really going to quit the band?"

He nodded. "Yeah, although I'm contracted to make another album so it seems I've got no choice but to wait another year or two."

"Look," said Evie, shaking her head, "although I don't particularly like the lifestyle you lead I wouldn't want you to give up your career because of me. You may think it's okay now, but you'd end up resenting me and I could never live with that. You see? It just won't work."

"For crying out loud, Evie. I'm not quitting the band because of you. I'd already made the decision and the only reason I haven't done so already is because of the damned contract. There are things going on that I can't go into right now but, trust me, there's nothing I want more than to leave and get my life back."

"But what would you do?"

"I'd love to have a go at producing. That way I'd still be involved with music, but I'd be behind the scenes instead of in the limelight. That's the dream," said Aaron, his eyes shining with optimism. "But that dream wouldn't be whole unless I had you."

Evie put the pizza box down and picked up her champagne. She needed a drink while she processed everything Aaron had just said. He wanted her, he really wanted her. She took a sip and closed her eyes as the bubbles tickled her tongue. When she opened them again Aaron gently took the flute from her hand and put it on the coffee table. "Let's see if this will help you to understand," he said softly.

He leaned toward her and brushed his lips lightly across her own.

"Aaron," she whispered.

"Shh." This time his lips locked firmly onto hers. With a deep rumble he pushed his tongue into her mouth and kissed her hard. Every last drop of resistance drained out of her as she responded to him. When he gripped her ponytail and held her head in place she groaned as she fell deeper under his spell. Finally, he let go and pulled away. "Do you get it now, Evie?"

"Yes, oh yes."

Smiling, he ran the tip of his finger over her lips then down her neck, sending little shivers of pleasure ricocheting across her skin. "Now, just to be completely clear. Will you be my girlfriend and submissive?"

"You want me to be both?" she drawled, deliberately teasing him. "Oh, Sir, what a greedy man you are."

He gripped her hair again and pulled her head back. "Answer me, you little minx."

It was hard to look serious when he was so clearly trying to contain his laughter. The combination of humor and dominance was irresistible and melted away any last doubts she might have had. He really did want her and, now that she'd finally managed to rid herself of the fear of heartbreak, she could admit that she wanted him too.

Oh, how she wanted him. "Yes, Sir. I agree," she said and closed her eyes again as he pulled her in for another kiss.

"We need to talk about your punishment." Aaron tried to hide his smile as Evie's pupils dilated and her cheeks flushed. She wouldn't be quite so keen later when she found out what the punishment was. "But first I want to talk about the kink. We can discuss limits later, but right now I want to get an idea of what you want from it."

"Okay," said Evie slowly, with a slight edge of apprehension in her voice.

"Is that a problem?"

She twisted a strand of hair that had fallen loose from her ponytail around her finger as she hesitated. "No, not a problem really..."

"But?"

"But I get embarrassed talking about my fantasies. You know?"

He smiled. Fuck, she was adorable. "Yeah, I understand. Take your time, but remember I already have a pretty good idea of what you like. I just want to make sure there are no misunderstandings. I can be a pretty strict Dom so I need to know you're happy with what I expect from you as my submissive. I will compromise on things that you might not be comfortable with, but that's why we need to have this chat. Okay?"

She nodded, her cheeks now a deep red. His stomach contracted as a myriad of emotions washed through him. How was it possible to experience such overpowering feelings of lust and longing mixed with tenderness and the need to dominate all at the same time?

He picked up the champagne flute he'd refilled a moment ago. "What do you want, Evie?" He held the glass to her lips and allowed her to take a sip.

When she'd swallowed the drink she coughed nervously then raised her gaze to meet his and said, "I want to be *dominated*. I want you to push me to my knees, pull my hair and make me do as you command. I want you to punish me if I don't please you and reward me when I do. I want you to put me over your knee and spank me until I'm begging for mercy…"

Aaron's mouth went dry at the passion burning in Evie's eyes as she spoke. This was what *he* wanted. He enjoyed most aspects of BDSM, but dominance and submission was what mattered to him the most and it seemed that Evie felt the same way. Unable to stop himself, he took her mouth again, this time more forcibly as he tested her words. As he'd hoped, her body went limp as she surrendered to him. He pulled away reluctantly. They needed to finish this conversation before they could go any further.

"Get on your knees," he ordered, the deep rasp betraying his overwhelming arousal.

"Yes, Sir," she murmured and slid off the sofa.

Once she was kneeling before him he stroked the top of her head and gazed down at her. God, she was beautiful. She had slipped into a submissive headspace with such ease that it was clear she wanted his firm discipline as much as he wanted to give it. "Good girl. Okay, let's set some rules. Do you like rules, Evie?"

"Yes, Sir," she replied without hesitation.

"Good. These rules will apply only when we're alone unless we're at a BDSM event. I don't want a twenty-four-seven dynamic and I don't believe you do either. Am I right?"

"Yes, Sir," she said with a strong hint of relief.

"Okay. First, when you are on your knees your eyes must be cast down toward the floor." As she started to lower her head he said, "Not now, though. While we have this chat I want your eyes on me. I'll let you know when to look down."

She nodded and waited for him to continue.

"Second, you're forbidden to wear underwear when we're together. Rule number three, you will call me Sir at all times unless we're around vanilla people. Number four, you will never come without my permission. These rules are to enhance our time together, to reinforce the D/s dynamic, and I may add to them as we go on."

He stopped and watched her reaction. She didn't seem to have any problems with this, as her eyes were now glazed and the corners of her mouth turned up just enough to give away her excitement.

"One more rule, Evie," he said, taking her chin in a firm grip. "I will expect you to use your safeword if anything ever becomes too much. I cannot emphasize this enough. Okay?"

"You have my word, Sir."

"Good. The only other thing I have to say right now is that this is meant to be enjoyable for both of us. I want us to have fun and, although I take D/s seriously, it's important that you get as much out of this as I do. When I ask how you're feeling about something we're doing I will expect you to be honest."

She nodded and, satisfied that she understood, he then said, "Look down now."

She obeyed immediately and lowered her head. She had already put her arms behind her back and locked her fingers together as she'd kneeled. He liked that, it made her look more submissive. His cock stirred—it was time to play.

"Get up, strip naked then bend over the armrest of that chair over there."

He folded his arms and didn't take his eyes off her as she pulled her T-shirt over her head. He wanted her to feel the intensity of his gaze as she bared her body for him. When she was naked she hesitated, looking a little uncertain, but as soon as he nodded toward the chair she walked over and bent over the armrest as he'd instructed.

Taking his time, he walked round to stand in front of her and rolled up his sleeves. Then he undid the buckle of his belt and pulled it off, making sure she could see what he was doing. "Eyes down," he ordered when he was happy that Evie knew what was coming.

"I'm going to spank you now, but this isn't your punishment. That'll come later." He chuckled. "No, this is for your pleasure. And mine, of course."

He ran his fingers down her back then over each cheek. Her skin was velvety soft and creamy white, a perfect canvas for him to redden with his hand. Then he smacked her, not hard, but with enough pressure for a satisfying slap to fill the still air. He rained a succession of similar smacks down on her buttocks until they turned a pretty shade of pink. She wouldn't be hurting yet, but would be warmed up nicely for what was coming next.

Without warning her, he delivered the first real hit on her right buttock. Her groan connected with his cock and he had to resist the urge to fuck her there and then. He spanked her hard, alternating the blows across both cheeks and the backs of her thighs. Her skin reddened and his hand stung. *Lovely*. He continued delivering the blows, hard and relentless, until he gradually fell into his own world of pleasure. His mind emptied and the only thing he became aware of was Evie and the scene they shared.

When her whimpers turned into gasps, he stopped and rubbed her bottom. So hot. So lovely. He kissed each cheek, his lips melting on her burning flesh.

"I'm going to spank you with my belt now. Can you take it for me?"

"Oh, yes please, Sir."

He chuckled and ran his fingers along the crack of her ass then down between her legs. "Fuck," he groaned as he made contact with her hot, soaking wet folds. *Best stop right there*. He removed his fingers and got a frustrated sigh from her. He smiled. This was just the beginning.

He looped the belt in his hand then hit her with it across the back of both buttocks. He didn't hit her too hard, as he had yet to get used to her pain threshold, but it was certainly enough to make her cry out. He hit her again, then again, with just enough impact to deliver a fiery sting.

She took the beating well, staying in the position he'd

demanded of her. Well, mostly. Now it was time to up the intensity. "Evie, I want you to count these last ten strikes. Be warned, they'll be harder than before."

The first stroke made her cry out and left a pretty red mark across her bottom. "Count, Evie."

"One, Sir," she moaned, her voice becoming muffled.

She continued to count as he increased the force with each strike. By the time he'd reached number ten her ass was lined with a series of red stripes, each one proudly displaying her pain. She'd screamed as the last two strikes had landed yet had refused to use her safeword. Aaron had watched her carefully, ready to stop if she showed any signs of distress, but he'd resumed when she'd asked for more. She was such a greedy sub—his favorite kind.

Satisfied that she had reached the peak of what she could take, he dropped the belt on the floor and scooped her up into his arms. As he carried her over to the sofa she wrapped her arms around his neck and held on tightly. It never failed to humble him when a submissive willingly gave him the power to control her. It was the most precious gift that he would never take for granted. He tightened his hold on her. The delicious musky scent from her pussy wafted up, seeped into his nostrils and sent shots of electricity down to his cock. He wanted her more than ever at that moment, but it was not the time. Right now, she needed his warmth and comfort then, when she was recovered, he was going to take her deeper into her world of submissive lust. Then, and only then, would her punishment begin.

# Chapter Eighteen

"Do you want some more water?" asked Aaron as he took the empty glass from Evie's hands.

"No, thank you, Sir."

He put the glass down then pulled her close to him again. They'd been snuggling on the sofa for at least half an hour since he'd spanked her and Evie seemed back to her usual self. She'd no doubt have marks from his belt tomorrow and, if she was anything like a lot of other submissives, she'd be happy and proud of them.

He tightened his arm around her. The longer he held her, the more his feelings for her intensified and the harder his cock became. It was straining against his jeans, throbbing impatiently as more blood rushed to it with every lustful thought of what was coming next.

"Are you ready for some more fun?"

Her head jerked and her eyes lit up. "There's more? Oh, yes please."

"Does the idea of sucking my cock excite you, Evie?"

"Yes, Sir, it does," she replied, her voice growing husky.

Aaron smiled and kissed her on the lips. Then he took hold of her chin and forced her to look at him as he growled, "Good. Then, afterward, you'll learn what your punishment will be."

She nodded and looked thoughtful. She'd no doubt be wondering what he had planned for her and when he would do it. He almost felt sorry for her but, hey, she had lied to him and had earned it. He had a feeling she would enjoy this next bit, though, nearly as much as he was going to.

"Get on your knees, hands behind your back."

As soon as she was in position he took some rope out of his jacket pocket and tied her hands together, just tight enough so she couldn't escape without cutting off her blood supply.

Standing directly in front of her, he unzipped himself and took his swelling cock out of its confines. The relief was soon outweighed by painful need as Evie licked her lips playfully.

She leaned toward him and licked the tip of his cock. The warm, moist velvety touch felt so sublime that he couldn't suppress the rumbling moan that escaped from somewhere deep inside him. Then she flicked her tongue over the slit, forcing a little pre-cum out, which she lapped up before very gently biting him, just hard enough to cause the smallest sensation of pain.

"God, Evie." He badly needed her to take him fully into her mouth, but the little minx ran her tongue along the length of his shaft until she reached the base then moved down to his balls. *Fuck!* Without the use of her hands she could only lick them, but she did so with so much ardor that he thought they might explode. When he could bear it no longer he grabbed her hair and moved her away so she couldn't reach him for a moment. He didn't want to come just yet. Looking down at her, he noticed she was grinning. So she was deliberately teasing him, was she? *Just you wait, little subbie.*

"Open your mouth."

Like a good girl she obeyed and he finally slid into what felt like a warm tropical haven. She sucked and massaged him, every now and again grazing him with her teeth, sending shock waves down to his testicles. Giddy with ecstasy, he groaned as he momentarily lost all sense of reality. *Fuck, I'm going to come.* He stepped back, badly in need of a little respite, and stroked Evie's hair as he gathered himself. When she smiled up at him his chest tightened. She was so beautiful, so perfect. *She's mine.*

When he was in control again he nodded at Evie, who took him eagerly back into her mouth.

"Can you take all of me?"

"Mmm," she mumbled sending little vibrations shooting down to his balls.

In a split second he was back on the precipice trying not to fall over the edge of a sky-high cliff. *Focus, man.*

Slowly he slid farther in until his cock touched the back of her throat. She gagged, but drew him back in again until she adjusted. Over and over she took him all the way, keeping him there for longer each time. It humbled him that she trusted him enough to let him do this. After all, right now, he was controlling her ability to breathe. But she clearly had no reservations as she took him back in after each time he'd allowed her to catch her breath.

Suddenly the slow pace wasn't enough anymore, he needed to fuck.

Grabbing her head with both hands, he said, "I'm going to fuck your mouth now. If you need me to stop shake your head from side to side, okay?" She nodded and, just to be on the safe side, he waited for any sign of objection. When there was none, he thrust in and fucked her face hard and fast until he drew dangerously close to the edge again then pulled out. His balls had tightened unbearably and he knew he wouldn't be able to hold on much longer. Still holding on to her head, he bent down and murmured in her ear, "Keep your mouth open when I come. I want you to hold onto any cum that lands on your tongue. Do not do anything until I tell you to."

She nodded, her eyes wild with desire, and parted her gorgeous lips. He managed to place the tip of his cock at the opening of her mouth just in time for the first spurt of cum to shoot out. He closed his eyes as his balls erupted, sending flashes of light across his eyelids and strong shudders through his entire body. When he opened them again he nearly came undone when he saw Evie waiting with her mouth open, trying to hold onto as much of his cum as she could. The rest had trickled down her face and onto her chest. A stream had pooled on her nipple before running down over her stomach and still she held onto what she could, obediently waiting for permission to swallow it.

He grabbed hold of a handful of her hair and growled, "Swallow it now, baby."

She closed her mouth and swallowed, then opened it again to show him that his cum was all gone. Fuck, he was getting hard again.

"Good girl." He reached between her legs and smiled as his finger made contact with her moisture, which was running down the insides of her thighs. She was so wet she was dripping. "Enjoy that, did you?"

"Yes, Sir," she said, her voice almost squeaking with excitement.

"Are you horny?"

Her eyes flashed with hunger as she nodded. "Oh, yes, Sir. Very."

"Good." He rubbed her moisture along her folds, marveling at how easily his fingers slid inside her. She groaned as he used just one finger to fuck her, but when she tilted her pelvis forward to give him better access he pulled it out again without warning.

Her moan of protest was adorable. "Sir, I need to come."

"I know."

"Please, Sir…"

"No. This is your punishment, Evie. You don't get to come tonight."

"What?" Confusion blurred the lust in her eyes then frustration when she saw that he meant it. "But…"

"If you're a good girl you'll get to come tomorrow, but, until then, you are forbidden to touch yourself. Am I clear?"

She glared at him, sparks of fire igniting in her eyes. "Aaron…"

"Sorry, but there's nothing to discuss. It's late. I'm going to make us a hot drink then you're going to sleep in my arms."

Evie stared at him in disbelief, clearly lost for words. Grinning, he held out his hand to help her stand. When she was back on her feet, he swatted her ass and said, "What time do you need to be up in the morning?"

* * * *

Evie didn't know whether she wanted to kill Aaron or hump him. She was so bloody turned on she could barely think straight. The spanking had been delicious and had put her in the right headspace from the onset. When he'd then ordered her to her knees to suck his cock, the rush of lust that had soared through her body had been overwhelming.

She had loved doing that for him and had reveled in his dominant hold over her. But she had also noticed the caring side that he had tried so hard not to show. She had seen him check on her and that had made her give even more of herself to him. Never had she trusted anyone the way she trusted Aaron.

And when he'd come in her mouth and ordered her to wait for permission before swallowing it... A wave of heat brought her out in a sweat as her pussy throbbed at the memory, and she squeezed her thighs together in an effort to create a little relief. She considered waiting for him to fall asleep then sneaking into the bathroom to sort herself out, but quickly discarded the idea. No matter how desperate she was to come, Aaron trusted her and she didn't want to let him down. And, anyway, she deserved the punishment. She *had* lied about her reasons for finishing with him. If she had been honest with him he would have been able to reassure her sooner and save her a night of tears.

The clock in the hallway struck midnight and she snuggled deeper into Aaron's arms. How lovely to bask in his warmth, to feel his arms holding her protectively. She felt safe, cared for. And fucking horny!

Then, without warning, Aaron practically threw her off him and rolled her onto her back. Pinning her hands down onto the mattress, he kissed her hard and nudged her legs apart with his own.

"Aaron," she gasped, when he freed her mouth. "I don't think I'll be able to stop myself if you…"

He put a finger over her mouth to silence her. "I said you'd be allowed to come tomorrow. Well, it's tomorrow."

"You tricked me," giggled Evie. "I thought you were punishing me."

"Do you really think I'd do all that to you and not let you come? And, for your information, I was punishing you. The punishment was to let you think you wouldn't get an orgasm tonight." He pushed himself up onto his elbows and looked down at her. His eyes smoldered and Evie shivered under their intense heat. "I think you've suffered enough."

He rained tiny kisses down her neck, over her chest until he reached her breasts. Then he took a nipple into his mouth and sucked until a sharp pain sent shocks down the inside of her body straight to her pussy. Arching her back to relieve the pressure, she groaned as Aaron bit down ever so slightly on the hard nub.

Pulling away, he grinned and said, "That was payback for biting my cock." Then he moved over to her other nipple and did it all again. By the time he stopped her nipples were swollen and sore and she was almost delirious with need. Her blood buzzed as it pulsed through her veins and her skin tingled with every touch of his lips as they moved down over her stomach toward her legs. Then they moved over her bare mound and found their way to the center of the raging fire. He kissed her labia then nibbled at her folds before finally thrusting his tongue inside her.

"Oh God," she gasped as he licked and sucked at her juices.

He brought his hand down between her legs and ran his fingers over her clit. His touch was too light, though. She needed more, and desperately arched her back for more pressure. Aaron chuckled and continued teasing her relentlessly. It was when he rubbed his rough stubble along her wet folds, though, that the agony really started. She lost herself between the pain of her need, his finger now fucking her pussy and his tongue flicking over her clit. She could bear it no more. The core of her body became rigid as the pressure inside her grew ever more intense until finally...

"Sir, I need to... Argh..." She screamed as she splintered into a million pieces, each segment of her body floating above her before falling slowly back into place. All the pressure, the desperate need for release, evaporated as she swam in the warmth of the embers still flickering inside her. The last thing she was aware of was Aaron's strong arms wrapping around her like a blanket of euphoria.

* * * *

"I've got a bone to pick with you," said Evie, and smiled as Christina coughed into the phone.

"You do?"

"As if you didn't know. I thought you were supposed to come and see me last night? You *really* needed to talk about something? And then, surprise, surprise, Aaron turns up instead. What a coincidence."

"Ah, yes. About that..." Christina paused, probably trying to work out if Evie really was pissed off or not. "Are you cross?"

"What do you think?" *Might as well let her suffer a bit longer.*

"Evie, I'm sorry if I overstepped the mark, but he's crazy about you and I know you really like him and I thought..."

"Don't worry, it's fine," said Evie, laughing. *It's more than fine.*

"Really? Oh, thank God, I thought you were going to kill me. So, what happened?"

"We talked and you were right."

"Of course, I'm always right. And did he put your mind at rest about him being a superstar and you a mere shopkeeper?" chuckled Christina.

"Oh, shut up. But, yes, if you must know, we did discuss

it and I realize now that I was a bit hasty."

"A bit?"

"Anyway, it's all good." Evie stretched her calf muscles as she spoke. She rarely sat down during a phone call.

"Did he spank you?"

"Uh-huh." Evie smiled as she recalled admiring her marks that morning.

"And did he fuck you?"

"Christina!"

"Well, you usually tell me everything so why not now? Did he stay over?"

"Yes. He woke me at six o'clock with tea and toast then…" Then he'd fucked her until she came screaming his name over and over. It was only afterward that she'd noticed Socks sitting at the foot of the bed giving them a very odd look. Evie sighed happily. "He did more than just spank me and fuck me. He *dominated* me. You know?"

"Yeah. So did you have to work today?"

Evie groaned as she recalled struggling to get through the day. When she hadn't been yawning she'd been daydreaming. At one point Julia had asked her if she was ill. "Yes, Saturdays are always busy in the shop, but I wasn't on good form today. It's a good job I'm the boss, otherwise I'd probably have been fired." Evie smiled. "It was worth it, though."

Christina laughed. "Well, I'm happy for you, honey. After that dickhead Vince you deserve someone who'll treat you right."

"Someone as kinky and perverted as I am, you mean?"

"Yep. So when are you seeing him again?"

Evie stopped pacing, turned out her feet and did a *demi-plié* as she replied, "Tonight. He's cooking me dinner at his flat."

"Cool."

"In fact, I've got to leave in about ten minutes so I can't talk for too long. So how about you?" asked Evie as she rose onto the balls of her feet. "What are you up to this weekend?"

"I'll be with Marco and Cleo at Dominion. Apparently I'm to be punished in front of everyone. Again!"

"Now what have you done?" laughed Evie.

Christina chuckled into the phone. "I slapped Marco's ass as he was picking up a box of glasses from the floor. He was so surprised that he dropped it and broke all the glasses inside."

"What the hell did you do that for?" *God, does that girl have a death wish or something?*

"His ass was poised like a target, I just couldn't resist it. But I then called him clumsy for dropping the glasses. He wasn't amused. I made it worse by laughing at him. That's when he decided I was to be punished. I think I might have pushed him just a teeny bit too far this time."

"Oh you think so, do you?" Evie was laughing so much now that she nearly dropped the phone. "Well, rather you than me. I wouldn't want to be punished by Marco Alessi and I certainly don't envy you tonight. Let me know how it goes, though, won't you?" Evie might not wish to be punished by Marco, but she loved hearing about what he did to her friend. She had to concede that she must indeed be a pervert.

When she ended the call it was time to leave. Aaron lived in Brixton, south London, and she lived north of the city so it would take a while to drive through central London, especially at seven o'clock on a Saturday night. She'd been surprised when he'd given her his address. Brixton wasn't exactly upmarket, not that she'd imagined him living anywhere posh, but Brixton?

She picked Socks up and gave her a cuddle. "I'll see you tomorrow," she said, kissing the top of her head. She had left her plenty of food and water, a massive pile of cat treats and a clean litter tray. She grabbed her overnight bag then checked her reflection in the hall mirror before leaving.

As she navigated through London, dodging buses, taxis and cyclists, she wondered what Aaron's flat would be like.

High-tech, all steel and chrome, no doubt. Not her style, but very befitting someone young, single and successful like Aaron. Well, not single anymore.

Her stomach did a little flip as she thought about the way he'd stormed into her flat last night and demanded that she listen to him. She still wasn't convinced that their lifestyles were suited, but at least she now believed that he wasn't using her. Did they have a future? Who knew? But they certainly had a 'now' and she was damned well going to enjoy it.

By the time she'd crossed the river her nerves were fraught with trying not to crash into the back of a bus or run someone over. She *hated* driving in central London. Why the hell hadn't she taken the bloody Tube? She would have been there by now. She glanced at the satnav. It said she was five minutes away. Thank God.

When she turned into his street she was surprised to find a row of huge Victorian terraced houses opposite a small park. For some reason she'd been expecting an old industrial warehouse or a modern complex or something. *"You have reached your destination."* Really? She doubled-checked the bit of paper she'd scribbled Aaron's address on. Yep, this was it. There was plenty of parking thanks to a residents parking scheme. Aaron had given her a permit before he'd left this morning, so she pulled into a space and turned off the ignition. Then she sat for a moment in the silence, trying to calm the influx of butterflies fluttering in her belly.

Just over two weeks ago Aaron Holmes had just been the guitarist in a band she had liked for years. She'd always thought he was the most attractive member of Decadence and had even had the odd sexual fantasy about him, but never in her wildest dreams had she believed that she would meet him. And now she was about to walk into his flat to spend the night with him. If he was anything like last night he would have her on her knees in no time, exerting his dominance over her before tying her to the bed and fucking her senseless. Grinning, she got out of the car, walked up to a black front door and pressed his buzzer. *Bring it on.*

# Chapter Nineteen

"Come on up. Top floor."

When Evie eventually made it up the four flights of stairs to the top floor she was shocked to find that she was panting. Bloody hell, maybe it was time to join the cardio class at the studios? Aaron was waiting for her, leaning against the doorframe to his flat with his arms folded and looking seriously sexy.

"What took you so long?" He grinned as she stuck her tongue out at him then he pulled her into his arms and kissed her.

"How do you cope with these stairs every day?" she said as soon as she got her breath back. "Bloody hell, I can do a two-hour ballet class yet this nearly killed me."

"It saves going to the gym. Come in." He held open the door for her and she stepped into his flat.

"Wow, this is lovely."

She'd been wrong about the steel and chrome, although the flat was certainly contemporary. Aaron had led her into a large living room with an open-plan kitchen at one end and, despite having been modernized, it had kept its Victorian charm with high cornices and a beautiful period fireplace. The cream carpets, black leather sofas and solid oak furniture were masculine and stylish. A bit like Aaron. Tonight he was wearing a pair of faded black jeans that looked like they'd been molded to his muscular legs, and a black Joy Division T-shirt. His hair hung loosely down his back, the ends slightly damp, presumably from an earlier shower. And his stubble was a little longer than it had been yesterday. She tried to hide the shudder that ran through her body as she remembered how that stubble had scratched as he'd rubbed it along her...

"Prosecco?"

"Oh, yes please."

As he handed her a glass of the sparkling wine she caught a whiff of sandalwood. She inhaled, wanting to capture as much of him as possible. Everything about this man tantalized her senses — his roguish good looks, his musky scent, the timbre of his deep velvety voice, his dominant touch, his taste... She licked her lips as her mind flashed back to last night. Mmm, his taste had been divine.

She took the glass. The moment her fingers brushed against his, electrical currents rippled up her arm, making her jolt. Startled, she searched his face for any sign that he had felt it too. Yes, the heated gaze he returned told her that he had. There was no mistaking the connection between them. It was almost tangible, as if they could reach out and touch the little sparks binding them together. They stared at each other, mesmerized, until Aaron looked away. Evie quickly took a sip of her drink to stabilize her thundering heartbeat. Wow, this was like the stuff she'd read about in romantic novels.

"Come on, let me show you around," said Aaron, his voice sounding more gruff. He headed back out into the hallway and she followed, taking in as much of Aaron's home as possible. It crossed her mind that she didn't know very much about him. He rarely talked about himself. Well, if they were going to be a couple, that was damn well going to have to change.

"That's the guest bathroom." Aaron pointed to a door as he passed it then headed toward another door farther down the hallway. When he reached it he stopped and turned to Evie. "And this is my bedroom."

He showed her into a large, airy room with a bay window and built-in wardrobes along the whole length of one wall. Evie glimpsed an en-suite bathroom through an open door, but it was the enormous wooden bed against the wall that really drew her attention. Although there was nothing obvious about it, the four posts were so perfect for tying up a helpless submissive that she could almost have believed it had been made especially for that reason. "Nice bed," she murmured as Aaron took her arm and led her out of the room again.

"You'll be getting better acquainted with it later tonight," said Aaron, grinning. "It's custom-made. There are hidden hinges that mean I can clip bars below the frame to make a cage. Perfect for naughty subbies."

"Oh." Evie didn't know if the shiver that ran down her spine was from apprehension or excitement. *He has a cage under the bed? Bloody hell.*

"And this is my favorite room." He opened the last door in the hallway and stepped into what looked like a cross between a cluttered study and a music room. A large desk covered in paperwork, magazines and a computer stood in front of the window next to a floor-to-ceiling bookcase stuffed with books, vinyl records and CDs.

A small two-seater leather sofa had been crammed into the space between the wall and chimney breast, where an iron wood burner stood surrounded by a stone fireplace. It was easy to imagine how cozy the room would be in the winter with a fire raging in that stove.

The rest of the room was full of keyboards and synthesizers, monitors and mixing boards. The walls were covered with gold discs, framed awards and photographs. It was stuffed full of too much furniture and paraphernalia, but Evie loved it. This room was a reflection of Aaron, finally showing her a glimpse of the private person behind the scenes. She walked over to the wall covered in frames and studied the selection of photographs, newspaper articles and mementos from his childhood. One of them was a certificate showing he'd passed his grade eight piano exam with distinction. And there was a picture of Aaron and Marco. They didn't look older than about twenty and appeared as wild as their heavy rock image portrayed. Another was a photograph of two young boys with their parents and three cats. Evie guessed that the taller of the boys must be Aaron. She'd recognize those eyes anywhere.

"Is that your brother?" she asked, pointing to the smaller child, who had similar features.

Aaron nodded, but his eyes clouded over and a haunted expression flickered across his face as he said, "Yes, Stephen. He was three years younger than me. He died when he was twelve."

"I'm so sorry." Shocked, she wrapped her arms around him and hugged him tightly.

"He had meningitis. By the time they got him to the hospital it was too late. They couldn't save him." Aaron's mouth was next to her ear as he spoke, with only her hair in the way of the emotional strain in his voice.

Evie was an only child and couldn't know how it would feel to lose a sibling, but she could imagine. Her heart went out to the smiling family in the photo, not yet aware of the heartbreak to come.

"Come on," said Aaron, his voice raspy. "Let's eat."

Dinner was delicious. Aaron had pan-fried large juicy steaks and served them with baked potatoes and salad. It was the sort of thing she would have chosen in a restaurant. And her steak was cooked to perfection — medium rare, just how she liked it.

"How long have you lived here?" she asked when she'd swallowed a mouthful of succulent meat.

"About three years now," he replied as he sliced through his rare steak as if it were butter.

"Why Brixton? I mean, don't get me wrong, there's nothing wrong with Brixton, but I thought you'd have lived somewhere posh."

Aaron laughed. "I'm not exactly the posh type. I grew up here. It was rough back then. But it's always had a soul — the streets are alive with people from all walks of life. Tomorrow I'll take you for a walk and you'll see what I mean. There are cafés, shops and restaurants from all over the world and the people who live here are eccentric and friendly. I love it."

"I can see that. It suits you. I can imagine you growing up here."

"We didn't live in a nice house like this, though. We lived in a small house on the council estate up the road. Marco's from around here as well."

"Oh. Did you know him when you were a kid?"

"No. We didn't meet until I attended an audition for his band. He'd placed an ad for a guitarist in the local paper and I was the only one who showed up." Aaron smiled. "It turned out he had been in the year above me in school. I recognized him because he was infamous for blowing up the science lab."

Evie giggled. "What? He actually blew it up?"

"Well, it was an accident. He put a large amount of caesium in some water, thinking it was sodium."

"What's caesium?"

"It's an extremely reactive metal that forms metal hydroxide and hydrogen gas when added to water. According to the stories that went around at the time, the glass container actually exploded. It made a right mess." Aaron grinned. "Marco was looked up to as a kind of god after that."

"I can imagine," laughed Evie.

"Luckily nobody got hurt, although Marco could have been if he hadn't been wearing goggles. He got away with a couple of minor burns and singed hair. The head teacher was livid."

Evie laughed as she pictured Marco's sheepish face as he tried to talk himself out of trouble.

"Were you a rebel at school?" she asked, curiously. She'd bet he was.

But he shook his head. "Nope. I was one of the brainy kids, but I was good at football so I didn't get picked on like some of my mates. I became a sort of protector for the geeks."

"A hero?"

"Nah, I just made sure everyone knew not to mess with my mates."

Well, he was a hero as far as she was concerned. She raised her fork to take another bite of the steak, but stopped before it reached her mouth when she saw Aaron staring at her. Suddenly the jovial atmosphere changed as his intense gaze sent goosebumps flurrying over her skin.

He gazed at her, his eyes effortlessly holding her captive. "One day I'd like to feed you from my hand while you're kneeling naked at my feet."

Evie nearly dropped the fork as Aaron's words sank in. *Bloody hell.* She frowned as she envisioned the two things she hated the most—being naked and him watching her eat. *Not happening.*

"Why are you frowning, Evie? Is that a problem?"

Oh God, now she had to talk about it. She tried her best to keep a neutral expression on her face as she shrugged and said, "Well, you know how I feel about eating in front of people. I'm not that keen on being naked either."

Aaron laughed. "You didn't seem to mind at Dominion. Or last night."

"That's different. I was in the right headspace."

"I fully intend to put you into that headspace here as well. What better way to embrace your submission than by kneeling naked at my feet with your hands bound behind your back and being fed by your Master?"

"My, er, Master?" Evie felt her eyes widen. Why did that thought send little ripples of lust through her body?

Aaron grinned. "I know it's early days, but you've no idea how happy I would be if you thought of me as your Master."

Evie swallowed, even though her mouth was empty. What was he saying? Did he want more than she was prepared to give? She thought they'd cleared that little matter up. "I think I'd like that too although...although I don't want to be your slave. Your submissive, yes, but not a slave. At least, not for real."

Thankfully Aaron smiled and said, "That sounds good enough for me. Like I told you before, I'm not interested in a twenty-four-seven relationship, just your absolute submission at our agreed times." He took a sip of his drink then sat back and studied her. "So, tell me about your problem with being naked. And while you're at it I wouldn't mind knowing what your issues are with food as well."

Evie sighed and put her knife and fork down. She knew she'd have to talk about it at some point, so she might as well get it over with. "Okay. I started ballet when I was four years old. All I ever wanted was to be was a dancer and I gave up everything so it could happen. I didn't do the whole teenage rebellion thing, never went clubbing or pigged out on junk food. I needed the body of an athlete and that's what I had."

Aaron nodded, his eyes focused on her as she spoke. She had his attention, so she continued. "When I had the accident I wasn't able to dance for nearly a year and, when I did start again, it had to be slow and gradual. Even now I'm limited in what I can do. Well, my body changed along with my recovery. I lost a lot of physical strength, the muscle tone that had taken me since childhood to build. I hate my body now. I know I'm not fat, but I feel it. I guess that's also why I feel so self-conscious about people watching me eat. A lot of dancers have a love-hate relationship with food, you know, so when the focus is on eating it sort of reminds me of what I lost." She stopped and took a deep breath. The words had come tumbling out, but they were from the heart.

"I'm sorry," said Aaron. "I never thought of it like that. For what it's worth, I think you have a perfect body. Strong and slim with sexy curves in the just the right places. You're gorgeous."

"Thanks." Evie's cheeks burned as she accepted the compliment. She hated talking about her body, but she knew it was something she needed to deal with. "I want to be the best submissive to you that I can be and if me being naked is important to you then I'll do my best to overcome my insecurities."

Reaching across the table, Aaron took her hand and squeezed it. "Thank you. Okay, how about this. Remember we talked about rules?"

Evie nodded as her pulse suddenly started racing.

"How about we set a rule that when you enter this flat on Saturdays you strip naked and wait for me on your knees by the front door? Only on that one day a week and only if nobody else is around. Would you be comfortable with that?"

Evie nodded slowly. "I think so. I'd like to try, but please be patient if I find it difficult at first."

"Hey, this is about both of us getting pleasure. Although I'd like to push your boundaries a little I wouldn't want you to do anything that makes you feel truly uncomfortable. I was thinking that if you're alone while you strip and then wait for me on your knees you can get into the right mindset in your own time."

"That sounds like a plan." Evie smiled. That sounded like a very good plan.

"When we've finished eating I want you to strip in the bedroom and wait for me on your knees. Okay?"

"Yes, Sir." Somehow calling Aaron 'Sir' seemed so right. It felt good, natural.

"By the way, do you like Solar Flare?"

Evie nodded. "Yes, I love them." Solar Flare was a successful rock group that had taken the charts by storm five years ago. They weren't as heavy as Decadence, but they were exciting and fresh. Evie had even downloaded one of their songs.

"Well, their singer, Jon Hamblin, is making a solo album and I'm going to be a guest guitarist. I'm going to the studios on Tuesday to record the track. Do you fancy coming along?"

"Wow, that's amazing. I'd love to, but I'm working."

"We couldn't get the studio booked until six o'clock, which was a pain at the time we booked it, but now it works perfectly. If you could ask Julia to mind the shop for the last half an hour you should make it. So what do you think?"

Evie grinned as she made her mind up. How often did you get to visit a recording studio and watch two massive rock stars perform a song? "All right, I'd love to come."

"Good. Now hurry up and finish that steak. I've got plans for you tonight."

When the time came for Evie to present herself in Aaron's bedroom she was ready and even a little excited by the thought of obeying his wishes. He was right. By pushing her out of her comfort zone just a little she was able to give him her complete surrender. He was aware of what it took for her to get naked before the heady highs of a scene kicked in and she knew he'd get great pleasure from that. That gave her even greater pleasure. What a funny thing D/s was. But it worked.

As she removed her clothes she had her back to the mirror, but once she was naked she turned slowly around and raised her eyes to meet her reflection. She pulled her tummy in and straightened her back. For the first time in years she looked beyond the slight bulge around her stomach and the rounded curve of her hips, and saw her body the way Aaron might see it. She was still toned, her legs were muscular, her neck long. Without thinking she turned her feet out into first position and did a *demi-plié*. She still had a pretty good turnout.

"Are you ready?"

Aaron's voice made her jump. "Er…give me a second," she called back and quickly made her way to the middle of the room. She sank to her knees, reached her arms behind her and locked her fingers together. Then she lowered her head and waited.

A moment later Aaron entered the room. "Good girl."

Evie kept her gaze on the floor as he padded across the

carpet and stopped in front of her. A tingle ran up her spine as he walked around her as if inspecting his property, and it was at that point that Evie knew she was already where she needed to be. She wanted to give him everything she could, her body, her mind, her soul. When he took a handful of her hair and pulled her head back, she looked up into the dark eyes of a Dom who was as powerful as he was caring. She'd found her heaven.

"Close your eyes." When they were shut Aaron placed a blindfold over them and secured it. She liked not having the choice of whether she could see or not. With her sight taken away she knew her other senses would compensate and tell her everything she needed to know. Like the fact that Aaron was kissing her neck as he held her head back by gripping her hair again. She'd always liked having her hair pulled. She loved the feeling of being controlled and the little bit of pain that came with it.

Aaron moved his mouth up to her lips and forced them open. He kissed her forcefully, demanding her compliance, and she slid further into her giddy world of submission. She'd not only handed Aaron all her control, but had given him her complete trust. She knew without a doubt that he would cherish it and that only made her even more willing to surrender completely to him.

She listened for any clues as to what he was going to do next. He'd let go of her hair and now his footsteps headed away from her. It was hard to hear exactly where he'd gone as the carpet was so spongy, but she guessed he was still in the room. Then the strike of a match suggested that he might be lighting some candles. When he returned to her he stroked her cheek softly before taking a handful of her hair again.

"I want you to crawl over to the bed on your hands and knees," ordered Aaron. "I'll lead you by your hair."

"Yes, Sir," whispered Evie. She was glad she didn't have to stand up. She wasn't sure her legs would support her at that moment. Aaron tightened his grip and gently tugged in the direction he wanted her to crawl. When they reached the bed Aaron tightened his grip and said, "Stop. Now, reach out for the bed and crawl onto it. Then lie face down."

"Yes, Sir." She obeyed immediately and climbed up onto the large bed. The mattress was soft and the sheets smelled of freshly washed cotton linen.

Aaron must have walked around to the other side of the bed then, because suddenly he took her right hand and pulled her arm until it was stretched out. He bound a soft leather cuff around her wrist, fastened it then attached it to some sort of chain that was secured to the corner of the bed. Then he repeated this with her other wrist then her ankles, until she was spread-eagled and unable to move. Her pulse raced as she tested the restraints. She was helpless. A rush of moisture warmed the exposed apex between her legs as she tried, in vain, to close them.

"Have you ever played with wax, Evie?"

She had to force her fuzzy head to focus on Aaron's question. After a few seconds she managed to reply, "Yes, Sir. A long time ago."

"Did you enjoy it?" he asked as he moved her hair away from her shoulders and draped it over her head.

She had, actually, but the candles had been made with special wax that had a lower melting point so they didn't get too hot. "Er, yes, Sir." She trusted him not to use anything that might burn or blister her, so she didn't elaborate.

"Good. I think you'll like this one. Rather than cooling into a crust on the skin this one stays runny and turns into massage oil. All you have to do is remain still and enjoy."

When the first drops of the hot wax landed on her back she gasped. It was hotter than she'd expected, but not unbearably so. Aaron poured the wax down each arm, across her shoulders and down to the small of her back, where it ran into a pool of tropical warmth. Then over her buttocks and down her legs. When she was covered in the spicy-smelling wax he kneaded his way up from her feet to her thighs with strong, firm fingers. First the right leg, then the left. When his fingers smoothed over the skin on the insides of her thighs they were tantalizingly close to her pussy and Evie held her breath as she waited for them to reach her throbbing heat. But instead Aaron moved his hands up to her ass cheeks and rubbed the oil in with firm sensuous strokes.

Then he moved up her back, tracing her spine until he reached her shoulders, where his grip became stronger. With each stroke Evie's body relaxed a little more until she felt as liquid as the oil being rubbed into her skin. By the time her neck and arms were done she was a puddle of warmth, so relaxed that she felt like she was sinking into the soft depths of the mattress. With her eyes closed and body restrained there was nothing she could do except indulge in the luxury being bestowed upon her, and her mind emptied of everything except the touch of the hands massaging her. Finally, she became weightless and floated above the bed as warm, comforting blankets wrapped themselves around her and kept her safe.

When Evie awoke she had been released from the restraints and the blindfold had been removed. She was lying in Aaron's arms. When had that happened?

"Hello, beautiful." He smiled and tightened his arms around her.

"I'm so sorry," she gasped as it gradually dawned on her why she hadn't noticed being freed from the restraints. "I fell asleep on you."

"That was the intention." He stroked her back, his fingers gliding over the still-oily surface of her skin.

"Mmm," she murmured into his chest. Could this man be any more perfect?

"And now I'm going to fuck you so hard you won't be able to walk for a week."

A frisson of excitement fizzed through her blood as he flipped her onto her back then straddled her, his strong thighs keeping her in place. He slipped a condom over his erect cock then took hold of her hands, reached them above her head and pinned them down with his weight. He glared at her with eyes that glowed from a raging furnace deep inside him.

"Beg me," he growled. "Beg me to fuck you hard."

"Just fucking fuck me," snapped Evie back, impatiently. She barely heard his chuckle before he thrust inside her. He hadn't been joking when he'd said he was going to fuck her hard. He overpowered her, took over her body with ferocious greed, and Evie loved every glorious minute of it. She wrapped her legs around him and clung to him with all her strength, desperate to get as close to him as was physically possible. The tension was building quickly, the passion close to peaking, when he suddenly pulled out and rolled onto his back.

"You get on top," he said, his voice gruff with arousal. "Ride me until you make me come."

"Oh, yes, Sir." Evie grinned and climbed onto him. As she lowered herself onto the solid steel of his cock she groaned as it reached new places it hadn't touched before. Oh yes, this felt good. Slowly, she began to grind herself onto him, until a need deep inside her drove her to move with more and more force and speed. Her clit rubbed against the base of his cock as she rode him and the faster she moved the more intense the mounting pleasure became.

"Good girl, I want you to come with me. Don't come until I tell you."

"Yes, Sir," she panted and rode him even faster.

Sweat ran down her back, her breasts bounced with every movement she made and her hair clung to her face as she threw herself down on Aaron's cock again and again. When it swelled it almost became too much. She needed to come. Fuck, she couldn't hold off for much longer. She groaned as little sparks inside her ignited and only just heard Aaron moan, "Now, Evie," before the explosion took over her entire body.

Aaron's cock pulsed inside her as he shot hot liquid into the condom and Evie's pussy contracted over and over as it squeezed every drop out of him. Finally, she collapsed onto his chest, breathless and exhausted.

After a few minutes Aaron rolled her gently off him then pulled her into his arms. She snuggled into him, content and happy.

"You're perfect," Aaron murmured softly in her ear. "I never want to lose you."

"Mmm." *I think I might be falling for you.* She wanted to say the words, but never quite got around to it before falling into a deep and blissful sleep.

# Chapter Twenty

Just before six o'clock on Tuesday afternoon, Evie pushed her way off the crowded train at Hammersmith and headed for the exit where she had arranged to meet Aaron. She'd never been inside a recording studio before and the fact that she would get to meet Jon Hamblin made today even more exciting. There were perks to going out with someone famous.

She spotted Aaron straight away, surrounded by several fans hoping for an autograph. She stopped and took a few moments to observe him, admiring his patience as he smiled and chatted to the fans. She loved that about him, the fact that he always made time for the people who loved his music. As if sensing her presence, he looked up suddenly and broke into a huge smile when he saw her. When he eventually managed to break free from the small crowd he hurried over and pulled her into his arms. Mmm, he smelled of sandalwood and freshly laundered linen.

"Come on," he breathed in her ear, "let's get away before someone else spots me."

Evie laughed as he grabbed her hand and led her away from the station. A few minutes later they stopped at an inconspicuous building that nobody would look twice at. Aaron pressed a buzzer and a second later the door opened automatically. As they entered the building a camera followed them with a smooth *whirr*.

Inside was as different from the exterior of the building as Evie could have imagined. They were in a large reception area furnished with several plush sofas and armchairs. The walls were lined with framed gold discs and newspaper clippings which were illuminated by fancy spotlights that changed color every now and again.

"Hello, Mr. Holmes." A security guard sitting behind a glass reception desk smiled as they approached him.

"Hi there, Steve," said Aaron. "How's your wife?"

"She's much better, thank you." He smiled at Evie and handed her a pen. "Would you sign in, please, miss?"

Once they had both scribbled their names in the book on Steve's desk he handed them a security pass each. "Jon is in studio one."

"Thanks," said Aaron and took Evie's hand. "This way."

Evie couldn't help noticing how quiet the building was as they made their way down a wide corridor. The thick carpet cushioned their footsteps, but it wasn't just that. There were no sounds of music, she realized. Until Aaron stopped by a door and opened it. The insistent beat of a rock song lured them into a small room surrounded by windows. An enormous mixing desk and several computer screens lined the glass wall directly in front of them. It looked exactly like she had seen on television. Two men looked up and smiled as she and Aaron entered.

"Aaron, mate, it's good to see you," greeted a small man with a head of long wavy curls. He reminded Evie of a hobbit.

"You too. George, this is my girlfriend, Evie," said Aaron, pulling Evie forward.

A tingle of something delicious ran through Evie's blood at Aaron's words. That was the first time she'd heard him refer to her as his girlfriend. It kind of had a nice ring to it. She smiled at George and reached out her hand. "Hello, George."

"George is the sound engineer on this project," said Aaron. "And this polar bear of a man is Per, one of the best producers on the planet."

Per grinned at her, revealing perfect white teeth. He looked like a Viking god. Tall, even taller than Aaron, he had long blond hair that was like the mane of a wild horse and his eyes were the deepest blue she had ever seen. Eyes that reflected the broad smile directed at her.

"Hello, beautiful lady," he purred in a sexy Scandinavian accent.

His muscles bulged under his black T-shirt as he towered over her and Evie couldn't stop a rush of heat from creeping into her cheeks. He exuded power and raw masculine sexuality.

"Hello," said Evie, trying to appear unaffected by this fearsome-looking warrior. She couldn't help smiling as George and Per moved to stand side by side. Per looked like he might eat George up in one mouthful.

"Where's Jon?" asked Aaron as he took his jacket off and threw it on a chair.

"He's around," said George. "Now, we've already laid down some backing vocals, but I want you two together for the actual recording."

"No problem," said Aaron.

"Who wants a coffee?" asked Per, heading for the door.

"That'll be good," replied Aaron. "Evie, would you like a coffee?"

"I'd love one, thanks."

"I think Sam has left for the day, so I'll make them," said Per. "Won't be long."

As Per left the room someone else entered. Evie couldn't stop her jaw from dropping as she found herself face to face with Jon Hamblin. Even Evie, who was usually never impressed by famous people, was star-struck. As the lead singer of Solar Flare, Jon Hamblin was probably one of the biggest names on the rock scene.

"All right?" said Jon, giving Aaron a friendly slap on the shoulder.

"Hello, mate," said Aaron. "Jon, I'd like you to meet my girlfriend, Evie."

Jon smiled, took Evie's hand and kissed it. "Hello, Evie. So you're the woman who has finally managed to tame Aaron Holmes. It's very nice to meet you."

Evie laughed. "You too, but I'm not sure Aaron can ever be tamed. I try my best, though."

Jon chuckled. "Well, it's good to see him with a smile on his face. He's been a right miserable sod lately."

"Okay, let's get started," said George. He pulled a chair up for Evie. "Take a seat, Evie. You can watch from in here. You'll be able to witness all the fuck-ups and bum notes that you normally never get to hear because of people like me." He grinned as Jon playfully thumped him on the arm.

Aaron kissed Evie then indicated that she should sit down. "It might take a couple of hours or so. I hope you don't get too bored."

"Per and I will look after her," said George. "Now get your ass in that studio."

Per came back with the coffees just as Aaron and Jon were about to leave, so they took their drinks and headed off through another door. As Per handed Evie her coffee he said, "It's not as good as the coffee we have in Sweden, but it's drinkable."

"Thanks. I'm sure it's fine," she said as she took the mug Per was holding out for her. She couldn't help noticing his enormous hands as she took her coffee. A naughty corner of her brain wondered idly if other parts of him were just as large. She had to stifle her giggle at the thought. Heaven help her if they asked why she was laughing.

As Aaron and Jon settled themselves on the other side of the screen, Evie watched in fascination. The two men clearly had a good rapport and soon found their rhythm. Jon's vocals matched the mood played by Aaron and the two of them sounded like they'd worked together for years. When Aaron strummed a complex guitar solo Evie's eyes became transfixed on his fingers as they commanded the instrument with the same expertise as they controlled her body. He had incredible hands that could do magical things.

As she watched the two men, the novelty of Jon's fame soon wore off, allowing Evie to see him as the normal human being he was. He looked a little older than he did in photographs and his hair wasn't styled in his usual quiff. In fact, he looked surprisingly ordinary in real life. His voice was anything but ordinary though, and he easily hit the notes and kept up with the beat. He and Aaron made a good duo—two perfectionists making exceptional music.

But despite the perfect performances from both Aaron and Jon, George had them playing the same bits over and over until he was finally happy. Evie couldn't tell the difference between first attempt and the last—it all sounded amazing to her. She slowly lost her sense of time as she became more and more drawn into watching Aaron at work. He seemed to have an affinity with his guitar, making the sounds come alive as his fingers strummed effortlessly over the strings.

She jumped when Per's voice snapped her out of the dreamlike trance she'd drifted into. "Are you okay, Evie? Not too bored, I hope?"

"Oh no, honestly, it's great watching them," she replied, smiling up at the giant Viking. "They're good together, aren't they?"

Per looked through the glass and nodded. "Yeah, I've been trying to get them to work together for a while, but Decadence always took up all Aaron's time and Jon was busy with Solar Flare. I'm hoping this will be the first of many collaborations together."

"Okay, boys, we're done. Nice work," called George through a microphone.

"That's it," said Per. "Only two hours. That's pretty quick for such a complex track."

Aaron and Jon burst back into the sound room, both looking very pleased with themselves. By now, Jon was just a regular guy to her. It was amazing how quickly the superficial cloak of fame wore away. Famous people really were just like the rest of them. It occurred to her that she had stopped thinking of Aaron as the great Aaron Holmes, famous rock star. Now he was just Aaron, her lover and Dom. Her belly flipped as she recalled his words earlier. She was his girlfriend. It had felt really good when he'd said that.

"Are you guys staying for a drink in the bar?" asked Per as he switched off the monitors.

"Are you up for a quickie?" asked Aaron, grinning at Evie.

"I'm always up for a quickie," she giggled, careful not to speak too loudly.

Aaron gave her bottom a playful smack. "Be careful what you wish for."

A few minutes later they were in a private bar on the first floor. They were the only ones there and had opened a bottle of expensive champagne to celebrate the successful session, except for Jon, who had taken a can of diet cola out of a small mini fridge.

"So what's the score with Decadence, then?" asked Per as they settled into the comfy armchairs.

Aaron shrugged. "Not a lot. It seems that I don't have much choice in doing that last album with them." He pulled a face that told them exactly what he thought about that.

"Are Jona and Jaymz still being complete twats?" asked Jon.

"Yeah," Aaron groaned. "They're complete time wasters. If they'd been here tonight I can guarantee we wouldn't have finished this side of midnight."

"How's Marco?" asked Per. "I hear he's finally got his shit together."

"Yep, he's running Dominion now," said Aaron. "He's back on track."

"I still haven't had a chance to go," said Per. "Marco keeps sending me invites, but I never seem to have the time. One day I'll go. I hear it's pretty cool."

Evie raised her eyebrows as Per spoke. Was Per kinky? Actually, that wasn't at all surprising. Now that she thought about it, everything about him screamed 'Dom'. He had that same air of command that Aaron did. She could well imagine him with a pretty submissive over his knee.

She looked up and colored again when she noticed Aaron

watching her. She guessed that he knew exactly what she was thinking.

"Per has been known to reduce the toughest of subs to quivering wrecks just from a spanking," chuckled Aaron. "He puts those big hands to very good use."

"Oh," said Evie, her face now burning hot.

"Okay, boys, I'm off," said George as he emptied the last of his drink into his mouth. "Evie, it was a pleasure meeting you." He leaned over and gave her a peck on the cheek.

"You too," she smiled.

"I'm going to make a move as well," said Jon, standing up. "It's been a long day."

They all said their goodbyes as George and Jon left.

"It was good to work with Jon," said Aaron as the door closed. "He's looking good."

"Yeah, he's a different bloke now that he's sober," said Per. "Looks ten years younger."

Aaron nodded then turned to Evie. "Jon is a recovering alcoholic. The pressure of his success made him ill and he turned to booze. He had the guts to do something about it, though, and now you'd never know."

"Oh, that's why he didn't have any champagne," exclaimed Evie. "I had no idea."

"No, it was never public knowledge," said Per. "So, Aaron, tell me more about Marco's place. Is the dungeon as good as I've heard?"

Aaron grinned. "Ask Evie."

Per turned his piercing blue eyes on her and, in typical Dom fashion, raised his eyebrows to let her know he was waiting for her response.

"Er, yes, it's amazing."

Then she noticed the look on Aaron's face. It was a look that she had learned to recognize as a sign that the Dom was taking over. *Oh crap.*

"Do you know, Per, Evie was five minutes late arriving tonight?"

Evie stared at him in surprise. *Was I?*

Per narrowed his eyes at her. "Was she, now? Poor punctuality should surely be punished."

Evie's heartbeat suddenly thundered in her chest. Punished? Oh God, what were they up to?

"The trouble is," said Aaron casually, "my fingers are sore from all that playing. I don't suppose you would help out, would you, mate?"

"I'd be honored to," said Per with a broad grin.

Evie couldn't quite believe what she was hearing. Aaron and Per were plotting to punish her. A wave of heat shivered through her body as that delicious melting feeling of submission settled over her.

Aaron narrowed his eyes at her. "Evie, do you agree that you should be spanked for being late today?"

She knew this was Aaron's way of letting her know that she didn't have to do this if she didn't want to. But she did want to. The idea of being spanked by Per in front of Aaron did funny things to her insides.

"Yes, Sir," she murmured, trying not to give away just how much she wanted this.

Aaron smiled and she knew he could see right through her. "Okay, lie over Per's lap."

Her breathing became ragged as she positioned herself over the Viking's solid thighs. She had no idea what to expect. How hard would he hit her? Would he pull her underwear down? Surely he wouldn't touch her sexually? Would he? But before she had time to dwell on anything else, the happy feeling of peace that always enveloped her when she was bent over for a spanking calmed her.

She wasn't afraid. Although she didn't know Per, she trusted Aaron to keep her safe. She'd never have agreed to this if Aaron wasn't there. Even though it would be Per spanking her, it was still Aaron who was her focus. What would he be thinking right now? Would he be excited seeing her draped over another man's lap, about to be punished for a crime she hadn't committed? Of course he would.

Per pulled her skirt up over her waist, but didn't pull her

knickers down. Thankfully she was wearing a sexy thong instead of her comfy cotton M&S briefs.

The first smack was quite hard and made her gasp. His hand was so big it felt as though it had covered both buttocks. She raised her head and stole a glance at Aaron. He was smiling, his eyes alive with sexual arousal. Yes, of course he would enjoy this.

"Eyes down," he scolded when he noticed her looking at him.

The reprimand sent a rush of moist heat straight to her pussy. She quickly lowered her head just as Per's hand landed across her ass again. This time he hit harder but, shit, it felt good. Then he started spanking her in earnest. He had a firm hand and was more relentless than Aaron, but it was still nice.

Per kept to a regular rhythm, allowing her to drift off to her own world where pain and pleasure became one. As Per delivered the strokes with more force, Evie closed her eyes and savored each hard slap as they rained down on her. She could imagine Aaron sitting opposite, watching her every flinch, listening to her moans and whimpers. It was important that he liked this too.

She had completely lost track of time when Per eventually slowed the intensity of the smacks until he just rubbed her burning skin.

"What a good girl you are," he said softly. "Aaron, your subbie is delightful."

"I know," chuckled Aaron. "Evie, you can get up now. Kneel by Per's feet and thank him for your punishment."

Her eyes shot open and she stared at Aaron in shock. *What?*

Aaron laughed. "No, you naughty girl, not like that. *Say* thank you."

"Oh," said Evie, with relief.

"You can thank me later," he added with a deep rumble of laughter.

Evie slid off Per's lap and settled on her knees by his feet.

This low down, he seemed even bigger. Raising her eyes to meet his, she murmured, "Thank you for spanking me, Sir."

Per reached out and took Evie's head in his huge hands then, holding it still, he said, "You're very welcome, beautiful girl." He bent forward and kissed her on her forehead.

He rose and stepped away from her. Evie remained where she was, instinctively knowing that that was what Aaron expected her to do.

"I'll leave you to finish disciplining your sub in peace." Per's footsteps headed toward the door and a moment later it clicked shut.

"Kneel up," ordered Aaron, "then spread your legs."

"Yes, Sir," she breathed and quickly obeyed as Aaron moved to stand in front of her.

He bent forward then reached down and slid his hand between her thighs. He slipped his fingers under the thin material of her thong and groaned when he touched the heat smoldering in her pussy. "Ooh, you're very wet, you naughty girl."

"Yes, Sir," she whimpered as rough skin on his finger grated against her clit. The lingering heat from her spanking ignited fresh sparks inside her and she shook with the effort of staying upright. He shoved his finger inside her, forcing the walls of her pussy to contract, then he started finger-fucking her hard and fast. Her body responded as Aaron played her the way he'd done with his guitar. He controlled the sounds she made, her movement and ultimately her pleasure.

"Sir…"

"Yes, Evie, you can come." He moaned as he thrust his fingers deeper inside her.

It took no time at all to tip her over the edge once she knew she had Aaron's permission to come. She let go and cried out as she tumbled into a glorious orgasm that took her on a flight of ecstasy over and over again until she finally fell forward and collapsed in Aaron's arms.

As Aaron held her, allowing her to recover in her own time, he murmured, "Well, I'm going to have to bring you to work with me more often."

# Chapter Twenty-One

*Three weeks later...*

Aaron wandered into Evie's kitchen after finishing a phone call with Bill. Their manager was too fucking persistent. Less than a month had passed since the US trip and the band were supposed to be having some time off, not being badgered about the new recording schedule. He soon forgot about Bill, though, as he watched Evie, wearing nothing but a loose T-shirt, bend down to put some plates into the dishwasher. Now there was a sexy sight.

He still couldn't quite believe that this beautiful, clever and funny woman was his. He had never felt so connected to anyone before—in fact, he couldn't remember ever being so happy and content.

They had fallen into an easy routine, seeing each other almost every day except Mondays when Evie had her ballet class. During the week they would stay at Evie's because she had to be in the shop just before nine o'clock to open up, then they'd stay at his flat at the weekends. He loved staying at Evie's, especially now that Socks had warmed to him. There was no place he'd rather be than with his two favorite girls.

Today was Saturday and tonight he was taking Evie to Dominion. They hadn't been back since that first weekend and he couldn't wait to get Evie back into the dungeon. Although he'd spanked her, tied her up and dominated her at home, there was nothing quite like the heady atmosphere of a BDSM club where he had room to swing a flogger and Evie could scream as loudly as she wanted without worrying about the neighbors calling the police. And tonight was special—he was going to tell her that he loved her and he was going to have her on her knees and helplessly at his mercy when he did. He wanted the delirium of subspace to make his declaration even more special. He just hoped she felt the same way.

"So what are you up to today?" she asked as she handed Aaron a fresh mug of coffee.

"Thanks." Aaron sat down by the kitchen table and took a sip. *Mmm, that's good, steaming hot and strong.* "Bill has asked me to start thinking about drawing up a schedule for the next album so I guess I need to start planning."

"You need a schedule?"

He nodded. "The record company needs to know when we're ready to begin recording because they have to book the studios in advance. We need to check when the producer is free, sound engineers, the cover artist, photographer, plus there are additional musicians and backing singers to organize." He took another gulp of his coffee then continued, "Hunter and I also need to book the cottage so we can lock ourselves away to write the songs."

"You have a cottage?"

"Well, the record company does. It's for song writing, rehearsing, escaping from the media and stuff like that. I need to book it today so we can get in and get started on some new songs in the next week or so."

"I thought they were going to give you some time off?" asked Evie with a cute little frown furrowing her brow.

"Yeah, but as this will be the last album Hunter and I are doing with Decadence we want to get it over with as soon as possible." He couldn't wait until he'd fulfilled his contractual obligations so he could finally be free to do his own thing. Now that he'd made the decision to leave it couldn't come soon enough.

"Do the others in the band know you're leaving yet?" Evie sat down opposite him and stirred a teaspoon of sugar into her coffee. For someone so body conscious it never failed to amuse him that she took sugar in her coffee.

Aaron shook his head. "No. I must admit I'm not looking forward to breaking the news to them. They could carry on without us, but none of the others write songs and, although Jaymz fancies himself as a singer, he can't actually sing to save his life. I feel bad about Levi, but he's a talented guy so I know he'll be fine."

"When are you going to tell them?"

"Bill wants us all to meet up next week, so it makes sense to do it then." He glanced at his watch. "What time do you need to go down and open the shop?"

"Not until nine o'clock. Saturdays are always quiet first thing so there's no rush."

"Leave the rest of the dishes, I'll clear them away before I go."

She smiled. "Thanks."

"So are you looking forward to going back to Dominion tonight?"

Evie's broad smile gave him her answer even before she spoke. "I can't wait."

Aaron decided to play with her mind a bit and gave her an evil look he knew would unsettle her. "I wouldn't be too excited if I were you. I've got something quite intense planned for you." He didn't really, but her expression was priceless.

"Really? Oh God, should I be worried?"

He grinned. "Yep." Before he could wind her up any further, though, Socks jumped onto his lap and nudged his hand away from the table with her nose. He laughed as the cheeky cat started licking the butter off his leftover toast. Evie had warned him the first time they'd had breakfast here that Socks was addicted to butter and she hadn't been joking. The clever cat knew just by hearing the toaster click that the butter wouldn't be far away, even if it hadn't been taken out of the fridge yet.

"Socks! Get down," scolded Evie then shrugged as Socks ignored her.

"You'd make a rubbish Domme," he said, grinning. "Even the cat doesn't obey you."

"Well, it's lucky for you that I'm not, otherwise I'd have to punish you for such cheek."

Aaron raised his eyebrows at her and they both laughed. "Nah, maybe not." She stood up and stretched. Then she picked Socks up and put her back down on the floor. "I'd better finish getting ready."

"Okay, I'll see you later," said Aaron, giving her bottom a quick smack while she was within reach. "I'll pick you up at seven-thirty. Be ready."

Still grinning, she turned around and saluted him. "Yes, Sir."

The drive back to Brixton was uneventful, with no major traffic jams. When Aaron pulled up outside his building he parked the car, got out and headed toward the steps to his front door. His mind was whirring with ideas for songs so he was too preoccupied to notice the woman approaching him as he reached into his pocket for his house keys.

Suddenly he found himself locked into a tight embrace as the woman gushed, "Aaron, hi. I'm so happy to see you."

Trying to breathe through stifling fumes of expensive perfume, he pulled away from the woman and stared at her, confused.

"Do I know you?"

The woman giggled then, unbelievably, she tried to kiss him with her plumped-up glossy red lips. He only just managed to turn his head away in time to avoid her kissing his mouth. Thankfully, she then stepped away from him and looked at him with a knowing smile, as if she expected him to know who she was.

"It's me. Roxy from L.A. I texted Jaymz to let him know I was visiting the UK and he said you'd be pleased to see me again. You know, maybe I could keep you company again?" she squeaked in a high, sugary voice.

"Look, Foxy—"

"Roxy."

"Er, Roxy, I think you might have me confused with someone else. Jaymz probably gave you the wrong address. Excuse me," he said and tried to pass her. He'd had enough of this over-familiar stranger and now just wanted to get rid of her as quickly as possible.

"We met at the awards, remember? I was a guest at your table." She batted her false eyelashes at him and pouted as though she believed it was sexy.

Ah yes, now he remembered. "Look, I'm afraid Jaymz was out of order for giving you my address. I'm not interested in any kind of company and, just for the record, I'm in a relationship. Please don't come here again. Goodbye." That was about as polite as he could be without insulting her.

Roxy, finally appearing to get the message, stepped back and shrugged. "Whatever. Your loss." Then she turned her back on him and walked off. Thank God.

He let himself into his flat and promptly forgot about the woman as he dug out the folder in which he kept his notes. He'd always preferred to handwrite his thoughts on paper rather than type them into a computer, and as a consequence the folder was bulging with pieces of paper, napkins and receipts he'd scribbled on over the years.

The day flew by quickly and by five o'clock Aaron had booked the cottage for next week and had made a few rough notes for song ideas. He was packing them away when his phone rang. He checked the display — it was Hunter.

"Hey, mate." He stuffed the folder into a drawer as he spoke, his mind still on an idea for a rocky number based on the divisions within the band.

"Aaron." Hunter sounded rough. Something was wrong. "I need to talk to you."

"Yeah, sure."

"No, not on the phone. Can you come to the cottage?"

"Sure. How about tomorrow afternoon?"

"No, *now*." There was an urgency in Hunter's voice that sent a chill through Aaron. It didn't take a brain surgeon to work out that this must have something to do with the threatening letters he'd been getting. He checked his watch. The cottage was in Surrey, so he could be there in forty minutes.

"I'm on my way," he said, grabbing his jacket even before he'd ended the call.

Should he call Evie to warn her that he might be late? He decided against it, as she'd be busy shutting the shop. No, he could always ring her later if he was running late.

The journey took longer than he'd anticipated. Damn traffic—even on a Saturday there seemed to be a rush hour in London. When he was on the motorway he was finally able to put his foot down while his mind worked overtime trying to prepare for what Hunter was going to tell him. It had to be bad for his friend not to want to discuss it on the phone.

Over an hour later, he pulled up in the secluded driveway of the cottage, turned off the ignition and hurried into the house. Hunter was sitting by the unlit fireplace, his face ashen. Next to him was a bottle of whiskey and a piece of paper. Without a word, Hunter picked up the note and handed it to Aaron. As he read the message the blood drained from his face and he slumped heavily into the chair opposite Hunter.

"Fuck!"

He reread the note. There was no mistaking the animosity in the words.

*U think u r so fucking hot don't u. U r nothing but a piece of shit. Decadence wuld be better without u and your fucking cunt of a wife. I'm gonna teach u both a lesson. If u survive you'll wish u hadn't.*

"Jesus." He dropped the note, picked up an empty glass and poured a large shot of whiskey into it. After taking a large gulp he asked, "When did you get this?"

"This afternoon. It was hand delivered to my house. Fucking hell, Aaron, the bastard knows where we live."

Hunter's face reflected his own shock. This was a new turn. The other letters had been sent to the record company's offices and had never mentioned Fabiana. This was way more serious. Fuck, if it had been Evie who had been threatened he'd be beside himself. And it just as easily could have been.

"What are you going to do?" asked Aaron before tipping the remaining drink into his mouth.

"Hand this over to the police then Fabiana and I are going away. I don't care about the fucking schedule. I'm sorry, Aaron, but I've got to get Fabiana away where nobody can hurt her."

"Of course you do. Screw the schedule." He reached over and picked up the bottle. It was still nearly full, but he knew it would soon be empty at this rate. He picked up his phone to call Evie. He had to let her know that he wouldn't be able to make it tonight, but the signal was too weak to connect the call. *Damn, I'll try again later.* He refilled their glasses then nodded at Hunter before drinking the whiskey down as if it were water.

\* \* \* \*

Evie checked her phone for the hundredth time while pacing from window to window. Where was he? It was nearly half past eight, an hour after Aaron had said he'd pick her up. What if he'd been in an accident? Panic gripped her as she imagined him lying in a pool of blood, and she had to take a couple of deep breaths to calm herself. It was too early to be concerned. He was probably stuck in traffic with a dead phone battery.

Half an hour later she rang Christina while she could still get hold of her. Dominion wouldn't be open yet, but once Christina had left to go down to the club she wouldn't be answering her phone until the morning.

"Hey, honey. Are you nearly here?"

"No, I'm still at home. I don't suppose Marco has heard

from Aaron, has he?"

"Hang on, I'll ask him."

Evie waited impatiently while Christina spoke in muffled words with Marco.

"Hi. No, he hasn't been in touch. Is anything wrong?"

Evie tried her best to sound calm. "No, I'm sure it's fine. He's just late, that's all. I'll see you later."

"Okay."

As soon as Christina had hung up Evie tried Aaron's number again. Every time it went straight to voicemail. By ten o'clock she finally accepted that Aaron wasn't coming. She changed out of her sexy PVC outfit into a pair of leggings and a T-shirt and tried to distract herself with some accounts from the shop. But she couldn't shake the feeling that something was wrong and the more she tried, the harder it became to focus on the numbers in front of her. In the end she gave up, put the TV on and checked the online news in case there had been any incidents in London that could explain Aaron's absence. At half past four in the morning she fell into a troubled sleep on the sofa with Socks curled up next to her.

* * * *

When she woke the following morning the first thing she did was reach for her phone, but there were no messages. What the hell had happened? Should she ring the hospitals? But Aaron was a famous person and she could start a media frenzy if she reported him missing. She made herself a cup of strong coffee, but couldn't bring herself to drink it. The flat was becoming claustrophobic. She couldn't breathe properly. She needed to get out, get some air and hopefully a fresh perspective. There *had* to be a logical reason for Aaron's disappearance.

As soon as she stepped out into the early morning sunshine she took in a big lungful of air then breathed it out again in an attempt to release some of the tension in her chest. It was Sunday so the streets were still quiet. She started walking toward Muswell Hill, keeping her phone in her hand the whole time. She didn't know where she was going, she just needed to be out of the flat so she could rationalize what was going on. What if Aaron was dead? What if his car had crashed on his way back from hers and he'd died a horrible, painful death? Her chest tightened as she fought back tears of panic.

"Morning, love."

She looked up to see Ali, the owner of the local convenience store, smiling at her. "Hi," she replied, trying her hardest to smile at him.

She was about to walk on when she spotted a stand filled with the Sunday newspapers next to Ali. Halfway down the selection of papers was a tabloid that was more known for being filled with half naked girls and celebrity gossip than actual news. Her world came to a shuddering halt when she saw the photographs and headline that was screaming out at her. '*Rock legend reunited with lover*'. Below the words were two pictures, one of Aaron and Blonde Bitch at the music awards and the other of the same woman kissing Aaron outside his flat. Her eyes blurred as she tried to take in what the next paragraph said. Something about his L.A. girlfriend arriving all the way from the States yesterday and surprising him outside his home.

Stunned, Evie turned away and walked on without another word. She had no recollection of where she went after that or when she got home. All she knew was that she had been lied to and betrayed. How could he do this to her? He had seemed so genuine. Had he really just been using her all this time until his glamorous girlfriend came for him? She looked down at her hands, wondering why they were hurting, only to find her fingernails digging into her clenched fists. Why had he lied to her?

She should have listened to her instincts not to trust someone like Aaron Holmes. She'd always known their lives were too different for a relationship to work and yet she'd believed him when he'd promised her that he wasn't interested in the celebrity lifestyle anymore.

It had taken weeks for her protective barrier to come down so she could allow herself to love Aaron. And she did love him. More than she'd ever thought possible. She banged her fist down onto the table as anger took over from the pain. How dare he treat her like this? Well, this was the last time any man was ever going to hurt her again. With shaking hands, she switched her phone off then threw it across the room, wishing it were Aaron it hit instead of the wall.

# Chapter Twenty-Two

Aaron groaned as searing pain jabbed his head. He reached out for Evie, only to find his arm hanging in mid-air for a split second before the weight of it made him lose his balance. He couldn't stop the roll that ended in a heavy thud on the floor. *What the fuck?*

He opened his eyes tentatively then snapped them shut again as the light in the room blinded him. Where the hell was he, anyway? Footsteps, heavy strides, not the light padding of Evie's feet, alerted him to the fact that someone had entered the room. Reluctantly he opened his eyes again and found Hunter frowning down at him.

"What the fuck are you doing on the floor?"

Aaron looked around him and slowly it all came back. He'd crashed on the sofa in the early hours after they'd finished the whiskey.

"Must have fallen off," he mumbled and tried to drag himself back up. "Why are you awake? You were more pissed than I was last night."

"I know. For some reason I woke up sober and without much of a hangover. Fuck knows why. Here." He handed Aaron a mug of something hot.

Aaron took a sip and scowled. "Jesus, what is this? Dishwater?" After Evie's rich strong coffee this stuff was disgusting. At least he assumed it was coffee—it was hard to tell.

"It's the only thing I could find," said Hunter, sitting in the armchair. "There's some paracetamol in the kitchen if you need it."

"Thanks."

"Thanks for coming over last night. You're a real mate," said Hunter.

"No worries. How are you feeling today?"

Hunter shrugged. "I could have dealt with this shit a lot better if it hadn't been for the fact that Fabiana was dragged into it. That's what's screwing with my head."

"Of course. I meant to ask last night, does she know?"

Hunter shook his head. "No, I just told her something had come up with the band and that she needed to stay at her parents' house for the night."

"You're going to have to tell her," said Aaron gently. "She needs to know if she's in danger."

"Yeah, I know, I'll tell her today." Hunter rubbed the stubble on his chin. He looked like shit. "I'm going to head off soon. I want to pick her up as soon as possible."

"Yeah, no problem. I need to head back as well." He took another sip of the so-called coffee and grimaced. "I have to get hold of Evie. I wish they'd fix the fucking landline here, it's been down for over a month."

"You must have tried ringing her about twenty times last night," said Hunter, grinning. "Is it getting serious, by any chance?"

Aaron smiled. Too right it was.

"Yeah, mate. She's special, you know? She's my version of your Fabiana."

"Shit, you have got it bad," laughed Hunter.

"Yeah, and do you know what?"

"What?"

"I can honestly say I've never been happier. She's the one, Hunter," said Aaron, unable to stop the wide smile stretching across his face. Just talking about her made him feel good.

"Well, I'm happy for you, mate." Hunter smiled back, looking genuinely pleased for his friend. "When all this shit is over and we're free of Decadence maybe we can all get together? Go to dinner or something?"

"That would be good," said Aaron, reluctant to drag the

subject away from Evie and back to their problem. "So what are you going to do about the letter? Do you want me to take it to the police so you can get away with Fabiana?"

Hunter nodded. "Yeah, that would be cool, thanks. I'll just go and run a copy off from the printer." He stood up, picked up the note from the coffee table and left the room.

When he was alone again, Aaron sighed. A leaden ball seemed to have formed in his gut that was getting harder and heavier by the minute, and he knew only too well why. What would he do if Evie were ever put in danger because of him? They had to find out who this asshole was and quickly.

"What the fuck?" Hunter's voice carried into the living room from the small study.

"What's up?"

Hunter came back into the room holding out a piece of paper. "I just found this jammed in the printer."

"What is it?" Aaron took the paper and frowned. At first glance it was just a bit of scrunched-up paper with a load of words blurred together near the top.

"Read it," said Hunter. "You can make out some of the words if you look carefully."

Aaron held the paper up to the light and squinted as fresh pain stabbed at his eyes. Then, slowly, the words became legible. Some were too smudged to make out, but others were unmistakable.

*...of shit. Decadence wuld ...your fucking cunt of a wife. ... both a lesson. ...you'll wish u hadn't.*

Aaron looked up at Hunter in shock. "How the hell did that get here?"

Hunter's face was white as he took the paper back and looked at it again. "Whoever did this must have written the note from this computer then sent it to print twice and not noticed when the second copy jammed the printer. Aaron, it's someone who was *here*."

"Jesus. Do you know who stayed here last?" Aaron was too stunned to take this in. This meant that they very likely knew who the culprit was.

Hunter shook his head. "No, but Bill will." Everyone had to go through Bill if they wanted to use the cottage. Hunter was the only one outside of management who had a key.

Aaron jumped up, his headache forgotten. "Come on, let's get out of here. We need to get back to civilization and a phone signal."

"We'll take my car," said Hunter. "I can smell the alcohol on your breath from here."

As soon as they were on the main road both their phones pinged with messages and missed calls. Aaron checked the display on his phone and frowned when he saw several missed calls from Evie. He pressed Evie's number, but it went straight to voicemail.

"Evie. I'm really sorry about last night. I'll explain everything when I see you. I've got some stuff to sort out this afternoon, but I'll be around as soon as it's done, okay? See you later." He nearly said 'I love you' before he ended the call, but he still wanted the first time he said it to be face to face and special.

Next he brought up Bill's number and waited for him to pick up. Bill was a night bird and was notorious for not surfacing until well into the afternoon. As it was still morning, well, just about, he'd probably still be in bed.

"Piss off, Aaron." Yep, he wasn't up yet.

Aaron put the phone on speaker so Hunter could hear then he said, "Bill, get your ass out of bed. I'm with Hunter and we need your help."

"Can't this wait?" groaned Bill.

"No," they both said in unison.

"Bill, listen carefully," said Aaron. "Hunter got another note last night, but this one is more serious. It was delivered to his home and not only threatened him, but Fabiana too."

"Shit." Bill finally sounded like he'd woken up.

"Have you got access at home to the online booking

system for the cottage?" asked Aaron.

"Yeah, I can log on from my laptop. Why?"

"Who has been to the cottage in the last few days?" asked Hunter without taking his eyes off the road.

"I can tell you that without checking. The cottage hasn't been booked out formally for about two months now." Aaron frowned. Bill's voice was more alert now, but this wasn't the answer he wanted to hear.

"Have you given the keys to anyone recently?" urged Aaron.

There was a pause then Bill said, "Yeah. Jaymz needed it for a day or so last week. Guys, what's that got to do with the letters?"

"Jaymz?" Aaron turned to Hunter in shock.

"Bill, that means that *Jaymz* sent the notes," said Hunter, his voice shaking with anger.

Bill laughed, clearly not taking them seriously. "Why would he do that?"

"That's what I'd like to know," growled Hunter.

"Look, Bill," said Aaron. "Don't say a word about this to anyone just yet. Can you get Jaymz to come to your house this afternoon? Don't tell him we're coming, we want to catch him off guard."

"Okay," said Bill, his voice now tinny with shock.

"We're coming straight to yours. We'll be there in less than an hour. See you soon," said Aaron and hung up.

"Jaymz?" said Hunter, looking dazed. "Why the hell would Jaymz send those letters?"

Aaron shook his head. "I don't know, mate, but we're damned well going to find out."

"I'm going to fucking kill him," snapped Hunter with a dangerous menace creeping into his tone.

Aaron thought for a moment before replying. "Look, don't touch him, Hunter, or you could end up in trouble yourself. Think about it, this could be our way out of the band."

Hunter seemed to catch on to what Aaron was saying as

he nodded. "Yeah, you're right. Let's go get the fucker."

By the time they arrived at Bill's house they were both calm and composed. Well, at least on the outside. Aaron had tried to call Evie several more times during the journey, but her phone kept going straight to voicemail.

The smell of fresh coffee — proper coffee — greeted them as Bill let them in.

"You both look like shit," said Bill as he closed the front door.

"Thanks, you don't look so hot yourself," Aaron replied and headed straight for the kitchen. "We need coffee."

"Help yourselves," said Bill as Aaron and Hunter grabbed a couple of mugs from the cupboard. "Jaymz is on his way."

Hunter nodded. "Good. I want to show you both the notes before he arrives." Hunter reached into his pocket and pulled out the letters. "Here."

Bill took the pieces of paper and read them. The more he read, the deeper the lines on his face became. "Jesus."

"It has to be Jaymz," said Aaron. He took a large mouthful of the coffee — it was good, but not as good as Evie's — then said, "If he's the only person who's had access to the cottage in two months it can't be anyone else."

"He'll deny it," said Hunter, his face grim.

The doorbell rang as Aaron was pouring a fresh cup of coffee for himself. He glanced at Hunter, whose jaw was rigid. "Come on, mate. Let's get this over with. Remember, stay calm."

Hunter nodded then followed Aaron out into the hallway. As soon as Jaymz spotted them he stopped in his tracks. The look on his face told them he hadn't been expecting to see them.

"Hey, guys," said Jaymz, his voice faltering as he took in their serious expressions. "Look, Aaron, if this is about the newspapers, I didn't know the fucking press were hanging around. I thought I was doing you a favor by pointing the girl your way."

What the fuck was he rambling about? "We know it was

you who sent the threatening letters to Hunter," said Aaron before Jaymz tried to divert their attention to something else.

The color drained from Jaymz's face. Yeah, the fucker was guilty as hell. "What letters?" he asked, his voice suddenly an octave higher.

"Cut the bullshit, Jaymz. We know it's you," hissed Hunter.

Jaymz glared at the three men, although he refused to make eye contact. "Fuck off," he said, his tone turning aggressive, "You don't know nothing."

"So you weren't at the cottage last week?" challenged Aaron.

A hint of worry crossed Jaymz's face, but he stood his ground. "So what if I was? There's no law against staying there."

"No, but it is illegal to make death threats," retorted Hunter, his anger looking like it was about to boil over.

"Well, it weren't me. It was probably that tart of a wife of yours trying to get some attention," snarled Jaymz.

"What did you say?" shouted Hunter, now shaking with rage.

Aaron only just managed to grab Hunter before he could launch himself at Jaymz. He pulled him back and stepped in front of him to stop him going for Jaymz again.

"Jaymz, you might as well give in. We found the latest letter you wrote jammed in the printer and, as you're the only person who's been at the cottage in months, it *has* to be you." Aaron had had enough and just wanted this whole mess cleared up. He wasn't in the mood for Jaymz's pathetic protestations and was close to knocking the fucker out himself. "Just fucking admit it."

Jaymz was cornered and he knew it. He slunk backward as if trying to escape the inevitable, but still didn't say anything.

"I just want to know *why?*" shouted Hunter, looking dangerously close to losing complete control.

Jaymz took in a breath to reply then released it again as his body deflated in defeat.

Hunter took a step closer to Jaymz, his fist clenched tight.

"Hunter, don't," said Aaron, holding on to his friend's arm to keep him back.

Hunter didn't retreat, but didn't move any closer to Jaymz either. Jaymz tried his best to square up to Hunter, but he didn't stand a chance. He was smaller than either Hunter or Aaron in both stature and character.

"*Why*, Jaymz? What the fuck did I do to make you do something so vicious and vindictive?" Hunter's voice was calmer now, but it held a darker, more threatening tone that Jaymz would be wise to take notice of.

"You took my role in the band," he spat at Hunter. His words were loaded with venom and his eyes burned with hatred. "*I* was meant to be the frontman and singer of Decadence and then *you* turned up and I was pushed back to playing the fucking drums again."

Aaron laughed. "Jaymz, you can't fucking sing."

"Yes I can." Jaymz pouted like a sulky child. He turned back to Hunter. "I thought the letters would scare you off and then me and Aaron would make Decadence the biggest fucking band on the planet."

"Are you serious?" Aaron stared at Jaymz in disbelief. The guy was more deluded than he'd thought. "Jaymz, the reason Decadence is so big now is because of Hunter. Oh, and for the record, without him I'd have left a long time ago, and I can guarantee that Levi wouldn't have been far behind."

Hunter leaned back against the wall and folded his arms. "You'll be pleased to know, Jaymz, that I've decided to quit. I would have stayed for one more album, but there's no way I'm spending another day in your company."

"The same goes for me," said Aaron gravely. "I'm leaving too. With immediate effect."

"Hang on," gasped Bill. "You can't just leave, you're contracted to make another album."

"We were," said Hunter. "But I refuse to work with this loser anymore."

"Ditto." Aaron glared at Jaymz as he spoke, making sure his contempt was crystal clear.

Bill, who was practically frothing at the mouth now, raised his hands in an attempt to appease Hunter and Aaron. "Look, guys, I'll sack Jaymz. Just stay and do this album, *please*."

Jaymz spluttered as he realized what Bill was saying. "You can't sack me," he cried incredulously.

"After what you've done?" growled Bill. "You fucking bet I can."

"Bill," said Hunter. "I'm quitting and nothing will change my mind, and I think you'll find Aaron will do the same."

Aaron nodded in agreement. "Absolutely."

Bill's face darkened as his eyes narrowed on Hunter. Then he turned to Aaron and hissed, "For fuck's sake. The record company will sue you to the point of bankruptcy for breach of contract."

Aaron glanced at Hunter, who nodded. It was time to play their only trump card. "Ah, now here's the thing," he said, turning his back on Jaymz. "If the record company releases us from the contract they can keep the name Decadence and Jaymz can continue with the band."

"Yeah right, like they're going to agree to that," snorted Bill.

"Or," continued Aaron, "we can take the letters to the police and let them deal with it. The media would most likely get hold of the story, which would cause a right old scandal. A scandal that would finish Decadence anyway, and one that I'm sure our esteemed record company could do without." He raised his eyebrows at Bill and gave him an uncompromising glare. Bill was backed into a corner and he knew it.

"Look, it's not you that we want rid of," said Hunter more calmly. "When I get back from my trip I'm going solo and I'd really like it if you would manage me."

"And I'm going to be focusing on songwriting and producing and I'd be more than happy to work with you again," added Aaron. Poor Bill, he was a good guy, honest and hardworking, if a little brusque at times. "We know you can get the top guns at the record company to release us based on what's happened."

Bill sighed, then suddenly turned around and punched Jaymz right on his jaw. Jaymz fell backward with a grunt and landed on the floor. Aaron grinned. Served the bastard right. Then Bill turned back to him and Hunter.

"All right, I'll talk to them. I know they'll be keen to avoid another scandal."

"Thanks, mate," said Aaron. He had been counting on the company's run of bad luck lately. One of their leading artists had been arrested for drug smuggling a few weeks ago and another of their top-selling bands had broken into a major fight while on stage at Wembley Arena last month. The press had had a field day with them and videos of the incident had gone viral on YouTube.

Bill turned back around to Jaymz, who was sitting on the floor rubbing his jaw, and pulled him up by the scruff of his collar. "*You*," he snarled, "are fired. If I ever see your puny face again, I'll do more than just hit you the once. Got it?"

"Yeah, yeah," said Jaymz as he headed toward the door. "I never liked working with you talentless tossers anyway."

Aaron and Hunter laughed. "Ditto," they said at the same time.

After the front door had slammed Aaron finally allowed himself to relax. It was over. The mystery of the letters had been solved and he was free to go his own way. And, best of all, he had Evie to share his happy news with. He turned to Hunter and slapped him on the shoulder, but Hunter pulled him in and gave him a man-hug.

"Thanks, Aaron," said Hunter. "When I get back I'll call you and we'll get together. Maybe you can produce my first solo album?"

Aaron grinned. "I'd be more than happy to, mate."

Then Aaron turned to Bill. "Thank you. I meant it when I said I'd like to work with you again." He reached out to shake Bill's hand, but Bill gave him a stiff hug of sorts instead.

"You too, Aaron. And you, Hunter. And don't worry about the contracts, I'll sort it." Bill's voice was gruff, but his words were sincere.

"Right," said Aaron, rubbing his hands together, "I'm off to find Evie. I only hope she's still talking to me."

# Chapter Twenty-Three

Evie gasped for breath as she completed another set of *sautés* and *entrechats*. Her feet were cramping from all the jumps, but still she pushed herself to do more. Thank God it was her own shop below and not someone's home or the residents might have wondered if she was going to fall through the ceiling.

She needed to wear herself out, to get rid of the anger gnawing away at her. And she wanted the pain in her feet to numb the agony in her heart and the subsequent exhaustion to knock her out so she didn't have to think about Aaron.

Being the masochistic fool that she was, she'd gone back to Ali's and bought a copy of the newspaper that had shattered her world. Now it lay on the floor face down. How dare he treat her like this? He hadn't even had the decency to call her last night to let her know that she was dumped. And now her bloody phone was broken because she'd thrown it against the wall. "Arghhh," she shouted as she attempted another set of twenty jumps.

She didn't hear the buzzer at first, she was so focused on keeping count, but suddenly she became aware of the persistent drone. She stopped, panting, and waited for it to stop. But it didn't.

"Oh for God's sake," she grumbled and stomped out into the hallway to answer the entry phone. She glanced at herself in the mirror and scowled. She was dripping with sweat and her hair was sticking to her face, which was flushed with the exertion from the vigorous exercise. "Yes?" she snapped into the mouthpiece.

"Evie?"

Shit, it was Aaron. What the hell was he doing here? "Go away." She slammed the receiver back down and backed away from the door, shaking. Was it not enough that he'd dumped her for his glamorous L.A. girlfriend? Did he have to come and rub it in her face? He should have had the guts to face her last night. She would still have been heartbroken, but at least she wouldn't have spent the night desperately worried that he'd had an accident or been taken ill.

The buzzer persisted and Evie tried to ignore it. She stomped into the kitchen and poured herself a glass of water, but was too wound up to drink it. Actually, maybe giving Aaron a piece of her mind was just what she needed to exorcise the anger and hurt that were steaming up inside her like a pressure cooker.

She banged the glass down onto the table, marched back into the hallway and pressed the door release without speaking. He must have taken two steps at a time because a split second later he knocked on her door. Taking a deep breath to steady herself, she flung it open and glared at him.

"Evie," he said, sounding as if he were pleased to see her.

"You've got five minutes," she snapped and shut the door firmly once he was inside.

"I'm so sorry about last night," he said breathlessly. "I'll tell you everything that happened. You must believe me when I say that I tried to call you so many times, but I just couldn't get a signal."

Evie put her hands on her hips and tilted her head to one side. "Right, so you couldn't jump into your car and drive a few feet down the road?"

"No, something happened and—"

"Yeah, I bet it did," said Evie, her voice loaded with sarcasm.

Aaron frowned, looking confused by her reaction. "Anyway, I had too much to drink and I couldn't drive. We were at the cottage, you see…"

"You took her to the cottage?"

"Who?"

Bloody hell, did he think she was completely stupid? "Oh, never mind. You're a lying, cheating pig, Aaron Holmes. Just say what you've got to say and then leave me alone."

"Evie, why are you so angry? I know you must have been worried when I didn't get in touch last night, but I've told you that there's a damned good reason." Aaron looked genuinely baffled.

"Why am I angry?" retorted Evie. "Okay, let's see. I'm up all night worrying myself sick about you and then I find out the next morning that you're back with your fancy girlfriend. And you didn't even have the fucking courtesy to—"

Aaron held up his hand for her to stop. "Hang on. Girlfriend? What the hell are you talking about?"

*Oh, for God's sake.* She grabbed the newspaper from the floor and flung it at him. "*This* is what I'm on about," she hissed.

As Aaron stared at the tabloid, his face changed from confusion to disbelief. "What the hell?" He threw the paper back down and glared at Evie. "And you believed this shit?"

Evie lifted her chin defiantly. "Why wouldn't I? She was with you at the music awards and now there are pictures of you kissing her yesterday outside your flat. What exactly am I supposed to think?"

"Actually, I didn't kiss her, she tried to kiss me," said Aaron and laughed. He *laughed.*

"I don't know why you think it's so funny." Evie raised her head to meet his gaze straight on. She opened her mouth to tell him it was time for him to leave but, before she could comprehend what was happening, he grabbed her, pulled her to him and kissed her. Despite her anger, she couldn't help responding. Damn that man.

Finally, he let her go. Then he cupped his hands around her face and held her head still. "It all makes sense now. Evie, that woman is nothing but some model who was paid to sit at our table at the awards. Jaymz hooked up with her and gave her my address. Apparently he assumed I might appreciate her offer to keep me company. She practically assaulted me on my doorstep, but left after I made it clear that I wasn't interested. The paparazzi are always hiding outside our homes so they must have photographed the moment she grabbed me then put two and two together to make five."

Evie stared at him, her head still held prisoner in his hands. His eyes were sincere behind the concern clouding them.

"So she's not your girlfriend?"

"No, of course not. Evie, do you trust me? I mean, *really* trust me?"

Despite everything that had happened, Evie's gut instinct told her that he was telling her the truth. She did trust him, she realized. Slowly, she nodded as best she could, bearing in mind that he was still holding her head. "Yes," she said.

"Good, that's all that matters." He let go of her head then gently stroked her cheek. "I'll explain everything that's happened and it's quite a story, I can tell you, but first there's something I have to tell you."

Evie held her breath. Uh-oh, now what?

"I love you."

Did he just say what she thought he'd said? "Say that again," she said, not sure if she'd heard right.

He grinned. "I love you, Evie Lloyd. I think I fell in love with you the moment I laid eyes on you."

Evie was speechless. Joy bubbled up inside her as the words she'd never thought she'd hear from Aaron rang in her ears like church bells. He loved her?

"Evie, say something," he said, suddenly looking worried.

All Evie's insecurities melted away as her heart nearly exploded with happiness. Aaron loved her. "I love you too," she finally managed to say before he pulled her back into his arms and kissed her hard.

# Epilogue

"Evie, are you nearly ready?" Christina wandered into the bathroom where Evie was putting the finishing touches to her makeup. "Wow, you look bloody gorgeous."

"Thanks." Evie grinned at Christina's wide eyes. It was Saturday night and they were at Dominion getting ready in the suite Aaron had reserved. She was wearing a very short red latex dress, so short it showed most of her bum. Her breasts were exposed with the rubber cupping them from below and keeping them pushed together and pert. Even she had to admit that she looked pretty sexy.

"Come on," said Christina, "we've just got time for a glass of champagne before the boys expect us downstairs. We've got some serious catching up to do."

They went back into the main suite where Christina had already poured two glasses of champagne. Then they settled onto the sofa by the window and toasted the night ahead of them.

"I'm sorry I haven't had a chance to meet up this week," said Evie. "The shop has been really busy and then Aaron has been around every night."

Christina shrugged. "That's okay. As long as you tell me everything."

Evie took a sip then said, "Oh, Christina, I was so horrible to him when he came around on Sunday. Poor man, he'd had a really rough couple of days then, when he turned up at my flat I called him all sorts of nasty things. I was so angry."

"I'm not surprised—you thought he'd cheated on you. I didn't see the papers until Monday, which is why I didn't call you to see if you were okay. By then you and Aaron were back together and Marco forbade me to call you."

Evie raised her eyebrows in surprise. "Really?"

"Yeah, he said we needed to give you guys some privacy. Privacy, my ass. I want all the gory details."

Evie laughed. "And you'll get them—another time. I can tell you, though, that Aaron is going to punish me tonight."

"Ooh, goody. Can I watch?"

"I think it's going to be pretty public, so yeah, I guess so."

Christina frowned. "Is it for real? I mean, you had your reasons at the time to say the things you did."

"Don't worry," said Evie, grinning. "It's sort of for real, but I'm completely okay with it. He's not punishing me for calling him names—well, he is but that bit isn't serious. Last night, though, he asked how I felt about the fact that I hadn't given him the benefit of the doubt. I'd drawn the wrong conclusions based on information I should have known wasn't reliable. I said I felt really bad about that and then he reminded me that it wasn't the first time I had misjudged him. I was pretty rude to him when I first met him, if you remember."

Christina nodded and grinned. "Oh yeah. You thought he was an arrogant, self-obsessed rock star."

"Yes, well, I got that wrong as well. So that's when he asked if I agreed that I should be punished."

"Wow. And you said yes?"

"Yeah, I know this sounds strange, but I think I need it. I want him to punish me because I feel so bad about not trusting him when I should have done. I had absolutely no reason to overreact like that, but my own insecurities took over from my common sense. Thank God he loves me enough to forgive me."

"Well, I'm really pleased that it's all worked out in the end. I've never seen you this happy," said Christina, giving Evie's arm a squeeze.

"Thanks. We've just got to get you sorted now," said Evie.

"Oh, don't you worry about me. I'm a big girl now,"

laughed Christina, but there was a hint of sadness in her eyes that she couldn't hide.

Evie's phone buzzed with a text. "New phone?" asked Christina.

Evie nodded. "Yeah, I sort of threw my old one at the wall and broke it. Serves me right for being so stupid. Anyway, that's Aaron who just texted. They want us downstairs now."

"Okay. Good luck with your punishment. I'm so glad that, for once, it's not me."

They made their way downstairs to find Aaron and Marco waiting for them in the main entrance hall. After brief hellos Marco led Christina away, leaving her alone with Aaron. He looked overwhelmingly hot. Tight black leather trousers hugged his muscular legs and the only thing he wore on top was a leather waistcoat that exposed his hard chest and broad shoulders. And the tattoo sleeve that covered his right arm gave him an edgy look that Evie loved. His New Rock boots finished off the look, along with his long dark hair hanging loose down his back and rough stubble framing his chin. Her stomach flipped as she drank in the sight of him. He, in turn, whistled as he looked her up and down.

"Wow, you look stunning."

"Thank you, Sir." She couldn't stop the flush from creeping up her neck. One day she would learn to accept a compliment without being embarrassed.

Reaching into his pocket, he pulled something out and held it up in front of her. It was a black and red leather collar. Without a word he nodded at her to hold her hair up then he fastened it around her neck.

He took a step back and studied her. "Beautiful." Then he pulled out a leash from his other pocket and attached it to the D ring at the front of the collar. "Even better. You're mine now, Evie. Soon I want to formally collar you. Would you like that?"

She nearly swayed with giddiness as she managed to

reply, "Oh, yes, Sir."

"Right, here's the plan. I want to get started early, as it's going to be a long night. I want to get your punishment out of the way so I can spend the rest of the night rewarding you for being so perfect." He paused and looked thoughtful for a moment. "Do you know what has been the most common theme behind the scenes we've had so far?"

Evie shook her head, puzzled. "Er, no. Should I?"

"Punishment."

"Really?" *Now there's a thing.* Evie tried not to show her amusement and kept her face serious.

"Yes, really. If you remember, the first time I punished you was for being rude the night we met, then I punished you for lying about your reasons for finishing with me a couple of weeks later." Aaron appeared to contemplate what was next, although Evie knew damn well that he knew exactly what he was going to say. "Oh yes, there were the two punishments you incurred in the last fortnight because you were topping from the bottom. And tonight you're going to be punished again. I'm beginning to see a pattern here," he said with a wicked glint in his eyes.

Evie batted her eyelids and giggled. "Are you implying that I'm a brat, Sir?"

"I am, and don't you dare change. I love you just the way you are." He reached out and tapped her on the tip of her nose with his finger, his eyes brimming with affection as he did so. "Going back to tonight, don't think you're going to get away scot-free for calling me a lying cheating pig. You'll get your dues for that as well, but that'll come later."

She wouldn't have expected anything less and giggled as she wondered what he was going to do to her, but soon stopped when she noticed his stern expression. The joking was over and the guilt that had been nagging her conscience all week returned.

"Evie, I know you agreed to this punishment, but I want to be completely sure that you're happy to go ahead with it. It *will* be a punishment flogging," he said, his voice grim.

"I know, but I need to do it. I think it's the only way I'll stop hating myself for being so horrible to you. I *should* have trusted you. I'm so sorry." And she meant it. God, she could be stupid sometimes.

He nodded, his face solemn. "Okay. Let's go." He tugged on the leash and led her into the dungeon.

It was busier than she'd been expecting it to be. Quite a few people had already started playing and the atmosphere was warming up nicely. The slap of spanking, the thud of floggers and the groans of submissives all put her at ease as she breathed in the sexy scents of leather and rubber. Rather than it being intimidating as it might be for some people, it made Evie feel right at home. It was a good feeling.

As they crossed the dungeon she saw Per restraining a pretty redhead to the St. Andrew's Cross. He looked over and winked as they made eye contact. She had a funny feeling that the delicious spanking he'd given her that day at the recording studio wouldn't be the last time they'd play together. That was fine with her.

Aaron stopped by a spanking bench in the middle of the room, in full view of just about everybody there, and Per was instantly forgotten as he said, "Kneel, Evie."

She lowered herself to the floor and settled onto her knees by Aaron's feet. Then she reached her arms behind her and locked her fingers together before lowering her head so she was in the submissive pose she knew Aaron liked.

All she could see were his boots and the bottoms of his leather trousers, but his feet were parted and she could tell his stance was powerful without even looking up. A flutter tickled her belly as she allowed his dominance to take control of her.

"I'm going to punish you tonight, Evie," said Aaron, clearly so that those not already involved in a scene could hear. He took a handful of her hair and pulled her head back so she was looking up at him. "Tell me why you're being punished, Evie."

"I didn't trust you, Sir. I doubted you when I should have

known you'd never have betrayed me." Oh God, saying the words out loud made her feel even worse. She so needed to be punished.

"Tell me again what you called me?"

*Oh shit.* "I called you a lying cheating pig, Sir." As soon as she'd said it there was a murmur of giggles from the gathering crowd.

"Hmm. Yes, you did, you naughty girl. I'll sort you out later for that one."

"I'm sorry, Sir."

"I know, sweetheart," he said, softly. "But I'm still going to whip your ass."

A shudder ran through her body at his words. She was about to receive corporal punishment and it would undoubtedly hurt. "Yes, Sir."

"Stand up and bend over the bench," he ordered.

As soon as she was draped over the cool leather, Aaron fastened the cuffs that were attached to it around her wrists and ankles so she couldn't escape. She was thankful that she wouldn't have to concentrate on remaining in place without bondage. This way she could writhe as much as she wanted without leaving her position, and she had a feeling she would need the freedom to struggle tonight.

Once she was restrained Aaron moved around to stand in front of her. Grabbing a handful of her hair, he leaned forward and spoke in her ear, "I'm going to start by warming you up with a nice gentle flogger. The reason I'm doing that is so that you'll last the night. I don't want you being so sore that you can't take more later."

"Thank you, Sir," she whispered as she gazed up into his dark eyes.

"Although this is a punishment, I don't want to push you beyond what you can take, so use your safeword if it becomes too much. I will expect you to use it if you need to, okay?"

"Yes, Sir, I understand."

"Good. Enjoy the warm-up, because you won't like what

259

follows."

She knew he was deliberately putting her in the headspace that she needed to be in, but his tone was so serious that she almost regretted agreeing to the punishment. Almost, but not quite.

True to his word, Aaron started off gently by spanking her bottom and thighs lightly with his bare hand. It didn't hurt, but she knew her skin would be turning a little bit pink. Then he stopped and moved away. A couple of seconds later the first thud of the flogger swept across her buttocks. Not too hard, just enough for it to send a little shiver through her body with each impact. He flogged her for a long time, expertly directing the strands of suede so they didn't wrap around her thighs, and gradually she relaxed. As he increased the force of the blows her ass began to burn and the first sensations of pain started to build. But it was nice pain and Evie was warmed up enough by now to take it without any problems.

She was beginning to slide into her favorite headspace. The one that made her feel lightheaded and so happy she could cry. She needed this pain and she would take as much as Aaron wanted to give her. Her heart clenched as every thud brought her closer to him. How was it possible to be so happy?

Aaron stopped flogging her just as she was drifting further in her world of pleasure. He walked back to the front of the bench and bent down to talk to her. "Your punishment will begin now, Evie. I'm going to give you twelve strokes and you will count each one, do you understand?"

"Yes, Sir," she whispered as apprehension washed over her. Shit, what had she agreed to?

"I'm going to use a different flogger. It's leather, with thinner tails, so it'll sting."

The first strike was a shock after the heavy suede flogger that had felt more like getting a massage than a whipping. This one was mean. It bloody stung.

"One," she gasped once the pain had started to recede.

She was more prepared for the next two, although they hurt just as much. They came in quick succession so she didn't have a chance to recover between the strikes. "Two, three." Oh God she had another nine to go. Could she do this?

Number four landed across the backs of her thighs and she screamed as fire engulfed her. "Ow! Four!" *Fuck!*

He hit her again, and the pain seared its way through her skin and scorched her nerve endings. With each lash she tried to pull away from the restraints as her body jerked with the force of impact, but they kept her firmly in place.

As Evie took her punishment the guilt that had crushed her since last weekend started to ebb away. With each agonizing blow, the weight inside her lifted. By the time she'd taken ten strikes, tears were pouring down her cheeks. But the tears were a welcome release and she didn't try to stop them.

Number eleven felt like it tore through her skin and she groaned as she struggled to process the pain. "Eleven," she cried when she had enough strength to speak. The hurt was all-consuming now, her ass on fire as it throbbed intensely.

"One more, Evie."

"Yes, Sir," she hissed.

Number twelve took away her breath as it blazed across the backs of her thighs. She couldn't count this one, couldn't speak as relief and gratitude merged with the pain. When she was able, she cried, "Thank you, Sir. I'm so sorry."

"Shh," whispered Aaron as he stroked her hair. "It's over. I'm so proud of you. I'm going to untie you now, okay?"

She nodded through her hiccups and as soon as Aaron lifted her off the bench and picked her up in his arms, she buried her face in his chest and felt safer and more cherished than she'd ever felt in her life. He carried her through to the chill-out bar and found a sofa in a quiet corner. He must have called the waiter over because she heard him ordering a hot chocolate for her. Aaron held her in his arms and she savored every moment.

"You okay?" he asked as he tucked a stray strand of her hair behind her ear.

"Yes, Sir. I'm so glad you did that. I feel like I've been absolved of the guilt that's been eating away at me. I deserved it. I really am sorry."

"I know, sweetheart. You were very brave to take that. That flogger can be brutal. I wasn't even hitting you that hard with it."

Evie shivered and vowed never to earn another punishment with that whip again. A fun, playful punishment, yes, but…

"I'm going to make you pay for the rest of the night," said Aaron, nuzzling her neck. He chuckled then added, "I'll have you screaming for mercy and I'm going to have such fun doing it."

"I don't doubt it, you bloody sadist," said Evie with an irresistible mixture of trepidation and excitement.

Drake, the barman, came over with her hot chocolate then and Evie enjoyed every delicious mouthful. Her stinging buttocks were a constant reminder of her punishment. How was it possible that being whipped like that could make her feel better? It was crazy, but she felt even closer to Aaron now than she had before. He demanded certain behavior from her as his submissive and she had let him down. She had deserved the flogging and now that it was over, her behavior had been forgiven. There was no hidden resentment or bitterness. How she loved the uncomplicated and straightforward protocols of D/s. How she loved the fact that it was Aaron who had become the center of her world.

By the time Aaron told her to stand up she was fully recovered and ready for what was next. She was surprised when he led her out of the main dungeon and along the hallway. When they stopped by the oak door leading down to the real dungeons, Evie realized where Aaron was taking her. *Oh shit!* They made their way down the steep stone steps then followed the corridor until they reached the dungeon they'd been in last time. Aaron took out a key and unlocked the door, then he nodded for her to go through. Stepping into the darkened torture chamber was no less scary than it had been before.

Aaron took her over to some sort of wooden contraption that looked a bit like a pillory combined with a spanking bench. The space for the head and hands were at the top end of the bench and the ones for the feet were floor level at the rear. It was clear just by looking at it that there would be no escape once a victim was locked into it.

"Bend over."

She complied without hesitation and draped herself over the leather-bound bench so that her body was supported, but her ankles, wrists and head were encased in the pillory. Her legs were spread and her ass angled upward so he had perfect access to her. She was helpless and at the total mercy of whatever Aaron wanted to do to her.

"We're back in the original vaults of the house," said Aaron. "Marco has told me stories of what used to go on down here. All you need to know is that nobody will hear you scream."

Evie groaned as a powerful shudder surged through her body.

"You're helpless, Evie. Your pussy, your ass and your mouth are all available for me to use as I please. You can't escape."

Each word sent Evie's pulse soaring until her breath came in short gasps. Heat was building somewhere deep inside her, and an intense throbbing from between her legs made her press her hips into the bench to try to steal some relief.

Aaron moved to another part of the dungeon and seemed to be taking something out of a box, but she couldn't see what it was.

"They used to torture people down here, Evie," he said as he strode past her again. She tried to get a glimpse of what he was holding, but he'd moved it to the hand that was out of her sight. Damn. What was that he was carrying? Then he plugged something in behind her. A vibrator? "I'm going to torture you now."

"Oh God," she whimpered. Although she knew Aaron would never do anything to truly hurt her, he was so good at playing with her mind that she wondered if she could take whatever it was he had planned.

Then, to her horror, he switched on the thing he'd been holding and the sound of buzzing set every nerve ending in her body on fire. A violet wand. *Oh no!*

"Please, Sir," she begged, "I don't like electro."

He chuckled. "Oh, really? That's a shame, because I do."

"Please…"

Then she felt his breath on her ear. "Evie, I asked last week and I'll ask again, do you trust me?"

Ah, they were back to the trust thing again. "Yes, Sir," she replied without hesitation, because she did trust him. But electro?

"And do you trust me push your boundaries without going further than you can take?"

"Yes, Sir."

"Good. Remember the electro scene we watched upstairs a few weeks ago?"

How could she forget? "Yes, Sir."

"I was looking at you and your reactions more than what was going on up on the stage. You were fascinated by it, aroused even."

"But—"

"Shh, don't say another word."

He moved the buzzing wand up to her head and held it close to her ear. *Shit!* The ominous sound taunted her and she squeezed her eyes shut in the hope that that would somehow make her ears stop working.

She let out a big sigh of relief when he moved it away from her head. As the buzzing receded so did a little bit of her fear. She didn't even realize he had touched her with the glass bulb at first. It was only when she heard a change in the frequency that she became aware of a warm tingling running down her back. It was so subtle she could barely feel it. Okay, that wasn't so bad.

"Does it hurt, Evie?"

"No, Sir."

"Oh, I'll have to do something about that."

The intensity of the buzzing increased and Evie knew he'd turned the power up. *Damn*. But again, when the electricity touched her, all she could feel was the warmth again. It was almost like being tickled. It wasn't entirely unpleasant. Okay, it was quite nice, actually.

Aaron ran the wand along her legs, her arms and down her back and Evie found herself relaxing more and more as she grew used to the sensations. The buzzing, although louder now, as he must have turned it up again, was less ominous and the smell of ozone barely registered with her.

"How does it feel now?" he asked as he ran it over her shoulders.

"Mmm, nice. A bit like a pinwheel, it's sort of prickly."

He moved it down her back and over her sore buttocks.

"Ow," she cried and tried to wriggle away from the pain. "I'm still sore there."

He chuckled and moved it farther down to the moist heat gathering between her legs. "I know." He continued running the wand over her ass and thighs, clearly enjoying her struggle. The wand crackled and hissed every time it made contact with her and Evie got to the point where she didn't know which was worse—the slight pain of the static shock or the sound of the sparks as they flew off her skin.

She should hate this, but she didn't. Aaron had been right when he'd said that she could trust him to push her boundaries. Aaron controlled her world—he *was* her world. At that moment nothing mattered except pleasing him, so she embraced her fear and resolved to endure every moment the way she knew he wanted.

Finally, he switched the wand off and the dungeon was silent again. She waited until she heard his footsteps move away before opening her eyes. Oddly, now that the violet wand had been switched off, she almost missed its hum and the warm torture it had inflicted on her. *Get a grip.* Aaron, having put the wand away, returned and ran his hands down her back, stroking her sensitive skin. *Mmm, nice.* "That was for pleasure," he murmured as he massaged her shoulders. "Now it's time for more punishment."

"That wasn't punishment?" she cried in disbelief.

He chuckled and continued to massage her. "Tell me honestly, did you enjoy that?"

She couldn't lie, much as she wanted to. "Yes, Sir."

"So how could it have been a punishment?"

Point taken. "Okay, Sir, I understand."

"I'm going to let you up now. You'll have ten minutes to rest then, I'm going to restrain you to the St. Andrew's cross." He'd already released the top part of the pillory as he spoke and now moved to free her ankles. As he helped her up she stole a glance at his face to see if his expression might give away what he had planned. But his face was deadpan. He was too frigging good at this.

She drank the water he gave her and, before she knew it, the time had come for the next scene.

"I want you to crawl over to the cross," he ordered, standing over her with his arms folded. "Then wait on your knees."

"Yes, Sir." She slid off the sofa he had allowed her to sit on during her break and made her way to the cross on her hands and knees. If he wanted her in a submissive headspace he was right on target. When she reached it she knelt, head down, and waited for him to give her further instructions. All joviality had long gone as the seriousness of the impending scene loomed. Evie was very aware that Aaron intended to make her suffer some more and the anticipation made her belly flutter and heartbeat thunder. Submission had always been all-consuming for her, but now that her Dom was someone she loved it was on a different level.

"Good girl." Aaron's voice snapped her back to the here and now and she sighed with happiness when he softly stroked her head. Then he took a fistful of her hair and pulled. "Now, stand up and face away from the cross."

She complied straight away and raised her arms to the top of the cross without being asked. Aaron fastened the cuffs to her wrists then nudged her foot with his boot to make her part her legs some more. When he'd secured her ankles he stepped back and inspected her. "Beautiful," he murmured as he placed a blindfold over her eyes. "Now you can't escape."

His dark tone sent flutters through her entire body. Her need to surrender herself to Aaron was like an itch deep under her skin that could only be relieved by him taking her submission and using it as he saw fit. She trusted him more than she'd trusted anyone, and she knew he would keep her safe as he made her suffer. She didn't want to escape — ever.

"Do you remember the first time I punished you? After the double punishment with Christina I tied you to the cross and forced three orgasms from you."

"Yes," she replied slowly. Oh God, forced orgasms. Well, as long as she got to come she'd be fine.

"We're going to something similar now," he said. She could hear the evil smile in his voice. Damn, what was he up to? Then he pinched both her nipples and Evie's core contracted as if there was a direct connection between her breasts and her pussy.

"Sir, I think I need to come," she whispered as the sensations started building inside her. She was already aroused from the electro scene. All she needed was a little tweak on her clit and she'd be there.

"Do you, now?" There was a hint of sadism in Aaron's voice.

Then something cool, smooth and vibrating rested against her clit. "Oh, thank you, Sir," she cried as she tried to press herself closer to the vibrating wand. Delicious memories of the last time he'd forced orgasms on her with the wand wafted back. Ha, this time she could easily cope with coming multiple times.

"Don't forget to ask permission before you come," growled Aaron. "I'll be very displeased if you don't."

"Okay. Argh, I don't think it'll be long, Sir." The pressure built until her body stiffened in anticipation of the pleasure to come. "Sir, please can I come?"

"No."

He moved the wand away, leaving her quivering with the need for release. *Oh no, please don't let this be orgasm denial.* Aaron's words from a few moments ago drifted through her head, leaving her stomach to sink in dismay. *'Now it's time for more punishment'.* Oh shit.

She had only just stopped shaking when the wand returned to her aching clit. "Oh no, Sir, please…" she begged. She wasn't sure she could take too many near misses.

"Remind me what you called me on Sunday?"

The vibrations were taking hold again, sending fresh surges through her body. "I called you a lying cheating pig, Sir," she said through gritted teeth.

"So you did."

"Sir, I need to come. *Please.*" She wouldn't be able to hold off for much longer.

Again Aaron moved the wand away just before she was able to come. "Oh no you don't." There was a hint of laughter in his voice. The bastard thought this was funny. She clenched her fists, wishing her hands were free so she could grab the fucking wand and hit him over the head with it.

As soon as her body had recovered sufficiently, he placed the wand against her pussy again and turned the speed up. *Bastard!* The highs were quick to return and she was soon on the brink again, only this time she was beginning to really ache. She didn't bother asking permission this time as she knew he wouldn't give it anyway. Maybe she could trick him? But she was so desperate by now and he was so tuned-in to her reactions that she didn't have a hope in hell's chance of fooling him. As soon as the pressure peaked again he pulled the wand away, leaving her almost crying with frustration.

She lost track of how many times he took her to the brink and back, but by the time he eventually stopped the torture she was a complete wreck. When he removed the blindfold he was just a fuzzy image somewhere in front of her. Her legs were shaking, she had broken out in a cold sweat and she was dizzy with the need to come. As Aaron released her from the cross her legs buckled, but he caught her safely in his arms before she could crash to the floor.

Carrying her over to a sawhorse-type bench he said, "I'm going to fuck you now, Evie, and this time I'm going to let you come."

She almost sobbed with relief as she collapsed onto the bench. "Oh, thank you, Sir." She lay across it, face down, with her feet supporting her on the floor and butt slightly raised so he had easy access to her pussy.

"I'm not going to restrain you," he breathed in her ear. "I'm going to fuck you so hard that you won't be able to move anyway."

Moist heat gathered between her legs at his words and her blood sizzled through her veins as she processed their meaning. She could barely contain herself as she waited for him to sheath himself with the condom she'd just heard being ripped from its wrapper. Then he ran his finger along her soaked slit and she shivered uncontrollably as she tried to arch her back to give him easier access. He slid the finger inside her and it was almost too much. There didn't seem much room for his finger so how was she going to accommodate his cock?

"So wet," he murmured. "You're going to be very tender down there when I fuck you, sweetie. You're all swollen and puffy." Standing behind her, he finally slid his thick cock inside her and she cried out as her oversensitive pussy spasmed around him. Then he started fucking her, fast and forcible, hard and deep.

She cried out with pent-up lust as his cock went deeper

with each thrust, reaching her most intimate places. At the same time, he rubbed her clit with his finger, sending her mind and body into utopia. Stars twinkled across her eyelids as she gripped onto the bench for dear life. Her whole body seemed to be tightening, like elastic being pulled too taut. She was going to come soon. Oh God…

"Sir, can I come?" she gasped just as the elastic snapped and her insides convulsed with waves of euphoric pleasure.

Aaron groaned as his cock thickened inside her and only just managed to growl, "Yes," a split second before he exploded himself.

Their bodies became one at that point, soaring above the world as they rode the wind together. As she floated back down to earth Evie couldn't stop the tears from spilling as she reveled in the afterglow of the most intense orgasm she had ever had.

"Hey, are you all right?" asked Aaron, folding his arms around her and nuzzling her neck.

"Oh yes, Sir. I'm better than I've ever been in my life," she murmured.

"I love you so much, Evie," he whispered.

"I love you too, Master." She closed her eyes and imagined herself soaking in a pool of warm bubbles. She had never known such happiness or contentedness. She was so lucky to have found a man who was perfect for her — strong, dominant, caring, loving. Her Master. And to think she'd thought he was just another arrogant, selfish rock star when she'd first met him. She couldn't have been more wrong.

\* \* \* \*

"More?"

Evie nodded and opened her mouth as Aaron held the warm, juicy bacon sandwich to her mouth. She took a big bite and her eyes fluttered as the delicious salty flavor assaulted her taste buds. It had been a good hour or so since their intense scene down in the dungeon and she was now fully recovered. Aaron had held her in his arms as they'd cuddled on the sofa for what had felt like forever. Then he'd suggested going upstairs to the chill-out lounge in time for the bacon sandwiches and hot chocolate that they always served in the early hours.

To her own amazement she had agreed when he'd asked if he could feed her. She was sitting next to him on the sofa rather than kneeling by his feet, but she would happily have slid to the floor if he'd asked her to. And, somehow, she didn't mind being fed by him at all. It somehow felt right. Aaron had wrapped her in a blanket when they'd sat down and she was so glad that he had instinctively known that she'd needed a little discreet modesty.

Evie giggled as something Aaron had once said came back to her. "So, Sir, have we ironed out the kinks now?"

Aaron laughed then leaned down and kissed her again. "I'm sure we'll always have a few kinks to sort out, and I wouldn't have it any other way."

"Me neither."

"You called me Master downstairs. I liked that."

So he'd noticed. "That's what you are to me," she said and opened her mouth again as Aaron held the sandwich to her lips. Was it her imagination or did the bacon taste better because it had come from his hand?

When the food was finished they snuggled up together on the luxurious sofa and watched the crowd bustling with animated chatter. Several people waved at them as they walked past, others came over and said hello. The atmosphere was friendly, sexy and fun. She loved it.

"May we join you?" Marco had approached, carrying Christina. She looked so delicate in those strong arms, but also safe and cared for.

"Of course." Aaron nodded at the space next to them. "Did you have a good night?"

Marco chuckled as he lowered himself onto the seat, taking care not to drop Christina. She was out of it, deep in subspace. Marco made sure she was comfortable then kissed the top her head. Then Cleo approached with a bottle of water.

"How is she?" she asked, handing Marco the bottle. "This is for our little kitten when she wakes up." She sat down next to Marco and softly stroked Christina's head with her long fingernails.

"She's good," replied Marco. "I'll take her down to my apartment soon. I think we might have worn her out."

Cleo grinned. "Hmm, yes, we did give her a rather good seeing to, didn't we?" Then she turned to Aaron and Evie. "You two look like you've had fun too."

"Oh yeah," said Aaron, his eyes flashing dangerously. "I doubt Evie will be able to walk tomorrow."

"It looks like you found yourself your perfect subbie," said Marco, his voice unusually soft.

Aaron looked down at Evie with such open devotion that she almost cried with happiness. "Oh yes," he said, tenderly. "This gorgeous lady is the love of my life."

Christina looked up at that moment and winked at Evie. She grinned back at her friend, who was clearly beginning to come down from her high. It was thanks to Christina that she'd met Aaron. Aaron had done something she had never imagined anyone could. He had helped to mend her shattered dreams and put everything into perspective. She could still dance, albeit only on an amateur level, and she owned a business that she loved. And to top all that, Aaron had made her see that she was worthy of his love and, just as importantly, that he was worthy of hers.

# More books from
# Katy Swann

*Rachel Porter's dreams of being dominated are finally about to come true. But can she live up to the demands of a real-life Dom?*

*Should Rachel stand her ground and tell Adam that she won't be his slave? If she does, she'll lose him and if she doesn't, she'll lose her freedom.*

TOTALLY BOUND

KATY SWANN

BOUNDARIES

First she submitted, then she learnt to trust, but can
Rachel finally promise to obey?

TO LOVE &
OBEY

*First she submitted, then she learnt to trust, but can
Rachel finally promise to obey?*

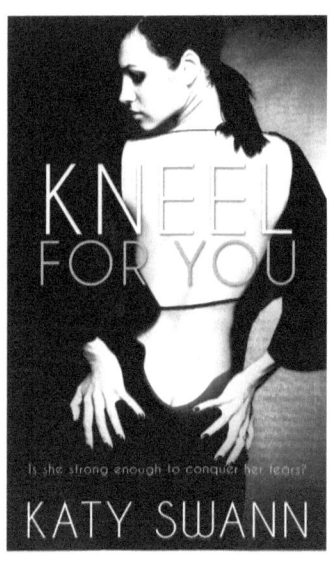

*Should she agree to be spanked? Just the once? It would all be in the name of research, of course…*

# About the Author

## Katy Swann

Katy Swann is in her forties and lives near London, UK with her husband, three children and two cats.

Katy writes BDSM romance with an emphasis on D/s. She finds the D/s dynamic the most exciting and erotic aspect of BDSM although a good spanking or flogging comes a close second. Her books are first and foremost love stories with a large dose of D/s and kinky sex.

The Boundaries Trilogy (To Love and Submit, To Love and Trust & To Love and Obey) was published in December 2013 and was her first release. She is currently working on a new series of standalone BDSM romance novels called Dominion.

Coffee, chocolate and cats are her favourite things and are often close by when she sits down to write.

Katy Swann loves to hear from readers. You can find contact information, website details and an author profile page at https://www.totallybound.com/

Home of Erotic Romance